Sword of Neamha

By
Stephen M. England

ISBN 978-0-557-16394-6

Copyright © 2009 by Stephen M. England

This book is dedicated to my parents, my friends, and all those who helped make this dream a reality. Thank you all.

Special thanks go out to the historians of the Europa Barbarorum project, without whose help this story could never have come into being. And to Louis Vaney, whose brilliant map-making brought the world of ancient Britain to life.

Glossary

Warriors

Brihentin(**Knights**)—these members of the Aeduan nobility form the bodyguard of a prominent chieftain.

Botroas(**Sword Soldiers**)—the basic medium infantry of Britonic and Gallic armies, these men often hire themselves out as mercenaries.

Cladaca(**Sword Carriers**)—light swordsmen of the Goidilic Irish, well-trained and fierce in battle.

Dubosaverlacica(**Blackened Fighting Ones**)—these elite Goidilic warriors come from one tribe— the Ebherni, descendants of the Vasci, ancient Spanish invaders of Ireland.

Eiras(**Nobles**)—the nobility of Goidilic Ireland, these chieftains are equipped with the best of equipment and fight at the head of lesser men.

Gaeroas(**Spear Soldiers**)—well-disciplined Gallic spearmen, the rock of an Aeduan battleline.

Iaosatae(**Slingmen**)—warriors are drawn from the young of Celtic society and armed with one of the cheapest and most effective missile weapons available in ancient times.

Lugoae(**Levies**)—the militia of Celtic society, these men are predominantly young and poorly equipped, often with a crude spear.

Ordmalica(**Hammer Fighters**)—wealthy and seasoned, these warriors emulate their god, Dagda, by carrying mighty war hammers into battle.

Teceitos(**Axe Soldiers**)—Although references to the axe are not prevalent in Celtic history, many have been found in the graves of warriors of the time period.

Vellinica(**Swift Fighters**)—lightly armed and armored, these men form the militia of Goidilic Ireland, levy fighters called up in the hour of need.

Places

Attuaca: A word roughly translated "fort", this stands as representative of the Caledonian settlements of ancient Scotland.

Caern-Brigantae: Near Aldborough, England.

Camulosadae: A prominent city of the ancient Britonic tribes, near modern-day Colchester, England.

Emain-Macha: The traditional capital of the Ulaid and founded according to legend by the goddess Macha in the 5th-century B.C., the ancient site is located less than two miles from modern-day Armagh, Northern Ireland.

Ictis: The capital of the Dumnonii even through Roman times, it is the site of Exeter, England today.

Ivernis: Near modern-day Sneem, in County Kerry, Ireland.

Yns-Mon: A settlement of the Cyremniu on the west coast of Wales, near the modern-day island of the same name.

Prologue

Once we had been a nation, a people great and mighty, beloved of the gods, a federation of the Keltoi stretching from sea to sea. All that was gone now, as though washed away by the surging tides of the sea behind me. The past.

Our brothers, the Arverni, led by their heathenous god-king, had turned against us, driving their sword deep into our ribs while grasping our hand in fellowship. Over the last few years, they had succeeded in driving us from our lands. They had robbed of us our birthright, backed our people to the wall. Over a year ago now, our Vergobret, a wise man named Cocolitanos, had made the decision. My people would flee.

We had abandoned our towns and settlements before the Arverni onslaught, fled northward to the sea, to the place we had prepared a small fleet for our departure. Many of the Aedui left immediately, over a thousand fighting men with their wives and children.

I, Cadwalador, son of the Wolf, had not left. I was one of the horsemen detailed to stay behind with Tancogeistla, one of our chieftains. Another detachment was working its way up from the south, from the settlement at Mediolanium. We must wait for them.

I and my fellows formed the *leuce epos*, the light horse of the Aedui. Taught from childhood to throw our javelins from the backs of our rapidly-moving steeds, to close with spear for the final charge. None of us had passed our thirtieth year. Many of us might never live to see it.

Tancogeistla was a volatile man, fond of his drink and of fighting afterwards. He grew weary of our enforced stay on this barren headland, as did indeed all of us. But he most of all. The ships were back from the land to the north, from Erain as it was apparently called by the natives. He was impatient to be gone.

Rumors ran through the cavalry, stories told by those that said Tancogeistla was preparing to leave immediately, in defiance of the orders given us by the Vergobret. In the end, who would know the difference? We were leaving our homeland for the last time.

I was never to find out if there was any truth in those rumors. *Ogrosan* closed upon us before he made up his mind and stranded us upon the cliffs, foraging through the snow every day for food for both us and our horses.

One day, as I was out on a scout, I glimpsed men through the trees. I took my javelins in one hand, watching as the column marched forward, all of them on foot. Many of them were bandaged and limping, leaving stains of blood in the snow as they advanced.

It was the column from Mediolanium. But something was wrong. I kicked my horse in the flanks, urging him forward as I rode toward the body.

The men halted as I moved into the clearing. I could see the suspicion in their eyes. There couldn't have been more than one hundred and fifty. Less than a third of their reported strength.

"Who is your leader?" I demanded, riding to the head of the column. A tall, red-bearded man stepped from the column, an unsheathed sword in his right hand.

"Who asks?"

"Cadwalador, son of the Wolf, a member of the army of Tancogeistla. I was sent to look for you."

A look of relief spread over his swarthy countenance. "Lead me to him. I am Cavarillos, captain of this detachment."

"Then the rest of the army follows behind you?" I asked, praying to the gods that he would answer in the affirmative.

He suddenly looked tired, sheathing his sword with the motions of an exhausted man. "We are the army. All that remains of it."

"The Arverni?"

He merely nodded. I wheeled my horse to the north and commanded him to follow. The rest of the men fell into step behind him, moving sluggishly, wearily. Bloody footprints in the snow. . .

Chapter I: Across the Waters

I never heard all that passed between Tancogeistla and Cavarillos, but we would soon learn most of the story. That Catamantaloedis, the young chieftain from Mediolanium, had been killed in a surprise attack by Arverni warbands just north of the great mountains. He had died fighting, along with most of his men. All those that survived were here with us now. An incredible blow to our dreams.

We stayed where we were for the rest of *ogrosan*, waiting for the warm months to come, when we too could sail north.

Over the following months, I grew to know Cavarillos well. This was the first time he had been this far north. He was one of the *botroas*, or sword soldiers, a mercenary employed by Catamantaloedis.

A man who had seen much fighting. He was unmarried, without children, as myself.

We had much in common, though he was ten years my elder. As the warm months approached, he borrowed a sword from one of the warriors and taught me its use. I had never felt a blade in my hand in all nineteen years of my life, but it was a simple weapon and I learned quickly. Still, I felt more comfortable astride my horse.

In the month of Giamon, we at last set sail for the unknown land to the north. None of us knew what lay ahead. The army sent ahead might already lie dead, slain by the natives. We might be sailing into a trap.

Our boats posed a threat as great as the unknown that lay ahead. They were light craft, hide stretched over wood frames.

We bound the feet of our mounts so that one of their hooves could not pierce the hull, and were very careful in stowing our weapons. At finally, we were off, sailing north. I could scarce help trembling as we hove out of sight of land. It was the first time in my life that I had ever been surrounded by water.

For three weeks we continued, fixing the sail to the mast whenever there appeared to be a breath of wind, rowing till our backs felt fit to break.

I was seated beside Cavarillos on the bow oar of the ponto on the first day of the fourth week when suddenly he grasped my arm. We hadn't spoken for several hours, just bending steadily to our task, and his action surprised me.

"What is it?" I demanded, nearly losing my grasp on the oar. A strange pallor had come over his dark countenance, contrasting oddly with the fire of his beard.

He gestured wordlessly to the sky, off to the south. A dark cloud about the size of a clenched fist was rising, moving toward us. It did nothing to answer my question.

"What's wrong?"

Clearly some of the others were considerably more knowledgeable in the ways of the sea than I, for already some of the sailors were engaged in stripping the sail from our mast. Cries to the gods rose from among us.

"It is the squall, the storm," he responded fearfully. "I have seen it destroy the ships of my homeland."

A chill gripped my heart. He had told me of the seafarers of the south, and their ships. Any one of which would dwarf the small vessel that was now carrying us to our destination. We didn't stand a chance. . .

The squall was upon us almost before we could react, darkening the sky, rain lashing the boat. We lost sight of the rest of the flotilla.

We took our helmets and began bailing water from the boat. They were the only containers we had. My clothing was plastered to my skin, water dripping into my eyes.

Cavarillos cursed and prayed alternately, clearly wishing himself elsewhere. As did I.

The storm had not yet abated when night fell, nor when morning broke the next day. The wind ripped at our tiny craft, water poured over the gunwales in a flood. My arms and hands felt like they were on fire, yet to cease bailing was death.

Day and night blurred into one, a dark void into which our vessel was cast. Several of our men had been swept overboard, dragged screaming to their deaths by the merciless waves. There was nothing we could do. We were all alone. Us, the sea, and the gods. Alone on the water.

An eternity later, one of the sailors cried out. For a moment, I paused, the helmet full of salt water still clutched in my raw and bleeding hands.

He was pointing, and in the darkness my eyes followed his outstretched finger. With an angry curse, I flung the helmet into the bottom of the boat. It no longer mattered. Nothing did. All our efforts had been in vain. The caprices of the gods had decided our fate long before we set sail.

Cliffs towered over us, mighty and high. The sailor had glimpsed the white foam of the waves breaking against the rocks. Our destruction was certain.

A breaker lifted our ponto on its crest, tossing us into the air. I glimpsed the look of terror in Cavarillos' eyes, fear on the countenance of a man who had witnessed countless deaths in his short life. The next moment we came down, slamming into the rocks. I felt myself falling, hurtling through space. Darkness. . .

When next I awoke, the sun was high in the heavens, beating mercilessly upon my exposed body. I was ashore—somewhere. . .

Every fiber of my body was aflame, my muscles wracked with pain. I raised myself gingerly on one elbow and looked about. The rocks I had seen just before the wreck lay exposed now, jagged pinnacles pointed like daggers to the sky. How I had survived was anyone's guess.

A body lay only ten feet from me, prostrate on the sand, the clothes stripped from its back. I staggered to my feet, grasping for the sword at my waist. It was gone, washed away in the chaos of the previous night.

I recognized the corpse. A warrior from my village, one of my boyhood rivals. As I gazed down into his dead, unseeing eyes, I remembered. We had fought over a girl once. Knives had been drawn, my javelin had been in my hand. The elders had intervened before we could do each other harm.

I had wanted to kill him, then. I felt nothing but pity for him now. He deserved better than this.

His wife awaited him in Erain, with the rest of the women and children of the tribe. The girl who put us at each other's throats.

The thought that once again she was a free woman gave me no joy. He was now nothing more than a comrade, slain by the pitiless designs of the gods.

He had deserved better.

"Cadwalador!" The voice slowly penetrated the haze that seemed to surround me, its tones strangely familiar.

I looked up. Cavarillos limped toward me, a ghostly apparition. He had apparently gashed his head on one of the rocks. What had remained of his clothes was wrapped around his head to form a bandage. In his condition, he looked for all the world like one of the *gaesatae*, the naked, drugged warriors who had so often served in the warbands of the Aedui. His sword was clutched in his right hand. There was no sign of its scabbard.

"Cavarillos!"

We embraced like brothers there on the beach, hugging and crying in the sheer joy of being alive.

"Have you seen any of the others?" he asked, pulling away from me. I gestured to the corpse that lay at our feet.

"Only he. And you?"

"I saw movement on the cliffs. Perhaps we are not alone."

I smiled grimly. "I only hope they are ours and not the natives."

"Then prepare, my brother." It was the first time he had ever called me that. Perhaps it was true, what the druids told us, how chaos, how *crisis* binds men together in a relationship unknown to any others.

I shrugged. "How? My sword was washed away."

13

Cavarillos gestured to the body of my fellow villager, in an instant reverting to the professional he was. "Take his. He has no more use for it."

I hesitated, glancing up through the morning mist at the rocks towering above us. There was something moving up there. Friend or foe, I knew not. With a quick motion I bent down and jerked the sword from my rival's sheath. Cavarillos was right. He had no more use for it. In a few more hours, I might not either. . .

Chapter II: A New Land

We waited, crouched motionless beside a cliff trail as the sun rose higher in the sky, burning away the fog that surrounded us. Had it not been for the determined look on my comrade's face, he would have looked quite ludicrous, stripped as he was.

However, despite his decided lack of armor, I had reason to pity whoever came to attack us. I had seen his skill with the sword evidenced back on the headlands of northern Gaul. He had taught me only a bare fraction of what he knew.

The sun was almost directly overhead when a pebble came rolling down the path from above us. Cavarillos tensed himself instinctively, the sound of footsteps following the small slide.

He looked across at me and nodded. My hand closed around the hilt of my sword. Sweat dripped down my brow and the palms of my hands were slippery as a new sensation gripped me. Perhaps it was fear, I had no idea.

The footsteps were moving faster now, there was more than one man descending the path. For all I knew, we were outnumbered.

I glanced over at Cavarillos, watched as his lips slowly formed the word *Now!*

He sprang from behind the rocks, his sword brandished high above his head. I was two steps behind him, moving swiftly to his side.

A surprised cry broke from the lips of the men on the path, then a long, quavering yell. I grasped Cavarillos' wrist before his blade could descend, recognizing the Aedui war-cry.

Tancogeistla stood facing us, his hand on the sword in his scabbard. Three of his bodyguards surrounded him, their bodies poised for the defense.

"Cavarillos," he acknowledged. I could see that he was searching for my name.

"Cadwalador, my lord," I introduced myself. It was the strangest of moments, Tancogeistla standing before us, surrounded by his bodyguards, his clothes still dripping of saltwater, Cavarillos naked save for the cloth wrapped around his brow, I with the longsword clutched unfamiliarly in my hand.

"I remember you," Tancogeistla said at long last. He spoke to his bodyguards, ordering them to sheath their weapons.

As we conversed with the great chieftain, we learned that his party had been swept ashore a few miles up the coast. He had no better idea where we were than we did.

But he was our commander, and so we followed him, encamping high on the cliffs. Days passed and more survivors appeared, arriving in various states of disarray. Several came in leading the few horses which had survived the disaster. Eventually, enough arrived to equip Tancogeistla's bodyguards. I was relegated to the *botroas*, to serve in the ranks beside Cavarillos. I had an idea that my stern friend found something humorous in my demotion, but he would never own it. We would march together from now on. The question was, march to where.

As it turned out we had lost almost fifty men in the storm, and almost as many horses. Many of my comrades in the *leuce epos* were drowned or missing, and those of us that remained were either made infantrymen or promoted to Tancogeistla's bodyguards. We now numbered less than two hundred men, little enough in this strange land we now traversed.

At the time of the next full moon, we set out for the north, having gathered weapons and clothing from many of the corpses which had washed up on the beach.

Several of the general's bodyguards rode ahead of our column, scouting out the territory before us. On the third day, they came galloping back into camp at sunset, their steeds panting and lathered with sweat.

Cavarillos was close enough to hear their conversation with Tancogeistla, and a few minutes afterward he came over to where I sat beneath a towering oak tree, laboring over a small fire.

"The scouts report a village ahead of us," he announced without preamble. "It's name is Ictis."

"Perhaps we can get supplies there," I said, gently blowing on the flames.

"Tancogeistla thinks so."

There was a note of uncertainty in his voice and I looked up in surprise. "You don't?"

"I believe they will show us nothing except the sharp end of the spear."

"Why should they? We are no threat to them. They have never even seen us before."

"Listen to your own words, Cadwalador, listen to the echo of your voice. They have never seen us before. We are alien, strangers. It is the nature of man to suspect what he does not know. We number less than two hundred men, but we are all armed. We are an invading army. How are they to know that we are alone, and not merely the advance guard of more to come?"

"Tancogeistla will be able to convince them otherwise."

There was no smile on the mercenary's face as he gazed into the fire. "I pray to the gods that it will be as you say. Until then, Cadwalador---make sure your sword is sharp on the morrow."

Chapter III: Dead Men Walking

At daybreak, we were up and moving. Breakfast was perforce light, consisting of a mere few handfuls of berries. Once again our scouts rode out ahead of us, cantering up the trail. I swung into step beside Cavarillos at the head of the *botroas*.

I had been marching for days now, but I still had trouble keeping up with his powerful strides. He glanced sideways at me as though to assure himself of who accompanied him. "Did you sleep well last night, Cadwalador?"

"Tolerable," I replied, surprised by his solicitude. It wasn't like him.

"Good," he retorted gruffly. "It's liable to be the last good sleep any of us get."

I nearly stopped marching, looking over at him surprise. "What do you mean? With any luck, we'll sleep with full bellies tonight."

"Luck is a fickle wench. Tancogeistla's been drinking," was his short reply.

"What? Where did he get liquor out here?"

"Ask the gods," Cavarillos shot back. "And while you have their ear, pray that they'll take it away from him."

18

I nodded, my cheer suddenly ripped away from me. I had seen Tancogeistla drunken before, back on the headland of Gaul. He had gotten into an argument with one of his subordinates and ended up killing three men before his bodyguards could restrain him. Just the man we needed to conduct diplomacy with the people of Ictis, the Dumnones, as they were called.

Just then, Tancogeistla rode by, as if an embodiment of our thoughts. Cavarillos was right. Our general's face was flushed with the fire of liquor and he was unsteady in the saddle. Passing the *lugoae*, the levy spearmen, he cursed their leader and ordered them to march faster.

"If he lives to see the end of this march, I will own that the gods are protecting him," Cavarillos stated quietly. "If he does not lose his drunken head to the natives here, he will insult one of his own men to the point of killing him."

"He is the anointed of the Vergobret," I replied hotly. "They wouldn't dare!"

"Once again, Cadwalador, hearken unto your own words. We are all alone here, far from the magistrates of the tribe. We may never see our tribesmen again. In this case, the men may decide that one as volatile as Tancogeistla is not fit to lead. A knife in the darkness, a sword thrust on the field of battle. That is all it would take."

I glanced into the mercenary's dark face, the man I called my friend. "You speak of treachery as though it were a light thing!"

He shook his great head slowly. "I have lived longer than you have, my brother. I have seen many men die, felt their blood run over my hands, watched their eyes as life fled them. We number scarce two hundred men. Are we all to die because of the foolishness of one? Or is it better for that one man to die that we all be preserved?"

I couldn't answer him. I could scarce believe what I was hearing. And yet his words made a strange, twisted sense.

The sun was directly above us when we arrived in the clearing before the village of Ictis. A small wooden palisade about the height of a man's shoulder encircled the small settlement. Behind it one could see the homes and buildings that housed its inhabitants.

Tancogeistla rode to the front, his bodyguard of *brihentin* or knights encircling him. Very few of them now were of noble blood, most being replacements from the night of the storm.

The king of the Dumnones, a man named Drustan, came out to meet Tancogeistla. He was on foot, surrounded by the champions of the tribe.

I heard our general ask him for food and supplies for his men. Perhaps Tancogeistla had sobered up since his morning binge.

"Why should we give you succor, since you come before our gates with armed men?" Drustan demanded. "Are not there more warriors behind you, to march in once you have spied out the land?"

Cavarillos tensed at my side, his hand going instinctively to the hilt of his longsword. "I pray you followed my instructions, Cadwalador," he hissed in my ear. "Is your blade sharp?"

I nodded silently, my eyes focused on Tancogeistla. The reply he gave would determine our fate. I silently asked the gods that he would be sober enough.

"A month ago, we were washed up on the shores of your land," Tancogeistla replied angrily. "We are the lone survivors of the wreck, yet you would turn us back in the wilderness to starve!"

"The lone survivors?" Drustan asked, his eyebrows going up suggestively. "Ten score of heavily-armed men? Nay, but to spy out the weaknesses of our defenses are ye come. Go find your food elsewhere, and get from my sight."

Tancogeistla drew himself erect in the saddle, towering over the Dumnone chieftain. I could see the flush of liquor upon his cheeks and he was unsteady on the horse's back. "If it is not within your will to give us food, then by the gods, we will take it! Fall upon them, warriors of the Aedui!"

His naked sword gleamed in his hand and he lashed out at Drustan before any of us could react. With an agility few would have suspected, the chieftain leaped back and Tancogeistla's blow fell upon one of the champions, laying the man's shoulder open to the bone.

Cavarillos swore furiously at my side. "He has done it! He has slain us all. See, Cadwalador, he has slain us all!"

As one man, our warriors advanced toward Drustan's bodyguard, to shelter our general. Seeing our numbers, he began to fall back, toward the gates of the palisade.

Waving his sword in the air, Tancogeistla swung his horse to follow them, but two of his nobles reached out and grasped his bridles, turning him away from the enemy.

It was too late. The damage was done. We could no more stop the battle which was to come than we could stop the chill winds of Imbolc blowing through the trees. Once again, Cavarillos was right. We were all dead men. Only our bodies didn't realize it—yet. . .

That night we encamped in the plain facing Ictis, preparing for the fight to come. Several of the nobles had counseled flight, but Tancogeistla, although now perfectly sober, was still adamant. We were the warriors of the Aedui, and we would remain where we were, stand our ground. Eventually most of the *brihentin* went over to his side of the argument.

"This is madness, Cadwalador," Cavarillos said as he joined me by the campfire. The flames danced into the night sky, casting strange shadows all around us. The number of our fires was pitiful in comparison to the light blazing up from Ictis. In the distance, torch-bearing runners could be seen hurrying through the woods, undoubtedly rallying the warriors of the Dumnones to the standard of Drustan.

"Tancogeistla actually believes we can win," he said a moment later, his tones full of disbelief.

"He was not appointed by the Vergobret for nothing," I said weakly. "Perhaps we can."

Cavarillos glanced across the fire at me. "Cadwalador, have you been pillaging the general's wine?" He shook his head derisively. "We have no more chance of winning than we do of taking wing like the birds. Several of the men are planning to run tonight."

"They are betraying us!" I cried, anger rising within me. My hand reached out for the longsword laying beside me. "Tell me who they are."

"I don't think I will," Cavarillos replied in a voice more amused than angry. His humor nettled me.

"Why do they run?"

"Because they are mercenaries like me, the merchants of war. A dead mercenary does not show up to collect his coin. It goes to another, just like his woman and everything else he possesses. That's not good business."

"Serving your country is not about business!"

His eyes locked with mine and all humor was gone from his voice. "These are not my people, Cadwalador. This is not my tribe. All of my tribesmen died in the mountains on our journey to meet Tancogeistla. This mythical country you speak of is but an ancient dream from the days of the Keltoi Confederation. Those days are gone, just as the men who leave camp tonight."

"Then why don't you go with them?" I shot back.

He shrugged. "As I said before, I am a businessman. Just as dying does not strike me as a good proposition, neither does running through an unknown land peopled by those hostile to me. There is safety in numbers, Cadwalador---even if those numbers are commanded by a drunken fool. Go to sleep."

I lay there for a long time as the flames danced high in the air above me, as Cavarillos snored noisily on the other side of the fire. I was seeing another side of my friend, and I didn't know what to think of it. Finally I fell asleep, there on my cloak on the hard ground. Deserters were not my problem, staying alive soon would be. . .

When next I woke, the sun was rising in the eastern sky, casting its rays over the camp. Cavarillos was stirring the ashes of the fire, apparently hoping to find some hot coals. Two fish lay at his feet.

"Where did you find those?" I demanded, raising myself on one elbow.

He smiled for the first time in days. "A stream back that way," he replied, pointing. "Our last meal should be a good one."

Just then a shout arose from the town. "What's that?" Cavarillos dropped the fish and sprang to his feet.

I was at his side in a moment, my hand going nervously to the hilt of the longsword at my waist. Before us, we could see the Dumnones issuing forth from the town, their warriors marching in formation.

Drustan was nowhere to be seen. Instead, a man rode out before them with a horn in his hand. "Hear me, outlanders!" He screamed, rising in his saddle. "Prepare to die!"

"He's not wasting his breath," Cavarillos observed dryly. He kicked the fire out and grabbed up his cloak and sword. "We'll fight on empty stomachs, Cadwalador. Perhaps it's just as well."

All around us, our warriors were scrambling to get ready. Behind us I could see Tancogeistla pulling on his armor as he called for his horse. The scene was chaos. We were encamped slightly below the town, and we knew without being told what would happen if the enemy charged down the slopes into us. Massacre.

The *lugoae* were already moving up to the ridge, their simple spears grasped in one hand. Cavarillos was gone, gathering his men. Together we ran to the high ground, barely a dozen of us. Thirty of the *gaeroas* moved into position behind us.

The enemy continued to pour from their gates, hundreds and hundreds of armed men. I tried counting the battle standards of the chieftains, but lost count. Cavarillos had been right.

The slingers began their fire from behind us, stones whizzing overhead to fall upon the bodies of the enemy. A number of the Dumnones had stripped off their cloaks and were completely naked as they marched against us. I had seen our own warriors do this, but it still unnerved me. They were completely without fear.

"What did I tell you?" Cavarillos appeared suddenly at my side. His javelins were clutched in his right hand, his longsword still sheathed. "We throw these first," he said quietly, reminding me of my duty.

I flushed hot, returning my sword to its scabbard and taking my own two javelins in my hand. In my excitement, I was forgetting the proper order of things.

I looked back to where Tancogeistla waited, with his band of *brihentin*. Perhaps they would be the deciding factor in this battle. The enemy seemed to possess no cavalry.

The slingers were taking a toll of the enemy, but I could tell it would not be enough. They would run out of stones before the Dumnones ran out of bodies to absorb them. Nothing would be enough.

To our left, the first enemies advanced, tossing their javelins into the ill-protected *lugoae* before charging home. I closed my eyes, hearing the sound of metal tearing into flesh, the screams of the wounded and dying.

"So the battle begins," Cavarillos observed quietly. He looked my way, a quizzical expression on his face. "Have you ever been in a battle, Cadwalador?"

I shook my head. "We raided a village—a year ago. It was just a skirmish."

"I see." His voice was studiously neutral, but I could tell he was hardly pleased.

A second band of the Dumnones suddenly appeared in front of us, charging into the *gaeroas* on our left. Once again the clatter of weapons and the shrieks of the dying filled the air. A new sound, hoofbeats to my right. Tancogeistla and the *brihentin* were circling around us. They were obviously planning to charge into the axemen that had attacked the *gaeroas*. Javelins slew several of the nobles even as they passed before us.

One could tell from where we were standing that our brethren were taking heavy casualties. The javelins seemed to tremble in my hand, as though they wished to bury themselves in the flesh of our enemy.

Cavarillos' face was impassive, unmoved by the carnage. Aloof. The *brihentin* slammed into the enemy flank, trampling many of the axemen.

For a moment, I thought perhaps they might succeed in routing the enemy army, in turning this debacle into a victory for our tribe. It was not to be. Their moment of glory was short-lived indeed, as yet another warband of our enemy descended, trapping Tancogeistla and his bodyguards.

We were the last uncommitted body of warriors. I glanced to Cavarillos. "Now?"

He looked 'round, saw the bloodlust in the faces of his men. Perhaps he felt our moment had come. Perhaps he merely realized he could restrain them no longer. "Follow me," he ordered simply, breaking into a trot.

We charged the enemy spearmen. I hefted my javelin in my right hand, hurling it ahead of me as I ran.

"*Rabo!*" we screamed, expelling the air from our lungs in the age-old cry of the Aedui.

"*Rabo!*"

My javelin caught one of the Dumnones in the arm, ripping him open. He lost his grasp of his spear and stumbled backward. One of Cavarillos' men was upon him before he could recover, nearly disemboweling the man with a single slash of the sword.

We slammed into the enemy ranks, swords drawn. We had never bothered throwing our second javelin. One of the spearmen tried to block my sword, but I knocked him backward. To my right, one of my brothers fell, his face covered with blood. I stepped over the corpse, driving my blade between the ribs of the man who had killed him.

A strangled cry rose from his lips, a strange, gurgling sound. His eyes seemed to glaze over, and he collapsed forward, his blood spilling onto my trousers, a dark red life-fluid. I pulled my sword from his flesh with an effort, raising it to protect myself as a blow descended toward my head.

The force of it nearly took me to my knees, but I recovered. I had lost all sense of what was happening around me. My world was now restricted to the few feet around me, which were filled with my enemies. We were badly outnumbered.

My comrades were dying all around me. We were dead men. I brought my sword's edge down on the wrist of one of the Dumnones, severing the hand. He screamed in pain, blood spurting from the stump as his shield fell to the ground. He tried to bring his sword up to block me, but I knocked it aside, ignoring the terror in his eyes. Another moment and he lay dead at my feet.

From behind me, I heard a long, keening cry of rage, resounding above the cacophony of the battlefield. A blade sliced across the bare skin of my back, opening a wound. I spun around, my longsword raised high. A boy my own age stood in front of me, a sword in his hand. A sword which was descending toward my head. I raised my shield to block it, but the force of his blow knocked me to the ground. I lost my grasp on the shield, rolled away to escape his next slash.

I saw his eyes in that moment of time, saw the hatred and agony there. Perhaps I had killed his father, his brother—none of that really mattered now. I raised my sword to deflect his, but he beat down my guard. I was losing for all the reasons Cavarillos had taught. Balance, mobility, I had lost both of those and now I stood to lose my life because of it.

I saw his eyes again as he aimed a final blow to my head, and I couldn't tell which fate was the more merciful. Mine, to die, or his, to live with the knowledge of his loss.

He screamed again, but in pain, not rage. Drops of something wet showered over me and I looked up. Cavarillos stood over me, a bloody sword clutched in both his hands. My opponent was sagging to the ground, nearly beheaded by the blow. I was covered in his blood. I staggered to my feet, starting to thank my savior. Cavarillos stopped me.

"Run for your life, brother!" he screamed in my ear. I glanced around. There were only four of us left. The *lugoae* had already broken and were running from the field. One of the Dumnones aimed a blow at Cavarillos and I blocked it savagely. My mind refused to believe this was happening. That we were losing.

Cavarillos took me by both shoulders and thrust me toward the rear. "Run, Cadwalador!"

I did as I was told, running for my life. It filled my heart with shame, but Cavarillos ran at my side, threatening to strike me down if I turned back. I kept running.

Behind us, Tancogeistla himself was fleeing, with only a few of his bodyguards remaining. They had been butchered.

Tears were running down my face, tears of shame and rage. Behind me, I could hear the cries of our pursuers, baying like wolves on the trail.

"Have the gods abandoned us, Cavarillos?" I cried. It was a stupid question, but for some reason, I had to ask it.

He struck me between the shoulderblades, forcing me onward. "The gods haven't been with us since we were washed ashore on this land! Don't talk—*run!*"

And we were all running, all those of us that were left alive. All the valiant tribesmen of the Aedui. Running from the enemy. Running in defeat. . .

How long we ran, I will never know. We ran until our legs ached, till the sun sank low in the western sky. Behind us we could still hear the cries of the pursuers. Drustan was a determined man.

Cavarillos stayed behind me, his sword still unsheathed. I glanced back once and caught sight of his face.

Saw the anger there, the bitterness of a man who had always played to win. And who had now lost. His bare chest was streaked with blood, whether his own or that of his enemies, I had no idea.

As night fell, we camped 'neath a towering oak, inside a dark forest. Perhaps we could rest there in safety. The night air was cold, reminding us both that *ogrosan* was coming. We dared not build a fire, lest the Dumnones spot it and come looking for us.

"I will kill him," Cavarillos whispered harshly, rubbing his bare arms to keep warm.

"Who?"

He shot an angry look toward me. "Tancogeistla, that's who! Next time we meet, I will kill him."

I looked away, into the darkness of the forest, hoping to avoid the conversation. It was a futile hope.

"Are you with me?" The question came sharp as a sword-thrust, his tones cold as ice.

"He is the anointed of the Vergobret," I replied weakly. "I cannot raise sword against him."

"The *Vergobret*!" Cavarillos hissed the title as though it were a curse. "He is not here. We will never see him again, nor your people. My tribe is dead. I am the last of my clan."

"Do you want their legacy to be that of a murderer?" I shot back angrily, regretting the words the moment they left my mouth.

He started to rise from his seat on the moss, then apparently thought better of it, his lips relaxing into a sardonic smile. "I should have killed him yesterday morning, before he had the chance to slay us all."

"How many do you think we lost?" I asked, trying to steer him off the subject of Tancogeistla's imminent demise.

"Fourscore, maybe a hundred, how am I supposed to know? I was too busy trying to keep you from getting yourself killed. And the first opportunity you find, you call me a murderer." He laughed humorlessly.

"I'm sorry," I replied, but my voice must have lacked conviction. At least he seemed to think so.

"I don't ask that you slay Tancogeistla," he went on after a moment. "Just help *me*."

"They are the same thing. If I help you, I am just as guilty as if I had plunged the sword within his heart myself."

Cavarillos' form came erect suddenly, and for a moment I thought he meant to fling himself upon me. Instead, he raised a finger to his lips and reached for the sword at his side.

"Quiet," he whispered. I looked quickly around us and suddenly saw torches flickering through the trees, the low hum of voices coming from perhaps forty feet away. The searchers.

We threw ourselves flat on the ground behind a fallen tree, watching as the search party went by. I counted fifteen men, all heavily-armed. They flitted along the forest path, moving effortlessly. Without doubt they were part of the Dumnone army that had chased us away from Ictis.

There was no question that Tancogeistla had played the fool. I knew that. But he was the *taoi arjos*, the "chosen superior" of the Vergobret. I would not—I *could not* have any part of a plot against him.

We watched until the men had passed, then Cavarillos grabbed my arm. "We can't stay here," he hissed. "Let's keep going."

I nodded, acknowledging the wisdom of what he said. My legs ached as I rose to my feet and I wasn't sure I could keep going. But there was no choice. . .

We kept going all through the night. How we did it, I have no idea, but about morning we met up with two of Cavarillos' mercenaries, the last survivors. They didn't know where the rest of the army was any better than we did. Their bodies bore fresh scars, the marks of a brush with a search party. Perhaps the one we had seen—I had no way of knowing.

Tancogeistla—for the moment he was beyond the rage of Cavarillos. We were all alone. We were fugitives. . .

28

Chapter IV: A Time for Choosing

Two days later, we ran into the remnants of the *lugoae*. They carried fresh weapons, the booty of a Dumnone search party they had overpowered. They added to our numbers. And more importantly, they brought news of Tancogeistla. . .

"Where is he?" Cavarillos demanded the moment they spoke of him. I thought for a moment that they would detect the anger in his voice, but they either did not, or ignored it deliberately. Perhaps they felt the same way.

"A day's journey toward the rising sun," their leader replied. "He waits with the nobles who survived, as well as a few of the *gaeroas* and slingers."

"Take me to him," Cavarillos instructed gruffly. I could see the look in his eyes, the look that assured me that Tancogeistla would die. I glanced away, into the meadows and fields that stretched before us.

A man would die, and I knew of it. A chieftain of my people. And yet to warn him would assure the death of a man I called my friend. I felt twisted inside, torn between what I knew was right and what I wished to do. The loyalties of tribe, and the stronger loyalties forged in the fires of battle.

29

"Cadwalador." I turned, suddenly aware that Cavarillos was speaking to me.

"Yes?" His eyes seemed to be looking right through me, as though he could see what I was thinking.

"You will march beside me."

I nodded. It was plain he wanted me where he could see me. And that was all right by me.

We didn't stop that night, kept pressing onward through the hills and valleys of this strange land we now wandered in. Cavarillos was pushing us like a man possessed. Tancogeistla was not far away. I looked on my left and right, to the men marching there. The last swordsmen from southern Gaul. Mercenaries. I had no way of knowing whether they were part of Cavarillos' plot.

If they were, I was outnumbered. If they weren't, I was outclassed still. There was no hope of my beating Cavarillos in a fair fight. I had no desire to. My only wish was to dissuade him from this mad plan that he had conceived, this plot to murder one of my fellow tribesmen.

By morning we had reached a ridge that rose steeply above the surrounding terrain. From its height, we could look down and see the scattered campfires of Tancogeistla. So few. The last of the Aeduan army. . .

"He is still here," Cavarillos observed quietly. I didn't respond. To answer in the way I knew he wanted would be to lie, to deceive a friend. To answer in the negative—I feared what would happen then.

I fingered the javelins in my hand. They were my one advantage. Cavarillos was not skilled in their use. If I could keep him at range—But I prayed it would not come to that. He was one of the few friends I had left. Loyalty to him, loyalty to tribe, to the clan of my fathers. . .

My heart sank when I saw Tancogeistla. He was sitting beneath a large tree, his back resting against its bark. His sword-arm was swathed in dirty, blood-soaked bandages, clearly the result of a battle wound. He had fought bravely, despite his drunken foolishness.

"Cavarillos," he greeted quietly as we came to a halt before him. Once again, he didn't remember my name, and I didn't expect him to. Cavarillos had been the leader of the warriors from Mediolanium. I was merely a foot-soldier.

"Is this all that's left?" Cavarillos demanded abruptly.

Tancogeistla nodded, clearly sensing the condemnation in the mercenary's voice. He was dead sober now. He nodded to the two nobles who flanked him, his bodyguards.

"Help me up." It was then that I noticed the bandages on his foot as well. They lifted him into a standing position and he faced Cavarillos.

"Let your men rest today," he said calmly. "We head north tomorrow. You can bivouac your men over there."

"My men?" Cavarillos asked, irony dripping from his lips. "All four of them? The four that survived the slaughter of Ictis?"

"I understand how you feel, my brother," Tancogeistla said softly. He was not a bad leader when he stayed away from the bottle. "I lost many good friends in the fight as well."

Cavarillos nodded, seemingly mollified. He turned and led us over to the place Tancogeistla had indicated. He stripped off his sword and scabbard and threw them on the ground, sighing heavily. The march had been hard on all of us, him not the least.

I waited till we were alone before I spoke. "You have abandoned your plan?" I asked quietly, hope in my voice. Hope that I would not be forced to confront my friend, to match myself against his skill with the sword.

He looked over at me, humor glinting in his dark eyes. "There is a time for everything, Cadwalador. Everything under the sun. Including his death."

"But he was nearly crippled in that battle!" I protested, keeping my voice down with an effort. "There's no way he can meet you!"

"So much the better."

"You would murder him?"

He turned on me, eyes blazing. All humor was gone now, replaced by a frightening earnestness. "Yes, if you choose to call it that. Else he will kill us all. His stupidity has already caused the death of too many." Once again I felt as though his glance was searching the depths of my soul.

"Are you with me, Cadwalador?"

My eyes met his, and in that moment I knew I had to answer him. It was a time for choosing, between the loyalties I held dearest.

I nodded slowly. "I will be at your side when the time comes. . ."

We rose at sunrise the next morning, falling into formation almost immediately. The foraging parties had been unable to find food, and I heard the men murmuring as they shouldered what remained of their belongings. I saw the *brihentin* helping Tancogeistla onto his horse. He appeared to be little stronger this morning.

Cavarillos seemed in unusually high spirits, despite the lack of sustenance. Another day, I would have been deceived into thinking he no longer harbored evil against Tancogeistla. But not now.

By the time the sun was high in the sky, we were marching northward, through rolling fields of tall grass. Several of Tancogeistla's bodyguards rode out in advance of the column, acting as our only scouts.

By this time, I was sure that the remainder of the *botroas* were with Cavarillos in his plot. I had seen them talking together earlier, a conversation which had abruptly ended at my approach.

Cavarillos apparently no longer trusted me. I risked a sidelong glance at him as we strode along, his powerful body moving effortlessly when other men lagged. His cloak had been lost in the battle and the muscles of his chest and arms were clearly defined. A formidable foe.

I thought back to the day we had first met, that day in the snows of northern Gaul, how he had stumbled in at the head of the army from Mediolanium. How in the months that followed he had taught me the use of the sword, striving to pass away the time.

I had never dreamed of needing to use that knowledge against him. As our friendship had grown, I had never thought that we would be separated so violently.

Early in the afternoon, one of the riders came galloping back in. He was a noble from my village, a calm, dignified man. I had never seen him so excited.

"There are houses ahead!" he cried to Tancogeistla, striving to get his horse under control. "A village!"

I could see the look in Cavarillos' dark eyes. The last village we had approached had been Ictis. His memories of that bloodbath were clearly visible.

I heard Tancogeistla demand the number of houses, the strength of the villagers. Clearly he was acting more rationally this time.

Before the nobleman could give a full report, however, another scout came riding in, his mount lathered with sweat. "We were discovered," he gasped, panting out his message. "One of the village women. She ran back into the houses before we could stop her."

Tancogeistla hesitated for but a moment. He knew, as we all, what had to be done. He turned to face the column. "Men, warriors of the Aedui," he began, raising himself in the saddle. "Before us lies a village of the natives. It is too late to go around them. They have already discovered our presence. The village is small and should not pose a problem to our army." He paused for effect, glancing at the weathered faces of the men he led. "In short, we must leave no one to carry word to the Dumnones. Kill them all!"

Tired though the men were, I saw the line surge forward, each man grasping his shield and spear more firmly. Men once about to drop dead from exhaustion now ran through the meadows, spurred on by the twin motivations of food and women. From the village ahead I could hear the shouts as the hapless villagers rallied each other in their defense.

"*Rabo*!" Our war-cry burst from the lips of the *lugoae* as they charged down on the defenders. I felt strangely sick. If the fight at Ictis has been stupid, senseless, then this was twice so. Only this time we were in the position of might.

I kept moving forward, as though lost in a dream. Cavarillos was running ahead of me, eager for blood. And other things, perhaps. He was a warrior, a man who lived for the fight. We were opposites.

I saw the sword of one of the *botroas* descend upon the neck of a villager, severing the man's head completely from the torso, sending it spinning into a pile of straw. A young woman, her hair the color of flame, ran from one of the houses toward the dead man, a high-pitched wail breaking from her lips.

The mercenary turned, the blood-red sword still in his hand. I saw him grasp her by the arm, a strange leer on his face.

I stood there numbly as he pushed the sobbing girl roughly up against the side of her home, wiping his blade on her garments. All around me the slaughter continued, but I could not hear it. The screams of the dying were a dull ring in my ears. My eyes were locked on the mercenary, on the girl.

He began to tear at her clothes and her sobs turned instantly to screams. I moved forward instinctively, barely considering the consequences of what I was about to do.

"Stop," I ordered in an unaccustomed tone of command, laying my hand on his shoulder. I didn't know what his reaction would be, I only knew I couldn't stand by. He would rape this girl and then kill my general. I could have no part of either. What had I told Cavarillos?

If I help you, it is as bad as if I had done the deed myself.

There was no difference. The mercenary turned angrily to me, lust glazing his eyes. "You can have her after I've finished."

He turned, ignoring me. My sword was unsheathed, carried in my right hand, down low as Cavarillos had taught me. I didn't want to kill him.

She screamed again, tears running down her cheeks. The sound galvanized me into action and I thrust my elbow into his ribs, sending him sprawling into the dirt of the street.

He rolled over on his back and lay there for a mere moment of time before scrambling to his feet, roaring like a wounded bull. My sword was already raised to guard myself.

I blocked his first thrust, frustrating him. He swung the longsword in a two-handed sweep toward my head. The ferocity of the blow took me off balance, nearly ripping my own blade from my hands. The point of his sword sank into the flesh of my forearm, which I had raised to protect my face.

I winced, forcing myself to ignore the pain, find the space Cavarillos had told me of. That strange state of mind where the combatant is no longer a participant, but the spectator of his own actions. I reeled backward into the side of one of the houses, with him following hard on my heels.

34

His sword bit deep into the sod of the house as I dodged the blow. I had reached it. It was as though I was above and behind myself, watching a dirty, bedraggled, bloodstained fighter carry out the dictates of my mind. Except that it was me.

I slammed the hilt of my sword into his cheekbone, breaking the flesh and perhaps the bone. He toppled backward, howling in fury. His blade was left stuck in the wall of the house.

He was defenseless, on his back in the dirt. The girl was still slumped where he had left her, maybe in shock. My blood was up and I followed him, striding down on him as he tried to roll away from my approach. An avenging fury.

The sounds of battle around me had faded to a low hum, punctuated only briefly by the screams of the vanquished and the shouts of the victors. It was he and I.

I glimpsed the terror in his eyes as my sword descended upon him one last time, lust replaced by fear. A crimson spray erupted from his body, spattering my clothes, bathing my sword. Sightless eyes stared back at me as I looked down on the corpse. One less in the plot against Tancogeistla.

The eyes I found myself looking into when I lifted my head were anything but sightless. I was facing Cavarillos.

"Can't you find a better way to occupy yourself, brother?" he asked, his face creasing into a strange smile.

He kicked aimlessly at the corpse as the slaughter around us continued. "He was a good man. I'm amazed you beat him." The smile vanished as quickly as it came. "All over a woman!"

The back of his hand came up like lightning, slapping me across the face. My head swam from the force of the blow. I could hear his voice dimly through the ringing in my ears. "Take her! Use her as you like. But never, Cadwalador, *never* kill one of my men again. I am warning you of this."

I nodded, striving to preserve my temper. The time would come soon enough. I turned back to the girl. She was sitting in the dust of the street, cradling the torso of the young man the mercenary had decapitated, tears flowing down her face. Whether husband or brother or lover I could not tell. Her language was unknown to me.

I took another look about the small village. Our men were out of control, looting and killing. I saw a man dash out of one of the houses, a loaf of bread in his hand. By the door he stopped, spotting a villager lying wounded nearby. He paused only to thrust a spear through the helpless man's belly, dispatching him. Then he was gone.

I reached down and grasped her shoulder. She fought against me as I tried to pull her to feet. "It's not safe here," I hissed, painfully aware she couldn't understand me. I'm not sure I understood myself fully. What had I hoped to achieve by rescuing her?

I bent down on one knee, sheathing my blood-drenched blade. Her eyes were a startling green, stained with teardrops. "I won't hurt you," I whispered gently, hoping something would get through. A glimmer of understanding flickered in her eyes and she slowly relinquished her hold on the body, allowing it to slump onto the hard-packed earth.

It was as we made our way down the street that I spied Tancogiestla. Afoot now, he staggered away from us sword in hand. He was singing wildly and swaying from side to side. Somewhere, gods help us, somewhere—he had gotten hold of wine. My heart sank within me and I looked back at the girl I had rescued. She didn't know it, but we were now all in worse trouble than we had ever been before. Tancogeistla was drunk again.

Chapter V: Consequences

The slaughter continued until nightfall and after darkness descended upon the small village I could hear the screams of the village women. I didn't even want to imagine what was happening to them.

The young woman lay huddled in the corner of the hut we had taken refuge in, curled upon her cloak. She wasn't asleep.

Who would be?

I crouched there by the door all night, my sword clenched in my fist. Once or twice I heard footsteps approach, but no one entered. No one tried to harm us. I must have dozed off in the wee hours of the morning, for I awoke to hear her scream.

For a moment, I thought someone had slipped by my guard and I sprung to my feet, ready to go to her aid. My bloodshot eyes slowly adjusted to the darkness and I could see more clearly. We were alone.

She was sitting bolt upright, her body shaking uncontrollably. Muffled sobs escaped her lips. A nightmare. Clearly reliving some of the moments of the previous day. I sheathed my sword and went over to her, gently wrapping my arms around her thin form. She didn't react to my presence at first, but I could feel her body slowly relax.

"Shhh. . ." I whispered, speaking gently, soothingly, as I would have to a little child. It didn't matter that I had no idea how to speak her language. Some things are universal.

When next I awoke, the sun was shining through the door of the small hut. Motioning to the girl to stay where she was, I left the hut. Viewed in the light of morning, the devastation was even more terrible. Flies were beginning to gather on the corpses strewn everywhere. The villagers had been massacred.

I found Tancogeistla and the *brihentin* on the edge of town, gathering the rest of the troops from their looting. Tancogeistla was still clearly under the influence of his drink and was cursing the troops as they staggered into formation.

Cavarillos was standing on the edge of the group, arms folded across his brawny chest. He smiled at my approach, his mercurial temperament once again asserting itself.

"Sleep well?" There was something suggestive in his tones. I shook my head, knowing what he meant.

"Where is she?"

"In the village," I replied. "I am going back for her."

"Why not leave her here?" he asked, clearly baiting me. I didn't like the look in his eye, the way he glanced over at Tancogeistla.

"You left no one else alive," I shot back angrily. "There is nothing left for her here."

"That's not entirely true," he retorted, amusement in his tones. He was always amused whenever I showed anger. "We left a few of the women alive, *but*—I'm afraid they didn't last the night."

I turned away, sickened by his humor. "You had better hurry," he instructed, still laughing. "One of the village men *agreed* to show us the way north. We will be moving soon."

I went back to the hut where I had spent the night and collected the few things that belonged to me. The young woman I had rescued sat motionless in the corner of the hut, her knees tucked up under her chin, eyes staring straight ahead. She didn't even seem to notice my movements.

There was no way I could leave her here. It wouldn't be safe. I wasn't sure taking her with me would be much safer, but I was beginning to feel a strange attachment to her, despite her aloofness, despite the barrier of her alien tongue.

Gradually, by use of signs, I managed to make her understand that we were departing, that I wanted her to go with me.

We picked our way through the ruins of her village, past the distended corpses of those that had been her friends and family members. I didn't wonder at her distance from me. I had saved her life, that much was true—but everything she had ever known had been destroyed by my people.

The noble warriors of the Aedui.

I spat bitterly into the dust. There was nothing noble about this, any more than the fight at Ictis. Slaughter. Massacre. We had been in the position of might, and we had never even stopped to question the justice of our deeds.

The two of us caught up with the column just as it was marching out. I spotted several of the men leering at the girl as we hurried past them to where Cavarillos was marching. Clearly Tancogeistla was not the only one drunk on this morning.

Our guide, as Cavarillos had sarcastically termed the prisoner, was mounted on a horse up with the *brihentin*. Maybe he knew the way, maybe he was just trying to save his own life. An atmosphere of butchery is a strange one in which to accurately judge a man's motives.

We marched for several hours, each step carrying us farther into country covered with rolling meadows of tall grass bordered by dense woods. The girl kept pace at my side, her face stoic. Each step carrying her farther from what she had known as her home. . .

Milk-white clouds drifted lazily across the sky, sunshine peeking between them. There was a slight chill in the air, but we hadn't yet seen snow. And it was quiet. Almost too quiet, the silence broken only by the step of marching feet. And Tancogeistla's drunken singing.

All at once the girl plucked at my arm. I turned suddenly, having almost forgotten that she was there. She was gesturing wildly, apparently trying make me understand something. A stream of unintelligible words came rushing from her mouth. I grasped her by both shoulders and tried to settle her down. Cavarillos had fallen out of column beside me.

"If she does not keep up, you will have to kill her," he stated coldly. "We cannot leave her to give word of our presence to the Dumnones. And we can't slow down the march just so you can have the pleasure of her company, Cadwalador."

I turned, angry, but the words died on my lips. I looked forward to Tancogeistla and the *brihentin*, saw the prisoner suddenly jerk his bridle from the grasp of one of the nobles, digging his heels into the side of his mount. The horse leaped forward, carrying him away from his captors with a single bound. It was a signal. Men emerged from the woods on our left, from the tall grass on our right.

The girl had been trying to warn me, something she had seen, something she had known. Cavarillos let out an angry curse, seeing the same thing I had seen. The battle standards of the Dumnones.

Our pursuers had caught up with us.

"What now?" I asked. Even with my recent mistrust of Cavarillos, he was a veteran. I would follow his advice. In this.

He snorted, calling to his fellow mercenaries. "Now, Cadwalador, we do what we should have done in the beginning at Ictis. We run." He sensed my hesitation and struck me angrily, shouting, "Leave the wench and run, brother! Now!"

I ignored him, reaching out as she took my hand. I had risked my life for her already. What was once more?

Our enemy was closing in on us from three sides. Out of the corner of my eye I saw Tancogeistla charge into the midst of the Dumnones, leading the *brihentin* in a display of foolhardy bravery. I didn't stay to watch the results, I had too many problems of my own to worry about. The path Cavarillos had taken was the only left to me. I took my javelins in my hand, leading her toward the gap.

Several of the Dumnones rushed towards me in an attempt to cut us off. I let go of her hand, drawing back the javelin until it was well back of my head, balanced in my hand.

Now! The shaft flew from my hand, flying straight as an arrow. It caught the enemy spearman in the left thigh, sinking deep into his flesh and twisting. He screamed in pain and went down. My second javelin found a resting place in the belly of his comrade. There was one more.

My shield was still strapped to my back. I had no time to remove it, but instead jerked my longsword from its scabbard with a quick motion, confronting the warrior. He feinted toward me with his spear, drawing blood before I could knock the shaft away. He countered my blow with his shield, nearly trapping my blade as it bit deep into the wood.

He hit me a glancing blow with the edge of his shield, taking me off-balance. His spear gouged a path along my ribs and I went down to the ground, hard, losing my grip on the sword.

I saw the same look in his eyes I had seen at Ictis. That look of triumph the moment before a kill. I rolled over on the ground, reaching for my lost sword, knowing in my heart I could never reach it in time.

I heard a scream at that moment, a woman's high-pitched scream resounding loud above the sounds of death all around me. My fingers closed around the hilt of the longsword and I looked back towards my antagonist.

He was holding his shield up to protect his face and as I looked beyond him, I saw the reason why. The girl stood not five feet from us, holding one of my javelins in her hand. She had screamed to get his attention.

The weapon looked strangely out of place in her small hands, but I didn't stop to think about it. I rolled to my feet, the blade in my hand. He heard me coming, started to turn. . .

I didn't give him a chance. All was fair now. It was a fight for survival. My blade sank into his side between his second and third ribs, driving into his body up to the hilt. He screamed, life leaving him as he crumpled into the tall grass.

I wiped the bloody blade on my trousers, motioning for the girl to join me. There was no time to thank her for saving my life. The Dumnones were closing in on all sides.

All around me our men were fleeing. Men once so brave in the slaughter of the villagers, now fleeing like rabbits. The *brihentin* had been massacred, pinned in after Tancogeistla's reckless, drunken charge.

We were defeated, not by our enemy solely, but by our own general. Wine was a mocker. And perhaps Cavarillos was right. . .

We ran for hours. It was becoming a way of life for me. Once I would have considered it shameful. The dead feel no shame.

The girl hurried along at my side, still carrying my javelins. Something had changed between us, something I couldn't place my finger on. She seemed less distant than she had been, as though the struggle had brought us closer to one another somehow. I was grateful to her for saving my life, but I knew no way of expressing my gratitude.

Night fell, and with it came the chill of the coming season. *Ogrosan*. Once, I would have prayed the gods that we reach our kinsmen before we were hindered by snows, but I had long ago lost faith in their power to save. The heavens were silent, deaf to our pleas.

I paused to strip off my cloak and give it to the girl, draping it over her shoulders to ward off the cold. She looked up at me in the darkness and whispered a word in her native tongue. It sounded like thanks, but I had no way of knowing. I smiled at her and pushed onward.

A chill breeze rustled through the trees surrounding us, raising gooseflesh on my bare chest. I forced myself to ignore it, as I had in the days of my boyhood, when I had bathed naked in the icy mountain streams of my homeland. It had been meant to harden me. Perhaps it had succeeded.

Ahead of us, I spotted the light of a small fire, flickering up from the mouth of a cave in the hillside. Something told me the Dumnones would not bother making such a small fire. Something told me that our men should not be so careless.

That left one option: Tancogeistla. I moved ahead of the girl, drawing my sword as a precaution.

The general lay with his back against a smooth rock, with several of the *brihentin* attending to him. I had no idea how many of Tancogeistla's bodyguards had survived. Not enough.

One of them glimpsed our movement in the darkness and called out. "Who goes there?"

"Cadwalador, son of the Wolf," I replied, advancing into the small circle of firelight, my hands empty. "From the army of Tancogeistla am I come."

The noble attending Tancogeistla rose to greet me. "Another sword is always welcome," he said, clasping me by the shoulders. "Only seven of us survived."

"None of you will be alive much longer if you keep that fire burning," I replied bluntly, surprising myself with my own boldness. "The girl and I were guided to you by its light."

I glanced behind me to see her coming into the light, advancing haltingly, as though unsure of herself. There was a haunted look in those beautiful green eyes, the same look I had seen in the wild deer, penned in by hunters.

I reached out to her, took her hand. She was trembling. The men surrounding us were the same men who had ordered the destruction of her village. I could understand her fright.

The noble held my gaze for a moment, then nodded. "We thought only of the health of the general. I did not realize."

"How is he?" I asked, aware that Tancogeistla was asleep.

"In no condition for the journey he must make," was the blunt reply. "His old wounds are bleeding again from his exertions and his shoulder was laid open to the bone. We were trying to keep him warm."

He turned away from me and quickly barked an order to the other *brihentin*, who immediately began to extinguish the fire, sending sparks flying into the night sky as they stamped at the flames with their feet.

I glanced around into the darkness. Seven men. Tancogeistla. Myself and the girl. Little enough. Danger lurked in the night, danger these men of the nobility knew not of. They thought only of the enemy army, the Dumnones.

But I knew. Another, a greater danger, was out there somewhere. Cavarillos. . .

One of the *brihentin* took the first watch of the night. I was to follow him, to stay on the alert for any enemies that might approach. I lay down by the smoldering embers of the fire, using the hilt of my sword to scrape out small hollows in the hard ground for my shoulderblades. That was another thing Cavarillos had taught me, in the days of our friendship.

I did the same thing for the girl and she stretched out beside me, rolled up in my cloak to keep warm.

43

I glanced over at her in the darkness, making out her slim silhouette only a few feet away. Stars twinkled through the canopy of trees overhead and she was gazing straight up at them. Stars which had shone down upon her people and mine for hundreds of years. Even for millennia.

I had a sudden yearning to know her name, a feeling, as though I would never have the opportunity to ask again. I rolled over on my back, longing to know how to ask her. The barrier seemed impenetrable.

"Cadwalador?" Her soft voice startled me from my reverie. For a moment, I thought I was dreaming. I glanced over to her to make sure.

She was propped up on one elbow, gazing earnestly into my face. A faint smile crossed her face as she pronounced my name again, hesitatingly, as though unsure of herself. She had a beautiful smile.

I nodded, tapping my finger against my chest, still afraid I was dreaming. She smiled again and a flood of words came rushing from her mouth. Nothing I could understand. But I had to know.

I pointed toward her. "What?" I asked, hoping my meaning would get through, that I could break the barrier that separated us. That I would at least know her name.

"Inyae," she whispered, smiling once more into my face. "Inyae. . ."

I reached over, clasping her small hand in mine and smiling at her through the darkness. It was enough, for now.

I rolled over on my back and went to sleep, two faces drifting through my mind as I slipped off. The smiling face of a beautiful, green-eyed maiden and the red-bearded countenance of a warrior. Two names: Inyae, and Cavarillos.
. .

I awoke during the night, something, a noise, a movement in the darkness that surrounded us. Something that didn't belong. Voices.

I raised up on one elbow, reaching out to where my javelins lay not a foot away. They were my weapons, fitting my hands far more easily than the still unfamiliar sword. The voices were coming closer, floating through the night. I recognized the voice of the *brihentin* who was to precede me on the watch. And another. . .

Cavarillos.

The sound of his voice struck a chill through my heart. I knew why he was here, why he had come. One reason and one reason only. Tancogeistla. . .

The nobles trusted him, they had no idea of his planned treachery. He would have no trouble. I rolled to one knee, gathering my weapons quickly, buckling the sword-belt around my waist.

Inyae stirred, throwing back the cloak which covered her. There was a strange look in her eyes, bewilderment not unmixed with fear. I placed my finger against her lips, motioning for her to remain where she was. I could only pray she would obey.

"You are welcome here," I heard the *brihentin* say. "We can use every good sword-arm. There's not many of us."

"How many of you survived?" I heard Cavarillos ask. A necessary question.

"Seven of us. A young man joined us just after dark," the *brihentin* replied, stirring the embers of the fire. "He is one of your men, I believe."

I could see Cavarillos stiffen, his face changing involuntarily. "Who?"

I took a step towards them, entering the small circle of light thrown by the reawakening fire.

"Here I am, Cavarillos."

"Cadwalador!" He replied, advancing toward me. "My brother. I feared the Dumnones had caught you and the wench."

His words were full of the same friendship I had known before. Yet something rang false. I couldn't lay my finger upon it. But I knew. The time had come.

He couldn't have helped seeing the javelins in my hand, the sword strapped at my side. As he advanced, I saw the glitter in his eyes, understood his gesture of friendship. It was a ploy. I took a step backward, my eyes locked with his. "I call no traitor my brother," I replied, taking one of the javelins in my right hand.

"Traitor?" the *brihentin* asked, coming up beside Cavarillos. "This man was the leader of the army from Mediolanium. He—"

He never got a chance to finish the sentence. Cavarillos turned on him with a quickness that even I never expected, drawing his sword from its scabbard and

45

disemboweling the man with it, one motion. The noble screamed and collapsed backward upon the hard soil, blood pouring from his body.

I drew back my javelin, hurled it at my friend, acting instinctively, without thought. The barbed head sank into Cavarillos' shoulder, twisting under the weight of the shaft.

With an angry curse he ripped the javelin from his flesh, tossing it away. He called to the two mercenaries with him, ordering them to kill the *brihentin*, just now rising from their beds. I looked back to where Tancogeistla lay, awake but helpless. He was my leader, my general, my kinsman. The die had been cast.

I dodged backward, ducking as Cavarillos tossed his own javelins in my direction. I could have taught him many things in their use, as he had taught me all my skill with the sword. I was glad I hadn't.

It would be little enough to save me. I caught a brief glimpse through the darkness as one of the *brihentin* fell, cut down before he could even grasp his weapons. Cavarillos had the advantage of surprise.

He was upon me before I could throw my second javelin. He knew my strengths and weaknesses just as well as I did. Perhaps better.

I jerked my sword from its scabbard, ducking his first slash. The advantages were all his. He still had his shield. I had lost mine at Ictis.

"I knew from the first that you would never stand with me, Cadwalador," he hissed, his blade ringing against my own. "You weren't fooling anyone."

I tried to ignore him. It was another ploy, a trick to throw me off-balance. He kept forcing me back, across the clearing, towards Tancogeistla. His attacks were relentless. He had never shown me the half of his skill.

His blade sunk deep into the flesh of my forearm, which I had tossed up to protect my head. A red spray erupted from severed veins, spattering my chest with my own life-blood.

I gritted my teeth, fighting against the pain, struggling to muster the force to meet his next blow. I was growing weaker. I saw one of the mercenaries fall behind him, killed by the swords of the *brihentin*. Tancogeistla's bodyguards, at first bewildered by the sudden attack, were rallying to my aid. It wasn't going to be soon enough.

His sword caught mine, clanging out with the clearness of a bell. I could see the look in his eyes. "You should have stayed with me," he whispered, twisting his blade suddenly. It wrenched the longsword from my grip, sending it spinning into outer darkness. There was no hope for me to retrieve it in time.

"I am sorry, brother." It was a prayer, a eulogy over my death. A death that had become as inevitable as the rising of the sun. A sunrise I would never live to see.

A blur erupted from the darkness to my right, a form flitting out of the night. Inyae. She threw herself on Cavarillos, small fists beating against his mighty chest. I grasped my final javelin, well aware I could never match him with the sword, even if I was able to find it.

She was a distraction, nothing more. A fly buzzing around his ear. A woman that had sacrificed herself for me. He jerked her around, pulling her arms behind her body, using her as a shield.

My javelin was poised to throw. He looked at me across her shoulder, that familiar, feral grin spreading across his countenance. "Go ahead," he invited me. "Throw it."

My hands trembled involuntarily. I looked into her eyes and saw the fear there once again, the terror I had saved her from once. His sword nestled against her throat, its blade still wet with my blood.

Time stood still. . .

Chapter VI: Treachery

My gaze lifted and I stared into the eyes of Cavarillos. The *brihentin* were still occupied with the last of his mercenaries. I was the only one who threatened him. But his cause was lost. And he knew it.

"I warned you not to stand against me, Cadwalador," he stated, a trace of sadness in his voice. "Together we could have achieved much."

"Treason is worse than death," I snapped back.

"All my life I have survived by choosing the winning side, going with it. It is the life of the mercenary. And I've never been wrong."

"Until now."

"That is your view. Now lay down the javelin, Cadwalador. Before I slay this woman."

I hesitated, and he moved the sword higher, until its tip pricked the skin of her throat. He wasn't bluffing. I knew him too well for that.

"Will you leave now?" I demanded. "I can let you go before they get here. Give me the girl and leave." I glanced over his shoulder to where the *brihentin* were fighting, bargaining with everything I had left. A lump rose in my throat, nearly choking me. If there was any way to save her, I must try it. She had saved me in the ambush.

He seemed to consider my proposition for a moment. "All right," he nodded. "Throw the javelin over here. *Under*hand."

I obeyed wordlessly, taking my javelin by the shaft and pitching it to him. He smiled as it touched the ground and released Inyae, shoving her toward me.

She had not taken two steps before he stepped up behind her, driving his sword into her body before I could cry a warning. She screamed, staggering toward me. I could see the tip of the sword protruding from between her ribs. It had gone completely through her.

I felt as though I was in a dream, as though when I had gone to sleep beside her a few hours earlier. When I had learned her name. This was all a dream. A sad, twisted dream.

In a haze I saw Cavarillos pull his blood-stained sword from her body and smile at me through the night. A death's head smile. The face of a killer unmasked.

She collapsed into my arms, sobbing with pain, her life-blood soaking her garments, staining my chest. Her breath was coming in short gasps, each one an effort. Her lungs had been pierced.

In the vision I saw Cavarillos spring to the back of one of the *brihentin*'s horses, straddling it bareback. He turned to wave a mocking farewell to me before vanishing into the night. A dark horseman.

I was crying too, with rage at my own foolishness, with fear at my helplessness now. She was dying, I could see it in the way her eyes were glazing over, the agony on her face.

Words came from her lips, but nothing I could understand. I had never been able to. Now I never would.

The nobles surged past me, their swords still drawn, past where I sat on the hard sod, cradling Inyae in my arms, to the place where Tancogeistla still lay. The drunkard she had been sacrificed for.

I looked down into her pale face, into the now-listless green eyes glazed with death. She lay still, her head lying limply against my chest, fiery tresses flowing over her shoulders.

Her spirit had departed. What remained was the shell of the woman that I had loved, the woman that had risked her life for me twice. And I had failed her. . .

A hand fell on my shoulder. I heard a voice through the mists that surrounded me. "Tancogeistla wishes to speak with you." One of the nobles.

I obeyed numbly, laying Inyae's corpse gently on the earth as I rose. But for the look of agony on her countenance, but for the dark-red stain of her torn garments, I could have imagined her asleep. With all my heart, I wished she were.

They had propped Tancogeistla up with his back against a rock. He looked up at me in the glare of the fire the *brihentin* had rekindled.

"Thank you, my son. I owe you my life."

I nodded wordlessly, striving to restrain my emotions. "But for you, he would have been accepted into my camp as a friend. And he would have slain me before anyone could stop him." He paused, seemingly to regain his energy before going on. The wounds had sapped his strength. "Three of my bodyguards died this night. The traitor Cavarillos stole one of their horses. I am giving you one of the others. You will ride in my bodyguard."

It was not a question, not a request. It was an order, reminding me of my station in life. He was the Chosen Superior.

"We ride tomorrow. First to rally what remains of our army, then north."

"Yes, my lord," I managed, still numb with shock. I glanced up into the sky, above the dancing flames, to where the silvery moon shone down upon us. Another eight hours separated us from the dawn. There would be no sleep for me this night, nor for a long time to come. It was all a terrible dream—but one from which I could never awake. . .

We rose on the morrow and pushed northward, joined by a few of the slingers and *gaeroas* that had survived. We were a small band of men, shadows of the once-great army that had been washed ashore what seemed like an eternity ago.

It had been months since I had felt a horse between my knees, and it would have felt good—if anything could have. I rode with my left arm wrapped in a sling, bandaged to stop the bleeding from Cavarillos' sword-cut.

Cavarillos. . .

·

We had seen nothing of him since he vanished into the darkness on that bloody night, riding a stolen horse. He might have joined the Dumnones, guided them in their pursuit. He might have fled to one of the other tribes that populated this wild land. There were a thousand possibilities.

We had buried Inyae at the spot of our campsite, along with the *brihentin* who had fallen. I still saw her, appearing in my dreams, reliving the last few moments of her life. Horror.

I had failed her. I couldn't get away from that. Failed her, and she was dead.

We rode north for weeks, slowed by the early snows of *ogrosan*. Foraging became harder and we slew the extra horse. The others would soon follow. It was them, or us.

Tancogeistla's wounds from the ambush were healing slowly. And he was still sober. I watched him from a distance, listened to his conversations with the nobles. I was not a participant in those conversations. I was merely his bodyguard, not his equal.

Some of the men were murmuring, whispering of mutiny. But they had nowhere to go. We were all equally lost, plowing through deeper and deeper snows as the weather turned colder. One of the men was found frozen to death in his blankets. His comrades ate his body.

I found some bugs under a rock, stripped them of their wings and ate them raw. I was too hungry to care.

One day Tancogeistla approached me soon after we had settled in for the night, sheltered from the angry north winds by a small wooded knoll.

"Cadwalador," he began. He had finally learned my name. I glanced up, popping a termite into my mouth. It had an unusually fruity taste, rather enjoyable in fact. Certainly there were enough of them under this log I sat on.

"Yes, my lord?"

He looked weary and cold. As were we all.

"Our scouts reported footprints in the snow to the northwest at midday. I need you to ride out and see if there are people in the area. One man will be perceived as less of a threat than the entire party of us."

I nodded slowly. "Should I find the area to be inhabited, do you wish me to make contact?"

51

"Yes. See if you can procure food and supplies, as well as the goodwill of the inhabitants. That will be essential."

"As you did at Ictis?" I snapped, speaking before I thought. Tancogeistla flinched as though I had struck him, but there was no anger in his eyes. Only a tremendous sadness.

"Their blood is on my hands, Cadwalador," he acknowledged after a long, awkward pause, holding those hands up to the sky and gazing into the palms. "Sometimes I think I can see it. That's what Cavarillos thought, wasn't it?"

His question took me off-guard. "Perhaps so—I really. . ."

"Come now, my son. You were his friend. You knew, else how could you have sounded the alarm that night? He blamed me for the death of his men, didn't he?"

"Yes."

"And he was not alone." It wasn't a question. It was a statement.

"No he was not, my lord."

"It must have been a difficult choice for you to make. Between your friend and your leader, between your brotherhood with him and your loyalty to the tribe of your fathers. Between a warrior who had taught you much of his skills, and a drunken imbecile who had led your army to destruction."

His frank self-appraisal took me completely by surprise. It was hardly what I had been expecting. "That is hardly my opinion," I remonstrated, "I have the—"

He cut me off. "It is the truth. I wonder at times, Cadwalador, if we will ever see our people again? Whether we are condemned to wander the rest of our lives in this desolate wilderness? I suppose only the gods know the answers to those questions."

I didn't respond. Telling him that I no longer had any faith in the gods of my people would hardly be diplomatic. I dared not abuse the sudden familiarity he had offered to me, strange though it was.

"And perhaps the people of this area," he added. "That is why I wish you to ride ahead."

"I understand," I replied, rising slowly from my seat. "I will endeavor to report back as soon as possible."

"I am counting on you, Cadwalador. Of all my men, your loyalty is unquestioned. That is why I chose you for this mission."

I nodded once again, taking my javelins in my hand and walking quickly to my horse. I carried no sword, had not since it had failed me that night with Cavarillos. I could not even see one without seeing a vision of his blade protruding from her belly. The image haunted my dreams.

Swinging lightly into the saddle, I took the reins in my hand and gently kicked my horse into a slow trot out of camp. What I found ahead would determine our future plans.

The wind whipped at me as soon as I moved out from the shelter of the hill, slicing through the thin, ragged garments I wore. I might as well have been naked, for all the protection they gave.

Soon my horse had slowed to no more than a walk, and I was unable to urge him to go faster. He was as exhausted and hungry as I was. His bones were clearly visible through his hide. I could feel them beneath me.

It began to snow, small flakes drifting down through the darkness of night. Whatever chance I may have once possessed of locating the tracks the scouts had spoken of was rapidly vanishing. If there had been any chance to begin with.

We wandered for hours, I and my horse. The snow was falling heavier now, accumulating on any surface that would stand still long enough. We were one of those surfaces.

I kicked my horse in the flanks, forcing it out of its languid walk. It had been full moon when I had left the camp, but all was white now, snow obscuring the moon, the stars. I had no guides left.

I was tired, incredibly so. And sleepy. So sleepy. I wanted to do nothing more than rest. Rest forever. Inyae, Cavarillos, Tancogeistla, the army; they were all a faint memory, fading from my mind. My mission, it no longer seemed important.

The reins slipped from between my fingers and I suddenly felt myself sliding, falling from the horse's back. I reached out wildly, losing my javelins. I hit the ground with a bone-rattling thud, feeling something snap in my lower leg. Pain shot through my limb and I sank back into the snow, gritting my teeth, fighting to keep conscious.

The snow opened up to welcome me, folding me in its pillowy arms. At first I struggled to regain my feet, but I found I couldn't. My leg was broken—at least it felt that way. Maybe it wasn't, but I no longer cared. Sleep. That was all I wanted to do. Lie back in the soft drifts of snow and rest. Forever. . .

Chapter VII: Rumors of War

I came awake slowly, dimly aware of an unfamiliar sensation that permeated my body, seeping even to my bones. It took me a moment to place what it was.

Warmth. I was warm. It was a strange feeling. My eyes flickered open and I began to take in my surroundings. I lay on my back on a blanket, only feet away from a small fire built within a hut. I started to get up, but pain shot through my right leg and looking down, I remembered. I had broken my leg. The snowstorm, the fall, all came rushing back to my consciousness. Someone had fixed a splint on my leg, straightening it.

Movement behind me. The form of a woman moved into the circle of firelight. Inyae. . .

Light fell upon her face and sorrow flooded through me as I remembered. Cavarillos, Inyae, Tancogeistla. That terrible night of betrayal and horror.

This woman knelt by my side and spoke gently to me. I shook my head, unable to understand her tongue. Where was I? How had I come here?

Her hand felt cool as she placed it upon my brow, apparently checking for any signs of the fever that often smote one so exposed.

She spoke again, but I could sense that she was no longer talking to me, but rather to another who had entered the hut behind me.

Another voice. That of a man. He moved into my line of vision, a tall, powerful figure, red-haired, but clean-shaven of face. Despite the weather, he wore only leggings and a cloak draped loosely around his shoulders. Strange designs were painted on his chest.

He spoke in the same language as the woman, apparently expecting me to comprehend. I shook my head in growing frustration. "I can't understand a thing you are saying!" I exploded, swearing in my native tongue.

The pair exchanged glances and the man spoke sharply to the woman. She disappeared behind me and I could feel sunlight stream in as she left the hut, closing the rude door behind her.

"Where am I?" I asked next, sensing something I had said had gotten through. I started to rise up, but the man bent down on one knee and laid his hand upon my shoulder, forcing me to lie back down.

"Wait," he said, speaking in Gallic.

I stared at him in shock. "Why—I mean, how—you know my language!"

He shook his head. "Wait," he repeated. For the first time, I noticed he carried my javelins in his hand. Apparently he was one of the men who rescued me.

"How did I come here?" He shook his head, apparently unable to understand my question. It baffled me. One moment he spoke my language clearly and the next he couldn't comprehend what I was asking.

The hide door behind me flapped open again and I could sense people entering, shadows thrown over my body.

It was the older woman and another, no more than a girl, maybe thirteen or fourteen years of age. She bent down beside me.

"I am Diedre," she said, once again speaking in Gallic, "a maiden of the tribe of the Belgae."

"Then how did you come here?" I demanded, interrupting her.

A faint smile flickered across her lips. "I could ask the same of you," she responded boldly. "But the Aedui are not unknown here." She went on before I could reply. "As for myself, I was taken prisoner in a raid by the Casse upon the mainland nine years ago. They sold me to these people in one of their trades north."

"Then you are a slave?" I asked, pity apparently coming through in my tones.

"I remember nothing else. They recognized the tongue you spoke as my own and brought me here to act as an interpreter."

"Who are these people?"

"They are the Calydrae, the tribe which controls the northern tip of this island."

"That's what this is?" I asked. "An island?"

She smiled again. "So say the druids. Everyone believes their word."

"What is this place called?"

"Attuaca. It is the chief town of the Calydrae. You escaped from the army that attacked here five months ago, didn't you?"

I was surprised, and apparently it showed on my face. "What army? What do you mean?"

Her dark eyes held mine for a moment, apparently trying to discern whether my surprise was genuine. "Five months ago, a small army came from across the waters, from the place where the sun sinks into the sea. They were led by a great, white-haired man mounted on a mighty horse. His companions were also mounted. They laid siege to this place, circled it round, demanded its surrender. A week later, the Calydrae sallied out against him, led by this man," she gestured to the man who had spoken with me.

"Who is he?" I asked.

"His name is Cinaed, the war-leader of the Calydrae. I sat by the wall as the battle was joined, and I heard the cries of the enemy army. It was the language of your people."

My eyes never left her face, I couldn't believe what I was hearing. "What happened?"

"Their leader charged his men directly into the Calydrae, cutting down many of our warriors."

"But he was outnumbered and Cinaed's men fought bravely, hamstringing many of the enemy horses and bringing their armored riders crashing to the ground. In the end, the enemy chieftain was surrounded by warriors. Blood poured from his body and from that of his steed."

I closed my eyes, the scene playing itself out across my mind. I could see it, images coming from my past, the sound of horses and men screaming in pain, terror. Pandemonium. My memories of Ictis, the ambush, that awful night facing Cavarillos. My life since I had come to this island. She was still talking.

". . . he fought on gallantly, slaying some of the mightiest men of Attuaca. His bravery was beyond question. Cinaed himself charged forward to challenge him and his arm was laid open by a sword-slash."

"And?"

She looked down into my eyes. "He died, the last of his army, surrounded by our warriors."

"His armor hangs on the palisade surrounding Attuaca. Cinaed ordered that he receive a hero's burial. That was the last we saw of them, until the men found you in the snow two days ago."

"Two days ago?" I asked in surprise. "I've been here that long?"

She nodded. I looked past her to where Cinaed stood, beside the woman I assumed to be his wife. "Do they know the origin of the men who attacked here?"

"That they were Aedui? No, I have only taught them a few words of your language. To my knowledge they have no suspicion. Just be careful what you say."

I acknowledged her words with a quick nod. "Can you interpret for me?" I asked. "I need to speak with Cinaed. I have comrades out there."

Tancogeistla arrived in Attuaca two days later, at the head of what remained of our army. The men were bone-tired, hungry. Had Attuaca been a smaller village, I would have feared a massacre like at Inyae's home. As it was, the clearly displayed weapons of the Calydrae served as a deterrent.

I spoke with Tancogeistla as quickly as I could without arousing suspicion. There was a strange look in his eyes as I told him of the men who had come across the waters, of the hero who had died before Attuaca. As though he knew something I didn't. . .

"Where was this armor the girl told you?" he asked, as I finished. I looked over at him, puzzled at his reaction. "On the town wall."

"Take me there," he ordered peremptorily. His voice was unusual, I almost feared he had been drinking again. But, no, his cheeks were free from the flush of wine.

I gestured toward my leg, wrapped tightly as it was with a crude splint. "I can't move. Not any time soon."

He cursed in frustration, acknowledging my injury. "I'm sorry. Where's the girl?"

"I don't know," I replied.

"Never mind," he retorted. "I can find it myself."

He stormed from the hut, leaving me laying there, my mind swirling with his reactions. There was no doubt in my mind about the identity of the army that had besieged Attuaca. They were my people, the army which had gone before us to Erain, the land across the sea. Had they been successful? Had they conquered that new land?

So many questions. So few answers. And now Tancogeistla. I didn't know what to make of his reaction. The armor. What mattered about the armor?

Night was falling when Tancogeistla reentered the hut. Deidre was kneeling by the fire, fanning the smoldering coals into flame. He extended his hands to the flame, his body shaking from the cold. His face was worn, I could read the strain of the journey in the lines of his brow. And something else was bothering him. . .

He waited until Deidre left, announcing that she would go get food. Then he turned to me, gazing down into my face as I lay there on the blanket.

"Cadwalador," he began. "I can trust you, can I not?"

His question took me by surprise. "Of course, my lord. With your life."

"Yes—yes, I know," he whispered distractedly. "You proved yourself on that night with Cavarillos. At great personal cost."

I didn't want the reminder. Inyae's death was still too fresh.

"And you will stand by me now, I know that." His eyes locked with mine, a powerful gaze. I could sense the magnetism, the charisma that had won him his position with Cocolitanos, his anointment as the Chosen Superior. Truly, he would have been a great man, save for the fruit of the vine.

"Yes, my lord."

59

"Cadwalador, I found the armor. It hangs near the gate."

"Aeduan?"

He nodded slowly. "And more than that, my son. Not just any Aeduan armor. It is the mail of Cocolitanos."

My mouth fell open. The shock. "The Vergobret?" I asked, unable to believe my ears. Our leader. . .

Another nod. "Our people are across the waters, my son. And that is where we must go, as soon as the snows melt. I must go and take my rightful place as their leader."

I had nearly forgotten. Of course. He was the *Taoi Arjos*, the successor of Cocolitanos. The reason I had stood against Cavarillos from the beginning.

There was a far-away look in his eyes as he stared into the dancing flames. "My people are leaderless now, Cadwalador. Scattered as sheep without a shepherd. I must go to them. . ."

Chapter VIII: Flight

The cold stretched on, vicious and unrelenting as *ogrosan* held the countryside in its dark grasp. There were days we never saw the sun, days of furious, blinding snow.

Tancogeistla was unbearable. I hadn't seen him this impatient since those days on the headlands of my homeland. It seemed so long ago.

Cinaed treated us kindly, but I knew he was suspicious. Tancogeistla's story of our shipwreck and subsequent journey seemed too improbable to be believed. I was hardly sure I would have believed it myself, had I not lived the horror. Still, we owed Cinaed our lives.

Spring came, and with it a wildly blooming purple flower that covered the hillsides surrounding Attuaca. My leg had healed almost completely and to exercise it, I took long walks in the hills with Diedre. On one such excursion, we walked to the cliffs overlooking the western sea. They made me think of the cliffs Cavarillos and I had huddled beneath on that first morning washed ashore. It seemed an eternity ago, but I knew that was just a figment of my imagination.

Diedre noticed my silence and mentioned it with her characteristic boldness. I shook my head. "Memories," I replied. "Just memories."

My eyes narrowed as I gazed out across the water, at a strange sight emerging through the mist. It looked like— it was a peninsula of land, jutting out into the sea.

I pointed it out to Diedre. "That is the land of the hero," she responded, speaking of the leader who had fallen before Attuaca. Cocolitanos.

My eyes fixed on that narrow spit of land—so close, yet so far. My people were there. I glanced over at the girl, wondering if she could read my thoughts. She was perceptive for one so young.

An unusual hunger rose inside me, a desire—to see my people, to live among them again. I had been a castaway for so long. Too much Aeduan blood had been spilled in this land.

Tancogeistla and I talked long into the night, in council with one of the *brihentin*, one of the last of the nobility. I felt honored to be part of such a council.

One thing was decided. We would split the men up into small parties, send them through the hills and forests looking for wood sufficient to build a raft. A raft we could sail across to Erain.

I didn't think it could be accomplished, but Tancogeistla was adamant. A strange fire had risen with him, perhaps another variation of the desire I felt, compounded by his knowledge that he was now the leader of his people. A leader who needed to return.

With my still-weakened leg, I was assigned no part of the woodcutting parties. Rather, it would be my job to occupy and deceive the man who had befriended us and spared us from the harsh blasts of *ogrosan*. Cinaed. . .

Over the time we had stayed in Atttuaca, I had come to respect and admire the leader of the Calydrae. Which made what I had to do all the more difficult. Still, if it would mean I could see my people again. . .

In the weeks which followed, I spent most of my time with Cinaed and his young warriors, matching myself against them in the use of the javelin. The accuracy which the Calydrae achieved stunned me. I was clearly not in their class.

But I was accomplishing my purpose, keeping them occupied. I accompanied Cinaed's son out on the hunt once, steering him away from our small groups of woodcutters.

Weeks passed. Looking up into the clear skies at night, I could see the moon grow full, then become dark. Two rafts were completed, but Tancogeistla felt a third was needed, if we were to carry all of us, and the remaining horses. They would be valuable in the new land.

The Calydrae celebrated the coming of the new moon with a feast, similar to that which some of the druids had observed back in Gaul.

I worried about the feast and the effect which the liquor might have on Tancogeistla, but he abstained, remarkably. He was drunk with something else these days— a fervor to return to his people, to take his rightful place as the Vergobret. And so no trouble arose from the feast. It was a blessing from the gods.

Two months had slipped by since the day I had seen Erain through the mists when Tancogeistla entered the small hut I had been living in ever since my arrival in Attuaca.

"We need to talk, Cadwalador," he announced abruptly. I gestured for him to sit down on one of the hides spread out on the floor, but he shook his head, glancing sharply at Diedre and one of the village women.

I rose from my seat on the earth, following him out into the streets of the village. Night was coming on, the sun sinking low into the western sky. "What is it, my lord?"

"One of the rafts," he whispered hurriedly. "It was discovered by the Calydrae. Smashed to pieces. We must leave at once."

I looked into his eyes. "Are two rafts enough for us all?"

"If we leave the horses, yes," he replied with a gesture of impatience, "quick, go spread the word among your comrades. Everyone must be at the top of the cliffs by the second watch of the night. We will set sail in the moonlight."

"I understand, my lord."

"Then, go! Quickly!"

I left Tancogeistla and hurried through the village, toward the houses where our men had been quartered, each of them with a family of the Calydrae. I was breathing hard as I ran from door to door, speaking briefly with our warriors, ordering them to depart as soon as they could without arousing suspicion.

A crescent moon shone down upon me as I continued on my mission, casting strange shadows over the town, flitting about me, each one of them a messenger from Cinaed, giving orders for our capture.

Tancogeistla and I had much ground to cover that dark night, but we managed, silently slipping from house to house, warning the men whom we had marched beside in our trek across this hostile land. Our brothers.

We were going home to our people.

It was an anxious group that gathered on top of the cliffs shortly toward the second watch of the night. Swords were unsheathed, held in sweaty palms, spears nervously leveled at every sound in the bushes. I clutched my javelins firmly, watching as several of the stronger men pulled the makeshift log rafts from the bushes along the beach. My leg was still too weak for me to be of much assistance.

Tancogeistla stood by the side as the rafts were launched upon the water, giving orders in his accustomed tone of command. No one minded tonight. His orders were too much in line with the desires of his men. They obeyed without question.

The work proceeded slowly, despite our best efforts. We had just dragged the second raft to the water's edge, pushing it out into the shallows. I had joined in the effort, leaning my shoulder against the raft and pushing as my bare feet scraped against the small stones that littered the shallow water.

It was just floating freely when we heard a shout from the lookout posted upon the cliff.

"They are coming!" he shouted, sprinting down the cliff path, fear giving wings to his feet. I turned and sprang to dry land, coming down on my bad leg. I fell to my knees in the sand, grabbing for the javelins I had laid aside. Tancogeistla shouted orders, drawing up his men in line of battle across the bottom of the path. Had we been facing swordsmen, I was sure we could have held men off on that path for hours, used it to bottleneck the Calydrae. But—I remembered their skill with javelins, and they would be throwing downhill. Flight was the only option left to us.

A body of torch-bearing horsemen appeared at the edge of the cliff, looking down upon us. A tall man with flame-red hair was at their head. I recognized Cinaed in the torchlight.

"Tancogeistla!" he called, his voice carrying far across the waters.

"Yes?" our king replied, standing in line with the dismounted *brihentin*, what remained of his retainers. I stood at his side, my javelins readied. After they were exhausted, I determined, I would grab a spear from the first man who fell. If I was not already dead.

"I wish to come down and speak with you," Cinaed retorted, swinging from the back of his horse onto the ground above us.

"You may come," Tancogeistla grudgingly assented, "but come alone."

"These many months, I have taken you into my village, fed you over the dark months, spared your lives. And now you treat me as an enemy?"

Cinaed had disappeared, but I could hear footsteps along the path coming toward us. After a few tense moments, he reemerged, standing in front of our line.

He stood before us unarmed, his scabbard empty, his javelins left behind somewhere on the clifftop. It was a gesture of trust I wasn't expecting.

"What has happened, my friend?" he asked, staring Tancogeistla in the eye. "I treated you all as my guests, yet you flee as thieves in the night."

Tancogeistla looked down at the ground for a moment. I could tell he was thinking. "A messenger came from my people at the time of the new moon," he lied glibly. "He brought word that our king is dead. I have been chosen to succeed him. We go now to rejoin our people."

Cinaed looked past our battle-line to where the rafts floated sluggishly in the shallows. "Why go by way of the sea? Did you not tell me that your people lived far away, on the main land to the south of this island?"

"Yes," Tancogeistla agreed, "but I also told you of the battles we fought with the tribes of the Dumnones. To pass their way again would be certain death."

"I understand," Cinaed replied, "however there was no reason for this stealth."

"You will make no effort to stop us?"

The chieftain of the Calydrae shook his head. "We destroyed the raft my young men found because we believed it had been left by the invaders we defeated months ago. Had I known it was yours I would have left it unharmed. Indeed, my brother, why should I try to stop you?" Merriment twinkled in Cinaed's eyes. "Every man of you that leaves is one less my people have to house."

"I thank you for your hospitality," Tancogeistla responded, honestly, I believe. Then we turned and began loading our weapons and what remained of our supplies onto the rafts. Cinaed sent some of his men back to the village for food with which to feed us on our journey. His generosity truly stunned me, and once again I felt a twinge of guilt for the deception we were perpetrating.

We did not get underway until shortly before dawn. We poled south, sticking close to the direction of our story until we were reasonably sure to be beyond the gaze of any watchers, then we turned west, propelling ourselves with crude homemade oars. To . To the new land of our people. To the land across the waters. . .

It is a rule of life. Things are always harder than they seem. What seems so close to the eye proves far to the feet, or the hands, as it proved in our case. The land that I, and the others, had seen from the cliffs of Attuaca, proved farther than we could have imagined.

Days passed as we rowed steadily over the waters separating us from Erain. Blisters formed on our hands and burst, causing great pain, only alleviated by slowly forming calluses. But I heard no word of complaint from the men. Each stroke of the oars brought us closer to rejoining our families. Each stroke brought us that much closer to ending our wanderings.

For eight days we rowed, aided by a patchwork sail we had made of the remaining clothes we had brought with us. There was little wind, perhaps a blessing in disguise. How our rafts would have fared in a storm, I shivered to think.

On the morning of the ninth day, the shoreline was close enough for us to descry the trees and lush green hills of this new land. It was everything the druids had described. Beautiful, I cannot create words to describe it. I only wished

66

that Inyae sat there beside me. As little as I had known of her before her murder, I felt she would have loved Erain. Perhaps that explained the strange pang I had felt leaving Attuaca, the island upon which we had wandered for so long.

By leaving the island, I was also leaving behind my last chance of revenging myself upon Cavarillos, slim though that chance had been.

His face still appeared before me in dreams, that last taunting smile of his as he disappeared into the night. The embodiment of evil.

One of the *gaeroas* came to relieve me at my oar and I went to the back of the raft, dropping down beside Tancogeistla. His eyes were focused on the hills before us.

"Just a little while longer, Cadwalador. Just a little while longer, and I will be the Vergobret of our people. The chief magistrate."

I nodded wordlessly, following his gaze, taking in the beauty of the place. He continued, apparently not noticing my silence. Or ignoring it. "I will not forget what you did for me that night, Cadwalador. You sacrificed much for honor. I will not forget, and neither will the gods."

"That is unnecessary, my lord," I replied. There was no way I wanted to accept rewards for an action I had long since regretted. The price of doing something I had felt was right. That would never restore Inyae to my side.

We touched the shores of Erain that night, built a fire on the sandy beach we landed upon. After the chill nights at sea, the warmth seemed to penetrate to my very bones. I looked around at my companions, thinking back to our embarkation on the headlands of Gaul so many months ago. This small band was all that was left.

A few of the *iaosatae*, the slingmen, remained. Old men and young, all skilled in the use of their weapons. A force not to be scorned.

The last of the *gaeroas*, the spearmen from Mediolanium that had accompanied Cavarillos northward.

And those of us who belonged to Tancogeistla's bodyguard, a few of the nobles and the rest of us freemen like me, who had been promoted to his side by virtue of some action on the field of battle, or because of the sheer need for his protection.

They looked little like they had when we had departed from Gaul, as they huddled around the fire, struggling to get warm. A rag-taggle band of warriors who had survived against incredible odds. In a strange way, I was honored to have been a part of it.

Morning came, and we were up with the dawn, marching after a perforcedly light breakfast of fish caught from the sea and berries plucked from bushes on the nearby hills.

We came upon a small village shortly after noon, surprising a man planting barley in the field. He attempted to run, but one of the fleet young slingers chased him down and brought him back to Tancogeistla.

The man struggled and twisted in the slinger's grasp, cursing us all in his native tongue, until the king spoke to him.

The expression on his face changed suddenly and he fell to the ground on his knees before Tancogeistla, still jabbering away.

"What is it, man?" Tancogeistla demanded, shaking the fellow angrily. He did not seem to understand, just kept up his endless chatter.

I glanced at the king and he met my gaze. "Take him under charge. We must be moving on."

I stepped forward and dragged the man to his feet, pushing him before me as we marched on, toward the village we could glimpse through the distant trees. I could sense the tension in the men around me, could feel it pulsating through my own body. Our captive had heard the Aeduan tongue before, even if he couldn't understand it.

We were at the end of our trail. Or, were we? Had our people taken this land as conquerors, or been repulsed in their invasion? Would we be welcomed, or driven into the wilderness? The next few minutes could answer all of this.

Spurred on by our growing excitement, we double-marched our tired bodies down the small path into the village. Men and women ran out of the houses to greet our procession with amazement and awe. Yet I saw no weapons in their hands.

Then I saw a door open from a slightly larger house at the end of the dusty village street. A man stepped out and strode toward us as Tancogeistla drew our column up in the middle of the street.

His walk was familiar to me, something about it. And his face, although slightly more aged than once I had known it.

"Berdic!" I called out, releasing my prisoner and running toward him. His mouth dropped open in surprise.

"Cadwalador?" he asked. "Is that really you?"

"In the flesh," I laughed, almost giddy with joy. I slapped my boyhood playmate on the back and hugged him close.

"Where did you come from?" he demanded, returning my embrace.

"It's too long of a story," I replied. "But, tell me, did our invasion succeed?"

"Succeed?" He threw back his head and laughed, his own good humor matching my own. "I am now the chieftain of this village. The cities of the Goidils are in our hands. We own Erain. It was more than a success, Cadwalador. It was glorious. I wish you could have shared it with me."

"So do I, my friend." Tancogeistla stepped up behind me and cleared his throat impatiently.

"My lord," I began, "I wish you to meet a boyhood friend of mine, Berdic."

My old friend was staring past my shoulder at the king. "Tancogeistla?"

"Yes," he replied gruffly. "What are you staring at, lad?"

Berdic shook his head. "I guess you would not have heard. . ."

"Of the death of Cocolitanos?" Tancogeistla asked. When Berdic nodded, he went on. "Of course. That is why I have returned, to take my rightful place at the head of my people."

The village chieftain turned away from us momentarily, as though trying to absorb what Tancogeistla had just said.

"That is not what I meant, my lord. You see— Malac reigns in Ivernis. . ."

Chapter IX: Erain

I stared at Berdic, unable to speak, unable to move. It was too much to comprehend. We had reached the end of the road, only to find that it was just the beginning.

Tancogeistla was the first to react, springing upon Berdic with the ferocity of a bear, slamming my old friend into the side of a village house. "What did you say?" he screamed, his hands around Berdic's throat. "What do you mean, Malac reigns? I am the Vergobret! I was the anointed of Cocolitanos!"

I reached Tancogeistla in another moment and grabbed him by the shoulder, pulling him off Berdic with the assistance of one of the *gaeroas*.

The villagers were gathering, stunned by the assault on their chieftain. Something had to be settled and settled quickly. I stepped between Berdic and Tancogeistla. "I am sorry, my friend. Your news came as a shock to us all."

My old playmate stood aright slowly, rubbing his sore throat. "I understand," he wheezed, still trying to get his wind back. He stepped past me and spoke a few words to his village in their language. Whatever he said, they dispersed quickly.

Berdic looked back at me and Tancogeistla. "I am sorry. Cocolitanos always held out hope that you would return. He was the only one. When he died across the sea, Malac took the throne with no one to stop him."

"Where was Dennoros?" Tancogeistla asked, speaking of his younger brother.

"He died in the beginning, trying to break the Goidilic army at the siege of Ivernis."

Tancogiestla turned away, a faint hint of sadness visible in his eyes. He would never show emotion in front of his men.

"He did not die in vain, my lord," Berdic went on awkwardly. "His charge turned the tide of the battle."

"Where is the nearest settlement?" Tancogeistla demanded abruptly, color coming back into his face. Berdic looked surprised at the sudden change.

"Three days journey," he replied. "The town of Emain-Macha. Why?"

The general looked back at me, at the men who had followed him, stayed true to him through the agonies of our journey. "There are those who will follow where I lead. Even to the throne."

Berdic shook his head. "It is no use, my lord. Malac has the council, the magistrates behind him. You would stand no chance."

Tancogeistla transfixed him with a hard glance. "If you would ever succeed in anything you set your hand to, then strike these words from your speech. *Never* and *no chance*. Cocolitanos is dead. Dennoros is dead. But *I* still live. And I will reign." He raised his voice, addressing all of us. "We will spend the night in this village. Tomorrow we march to Emain-macha. Tomorrow we set out to take the throne. . ."

Berdic had been optimistic in his prediction. Our men were footsore and weary, and it took us a week to reach Emain-macha. I was frankly overawed as we entered its gates. The one-time capital of the Goidils, it was an amazing place. Men hurried through its streets, going about their business. I had not seen such a populace since the day my father had taken me into Bibracte to trade when I was a boy.

From the gates, we could look north and see the holy hill of Teamhaidh, a place of worship for not only the

Goidils but for Celts from all over the world. I thought of the gods we worshiped, the gods whom I had forsaken in the wastes of the island we had come from. Perhaps living in the shadow of such a holy shrine would restore my faith. I doubted it.

Tancogeistla tried to rally support to his cause from the moment he arrived, but the results were lackluster. Apparently, Malac had already killed several nobles who had opposed him, had them executed on trumped-up charges.

Still, the charisma that had endeared my general to Cocolitanos was showing to full effect, and for a few short days, I thought we had a chance. I should have known better.

One of the detriments of our return to civilization. Tancogeistla's reaquaintance with the bottle. For several nights, his affinity for the bottle stood him in good stead as he frequented the taverns and alehouses, gathering support among some of the warriors who had been involved in the conquest of Erain. A good speaker when sober, he waxed eloquent under the influence of wine, swaying his equally-drunken audience with the power of his words. But it was not without its downside, and that was equally quick in coming.

He became short with subordinates and fellow nobles alike, alienating many of those who had pledged their support in the midst of their own drunkenness.

And then it all came to an end. Malac arrived in Emain-Macha. . .

It happened one night, three weeks from the day of our arrival in the city. I was standing in the gate of the tavern, listening to Tancogeistla's speech. He was already deep into it.

A shout in the street caught my attention, swelling and growing louder. Cheers. The tramp of horses. I ran from the gate just in time to see Malac riding slowly down the street towards me, flanked by several score of *brihentin*, clad in full armor. Malac himself wore a breastplate of elaborately woven mail, but no helmet, his red hair tousled by the wind. A sword was buckled to his side.

I left my post and hurried into the tavern, grabbing Tancogeistla by the arm. "Malac is coming," I whispered fiercely. "We need to leave. Quickly!"

He pulled away from me with a drunken growl. "Do you hear that, my people?" he demanded, raising his voice so that all in the tavern could listen. "The old woman who calls himself your leader is coming! Coming to die—by my hand! Let us arise and take our weregild this night!"

He jerked his longsword from its scabbard and unbuckled the scabbard from around his waist, tossing it into the corner of the tavern. I watched the reaction of his listeners. Drunk though they were, the mere mention of Malac's name had an incredibly sobering effect on them. I watched several get from their seats and hurry out, lurching toward the door. Fear was in everyone's eyes. And I knew there was no one that would stand with Tancogeistla, despite all their promises.

I tugged at his arm again, begging him to leave, to save himself. He *was* the rightful leader of my people, and dying here would end his bid for the throne.

He swung on me, fury in his blood-shot eyes. "Would you too betray me?" The hilt of his sword caught me on the tip of my chin and my head snapped back. I was falling. I felt myself hit the floor. My world was spinning, dark and sparkling. Dimly I heard Tancogeistla's drunken shouting, heard a crash as the tavern door came flying inward, the tramp of Malac's bodyguards. Then everything faded away. Darkness. . .

My eyes flickered open as I slowly returned to consciousness. I was still lying on the floor of the tavern, but this time sun was streaming through the window above me. I had no idea how long I had been there. I tried to rise, but a hand was on my shoulder.

Berdic's voice. "I wasn't sure you were going to come out of that, Cadwalador." He sounded worried.

I sat up quickly. "Where's Tancogeistla? What happened?"

"They took him away," he replied.

"Malac?"

He nodded wordlessly.

"How did it happen?"

"Malac's bodyguards stormed the tavern. There was not a man to stand with Tancogeistla. They all scattered like sheep. The general stood alone, fighting bravely until the sword was knocked from his hand. Then Malac took him prisoner. I imagine he will be executed, just like the others."

I closed my eyes, envisioning those last few moments before I lost consciousness. "I tried to stop him," I whispered futilely. "I tried to get him away from here before Malac came."

Berdic reached out and took my hand, helping me stand aright. I was still dizzy and wobbled as I walked. "Come with me, Cadwalador. You can find a home in my village. There is still a future."

A shadow was cast across the doorway as a figure clad in chain mail entered. It was one of the *brihentin* I had seen in Malac's retinue the night before.

He looked back and forth between Berdic and I, then his eyes settled on me. "Come with me," he ordered, beckoning. "Malac wishes to speak with you."

Berdic looked at me and I saw my own fear reflected in his eyes. A summons from Malac was anything but good news.

We found the Vergobret encamped outside Emain-Macha, beneath a spreading oak. Berdic and I followed the *brihentin* into the encampment. Berdic unstrapped his sword-belt and left it at the entrance. I had no weapons save the dagger concealed in the waistband of my leggings. I left it where it was.

Malac looked up at our approach. He was a tall, finely built man with orange-red hair falling about his neck, a neatly-trimmed mustache of the same color gracing his visage. Ruthlessness emanated from his gaze as he glanced into my eyes.

"Good morning, my son. Cadwalador, I believe is your name," he smiled. I replied with a silent nod.

"You were with the castaways of Tancogeistla?" He asked, his eyes locking with mine.

"Yes, my lord."

He indicated a seat beneath the tree. "Have a seat. I want to hear your story." I glanced over at Berdic before obeying. There was bewilderment in his eyes. Neither of us had expected this.

I took the seat as he had ordered and began my tale from the day we had set sail from the headlands of Gaul, leaving out only the plot of Cavarillos against Tancogeistla.

74

I intended to give Malac nothing that he could use against me. Tancogeistla might already be dead. I had no intention of going to my own grave to protect his drunken memory.

I talked for what must have been an hour or more, with Malac listening patiently. But as I told of our arrival at Attuaca, the Vergobret held up his hand to stop me. "This mercenary you spoke of—Cavarillos, I believe you said. What became of him?"

I hesitated only a moment. "He fell in the ambush of the Dumnones, my lord," I lied. "Fighting as only a warrior of Gaul can."

The words were bitter in my mouth, but I forced them out with an effort. Unbidden, Cavarillos' face rose in my mind's eye, that last moment before he had disappeared into the night. I closed my eyes as if to shut out the image.

"You were close friends?" Malac asked, apparently misinterpreting my face.

I nodded with an effort, forcing myself to deceive the usurper once again. "Go on," he said after a moment, and I continued my story, this time telling it as it was, from Attuaca until our coming unto Emain-Macha three weeks before.

"And your loyalties in this matter?" Malac demanded after I had finished. I looked into his eyes.

"My lord?"

"Do not pretend ignorance!" he snapped with a sudden show of anger. "You know what I mean. Tancogeistla—you followed him for months. Would you still draw sword for him?"

"I draw sword for no man," I replied truthfully. "I have seen enough blood spilled to last me for a lifetime. The life of a warrior is not one I desire to follow." It was clear enough that I was dodging his question and I continued before he could interrupt. "I followed and stood with Tancogeistla because I believed he was my rightful leader. I will follow any man who commands that position. You are the Vergobret."

He smiled, and once again his visage was full of cunning and deceit. "Cocolitanos knew. He knew that Tancogeistla's drink would be his undoing," he chuckled. "He tried to kill you last night—did you know that?"

I shook my head "no". All I remembered was him striking me with the hilt of his sword.

75

Malac nodded. "You—one of his most faithful followers. Only the entrance of my men into the tavern kept him from driving his blade through your belly."

I listened quietly, uncertain whether I should believe him. His objective was clear—to separate me from any remaining loyalties to Tancogeistla, but his words held the ring of truth. I thought back to the headlands of Gaul, when I had seen my general kill three men in a drunken brawl. In the power of liquor, he was capable of anything. I knew that. But I didn't want to believe this, that this was the end of the journey, the end of the man Inyae had been sacrificed for. I still saw her face in my dreams. Time had healed nothing.

Malac was speaking again. ". . .if you desire not the path of the warrior, then what are your plans?"

I wasn't sure I had heard him correctly. "My lord?"

He waved his hand impatiently. "What life do you plan to follow here in Emain-Macha?"

I shook my head. "I have given it very little thought, my lord. My days have been busy since my arrival. Perhaps. . .before our migration I worked in a gobacrado, as an assistant," I replied, thinking of my brief apprenticeship with the smith.

"Then return to that work," he replied, rising to indicate that our interview was at an end. Berdic and I rose as well.

"I thank you, my lord," I acknowledged, bowing low. The *brihentin* which had fetched me from the town returned and escorted the two of us to the edge of the encampment and bade us farewell.

My survival surprised me. Even more surprising was the lack of joy it brought me. I knew nothing of the fate of Tancogeistla, the rightful leader of my people. I had bowed and scraped before an impostor to save my own life.

But the dead can accomplish nothing. . .

Chapter X: Clouds of War

I went to work as Malac had instructed, in a gobacrado, or smithy. As the months passed, I saw Tancogeistla on several occasions. He had not been put to death by his rival, but ever he was accompanied by several guards. Clearly, whatever Malac's plans, they did not entail letting Tancogeistla out of his sight.

The smith's work agreed with me. We turned out mattocks, plowshares, picks with which to work the earth; as well as the implements of war. We dwelt in safety and peace. The Aedui now controlled only two cities, a sad decline from the glory days of the Keltoi Confederation, but more than I had ever dreamed we would possess after our flight from home.

I had no desires for further conquest and I naively assumed others shared my views. I had learned much in my sojourn on the isle with Tancogeistla, but I was still young. Yet to learn that the surest sign of immaturity is fancying yourself mature.

Berdic visited me often, riding in from his village with a girl riding sidesaddle behind him. Often a girl he wished me to take as my wife. There was little way for me to explain the lack of interest I showed in them. The wound was still too fresh, and my happy, carefree friend would never understand my continued grief for a woman I had known so briefly.

I visited the hill of Teamhaidh frequently, becoming close friends with one of the druids in charge of the sanctuary there, a holy man by the name of Motios. But the association did nothing to restore my faith in the gods which had abandoned us in the wastelands of the Isle of Tin, as Motios informed me it was called.

There was an emptiness I have no way of describing. I was searching for something, I knew not what. For a long time I concealed it from my friend. Then one sunny afternoon, it slipped out.

"Are the gods we worship real, Motios?" I demanded, glancing sharply into the face of the old druid. I don't know what I expected him to say. I could have hardly imagined that he would countenance my blasphemy.

A shadow passed over his face, something akin to sadness in his eyes as he regarded me gravely. "Why do you ask, my son?"

I shrugged helplessly, hanging my head in shame. "It was the Isle of Tin, father. The gods seemed to abandon us there. I lost a woman I loved, was betrayed by a friend I had held dear. I started to question." I looked up into his eyes. "Was I wrong?"

He seemed to be struggling with something and at first he didn't answer. Then he reached over and picked his staff off the floor, rising from his seat. "Come with me, son. I will show you what is true."

I followed him out of his dwelling and up the hillside. Despite his age, he was in good condition and I had to hurry to keep up with him as we trudged toward the top of Teamhaidh.

A circle of standing stones surmounted the crest of the hill, a place of worship, of observing the movements of the stars. A breeze was building, swirling over the mountaintop as clouds gathered from the western sea. A storm was coming.

We were alone.

Motios turned to me and once again I could see the struggle in his eyes. "Was I wrong, father?" I asked, impatient with his hesitation.

He shook his head slowly. "No, my son. The gods you see here, worshiped around here by these stones and the

78

altars below—none of them are real. None of them are divine."

His admission shook me far more than words can describe. All this time, I had assumed I was in the wrong, my faith beaten down by a series of circumstances. I had known of only one other man who shared my disbelief. Cavarillos, the profane, pragmatic mercenary. And now this.
. .

A thousand questions poured to my lips, but none of them could escape. I was speechless.

Motios sensed my dilemma. "You wonder why, my son? Simply this. We have lost the truth, abandoned it in the mists of our past. So we have had to invent, to fill the void with tales of our own making. The cycles of the druids confirm this. They show that at one time, long ago, before we even came to Gaul, that we worshiped one god."

The thought was completely foreign to me. "One god?"

A faint smile flickered across the old druid's face. "Yes, my son. One god who was supreme over all things—and invisible. No altars were built unto him. He was worshiped in the privacy of one's home."

"What happened?"

"That, my son, I do not know. The records I possess do not show."

"So there is no truth in the gods we worship now?"

"I did not say that, Cadwalador. I merely said none of them were divine. Cernunnos is an example I can use. He lived in those ancient days, as human as you or I. He was a mighty hunter and a conqueror in lands far to the east. The horns of the bull were a symbol of his aggression for it was said that he had wrestled with one and vanquished it in his strength. He rebelled against the worshipers of the one god and they put him to death for his blasphemy."

I still couldn't believe my ears. "And if this is all true, father, why have these gods been created—if they are all false, nothing more than the work of man's hands?"

He reached forward and grasped me by both shoulders, holding my gaze. "Because, Cadwalador," he whispered fiercely, "we have lost the truth. The records I possess are not sufficient to show us the right paths. Perhaps one day a man will come to once again restore us to truth. Until then—"

I interrupted him. "Until then, why deceive the people with these frauds?" The words came out with more anger than I had intended.

"Because we all must have something to believe in, my son. Something greater than ourselves. It is the fabric of our society. To destroy them will be to destroy our own selves."

"Then why were you honest with me?"

Motios shook his head, gazing steadfastly away from me, to where clouds were building, dark and forbidding. "I don't know. Perhaps because I realized that you were no longer deceived. That you were searching. That your unbelief was tormenting you."

"I thank you."

He nodded wordlessly and without further conversation we left the hilltop of Teamhaidh, both lost in our own thoughts.

Despite his words, I was more troubled inside than ever before. Little did I know that it was but a foretaste of things to come. Clouds were building, not only over the slopes of Teamhaidh, but in the hearts of the men who led my people. Clouds of war. . .

I had seen Tancogeistla in the square of Emain-Macha many times in the intervening years, but he was always accompanied by the *brihentin* of Malac, and I never spoke with him. All that changed on one bright day eleven years from the time of our departure from Gaul.

I was working steadily in the gobacrado, sweating from the heat of the forge as I hammered a sickle into shape. All at once, a figure darkened the doorway. "You prosper, my son," a voice announced calmly.

I looked up into the bearded face of Tancogeistla. His hair was growing gray, and he walked a little slower, but otherwise he was the same man I had known. "My lord!" I exclaimed, dropping my hammer with a crash.

He smiled, waving the *brihentin* in behind him. They were the same men who had accompanied him for years. "Cadwalador, my son," he whispered, embracing me. "I have come to enlist your help."

"In what, my lord?

"Raising an army," he retorted, watching for my reaction.

80

"I am no warrior," was my weak reply. I was amazed by his boldness in front of his guards.

He apparently sensed my hesitation. "These men are my friends, Cadwalador," he laughed, "you can speak freely in front of them."

I shook my head. "I still say, the warrior's way is not mine. You should know that more than anyone else. Raise your army. I will remain at my forge."

"The army is not mine."

His words startled me. "Then whose?"

"The Vergobret's. Malac's. He has decided that this island is not enough for us."

"Where does he intend to go? Back to Gaul?"

"He has not told me. But I need your help."

"I have helped you all I intend to," I replied, some of the old bitterness rising to the surface. That in itself disturbed me. I thought I had put that behind me.

"All the gobacrados in Emain-Macha have been called upon to provide weapons and armor for the soldiers being raised. I would be pleased if you would cooperate."

There was something underlying his words, a veiled threat. I stared into his eyes. "Why this sudden eagerness to help Malac?"

"Every man is duty-bound to aid his state in time of trouble," he replied piously. I could detect no sarcasm there, but I could sense something. Something was wrong.

But for now I saw no choice but to go along. "I will take your orders for weapons," I replied. "I presume I will be paid fairly."

He nodded, glancing at his guards. "It's time we were going. Good-day, my son."

"Good-day, my lord."

The orders came pouring in within a matter of days, swords, spear-tips, armor, helmets. Several of the requests pushed my skill to the limit, but I did my best. Troops were being raised from the native population, the Goidils, and numerous of them were in and out of the gobacrado constantly.

Many of the locals were levied into bands of *vellinica*, light spearmen who could hopefully be trusted to hold our line better than the *lugoae* I had fought with in the army of Tancogeistla.

Others, many of the younger Goidils, were formed into groups of *cladaca*, fast light infantry who could hurry from point to point on the battlefield to reinforce weak spots. They were armed with darts and short swords, many of which I forged.

I had seen many warriors, fought beside them in the isle of tin, seen them die beside me. But when a tall, flame-haired man stepped into the gobacrado about three months after Tancogeistla's visit, I realized that I had never seen one to match him.

He introduced himself as Lugort, and I realized almost right away that he was a native of the island, if the Goidils had any right to be called such.

I almost laughed when he told me his mission—to secure a number of large hammers. I was instantly glad I hadn't, for Lugort was not a laughing man.

"It is this army your Tancogeistla is raising," he replied in response to my query. "He has called on I and my warriors to aid him."

I just looked at him. "You use hammers to fight?"

"*Ordmalica*," he replied simply, which I was to learn meant "hammer fighters".

He went on, "It is the weapon of Dagda, with which he forged the creation and with which he punishes those who war against him."

My thoughts went instinctively to my conversation with Motios. Man warring against God. Utter foolishness.

". . .you can make what I need?" Lugort was asking, pulling me from my reverie. I acknowledged his question with a nod. "Easily." I gestured to a table full of forged swords. "Far more easily than I made those."

He sniffed perceptibly. "A sword is a fool's weapon. It will fail you in your hour of need."

I shot a sharp look in his direction, his words piercing to my heart. Did he know? There was no way that he could have, and yet he spoke the truth. Nine years had passed and yet I could still feel that sword being ripped from my grasp with the force of Cavarillos' blow, see Inyae rushing from the darkness to shield me.

"I know," I replied simply. He looked at me, a question in his eyes, but it went unasked. Clearly my reply was unusual for an Aeduan.

"I will return in two weeks. Your pay will be ready then."

"It is agreed."

Ogrosan was approaching and yet the task of preparing the army continued, more and more men pouring into Emain-Macha until I thought the city could not contain them all. I questioned every visitor to the gobacrado to find out the object of our invasion, but no one seemed to know.

One evening, as I was banking the fires of my forge, I heard laughter outside the door. Just as I was about to look out, the door swung open and Berdic lurched in, dragging a pretty tavern wench behind him. He was clearly in his cups, and she was well nigh as drunken.

"News for you, lad!" he exclaimed, clapping me roughly on the shoulder.

"Yes?" I asked, not expecting anything important. It was hardly his first such intrusion into my privacy.

"Malac rode in at sunset," he slurred, squeezing the girl tightly to him. She laughed at him and pulled away. "H-he was in the tavern, talking. Said we was going across the sea—to a place called Attu-something."

"Attuaca?" I demanded, my heart nearly stopping. Surely not.

He looked up at me through bleary, bloodshot eyes. "That's it, my old friend. Attu-Aca. You've heard of it?"

I pushed him aside roughly and strode toward the door. The girl giggled drunkenly at my hurry, but I had no time to heed her laughter.

My horse was tied in front of the gobacrado and I swung onto his back, grasping the reins in my hand. I needed to find Tancogeistla.

Visions of the hospitality we had enjoyed at Attuaca flashed through my mind. Now we were returning, to lay siege with fire and sword. It could not be. Not if there was any way to stop it.

I kicked my horse into a gallop as I rode out under the night sky, a premonition of doom enfolding me. The clouds of war were gathering. . .

I rode hard through the night, towards Tancogeistla's residence. A light rain was starting to fall, but I never noticed it. Too much else was on my mind.

An oil lamp was still burning inside Tancogeistla's house and I dismounted outside the door. Truly, I believe I would have gone inside had everything been pitch-black. I had to know the truth.

One of the *brihentin* answered my pounding on the door. "The night is late," he stated, glaring at me. His hand was on the hilt of the sword strapped to his side. Clearly he didn't take a welcoming view of visitors.

"Tell Tancogeistla that Cadwalador is outside his door," I replied. "I must speak with him."

"One moment," the *brihentin* replied, closing the door in my face. I could hear voices from inside and in a moment, he was back.

"You may come in," he acknowledged grudgingly. "Follow me."

I ducked my head to avoid the lentel and followed him inside. Tancogeistla sat at a low table near a fireplace, and rose at my approach.

"Cadwalador, my son," he greeted me. The look in his eyes told me he knew exactly why I was there.

"It's true, isn't it?" I demanded, gripping him fiercely by the shoulders, my eyes locking with his. The *brihentin* advanced to pull me off the general, but Tancogeistla waved him away.

"What, my son?" he asked, concern in his voice. "The night is raw and you're soaked with rain. You've ridden hard."

I nodded, seeming to realize my condition for the first time. He was right. But I had to know. "Malac is in town, isn't he?"

A silent nod. "And we are marching to take Attuaca?"

"Who told you?" Tancogeistla asked.

"Then it's true?" I demanded in return, still wanting to hear denial from his lips. Knowing I would not.

He nodded. "There's nothing I can do about it," he continued, as if sensing my next question. "Nothing at all."

I turned away, my mind still reeling. If only—I realized with brutal suddenness why Malac had been so interested in my story that bright morning I had been brought before him so many years ago. This had been a long time in the planning.

"How long have you known?" I questioned sharply, glancing back at Tancogeistla.

"A messenger from Malac. A week ago."

"They were our friends, my lord," I protested, endeavoring to find his loyalties in this. "They sheltered us in the dark months and saved us from perishing. How can we lift a hand against them now?"

"Ask Malac," Tancogeistla replied, his disgust seeming to match mine, "he cares nothing for the kindness shone us. And he will never heed the advice of the man from whom he stole the throne."

I looked over at the *brihentin*, surprised by the boldness of Tancogeistla's words. His guard was smiling.

The general smiled at my confusion. "Belerios is my friend. We have been together for so many years—he believes in my right to the throne."

The announcement stunned me. "If he believes," I asked, "don't others? Enough to stop this madness?"

Tancogeistla shook his head. "We stand not a chance with Malac in the city. I'm sorry, my son. But in a week, we march to Attuaca. I would be pleased if you would ride in my bodyguard."

The request took me by surprise, but Tancogeistla's requests had the habit of coming like that. And not leaving much room to refuse.

I nodded slowly. "I will join you."

We left Emain-Macha at the end of the week, as Tancogeistla had said. Malac drew the troops up outside the city and addressed them.

I was surprised by the change. The years had clearly wrought their work upon him. His once-flaming head of hair was now white as the snow cresting the far-off mountains of Erain. He looked now as old as Tancogeistla, who was a few years his senior.

"My people!" he began, "I am pleased to see so many of you here with me today. Pleased to see that you have answered the call of your state. The time has come to expand our borders, to wet our swords in the blood of our enemies, and to take more land for our people. Cocolitanos believed our destiny lay on the isle of tin, across the sea. That was where he died, killed by the people of a place called Attuaca. We march this day to avenge his death."

His eyes swept the ranks and I could feel his gaze rest upon me where I sat on my horse beside Tancogeistla. A faint smile creased his face, as though mocking me for the information I had given him. I stared coldly back at him. After a moment he looked away and continued his speech.

"A fleet of ships has been prepared at the coast. They will carry us to our destination. To our *glory!*"

Cheers greeted his words, a mighty, rousing cry of *Rabo!* swelling from the throats of the Aeduan warriors. The war-cry took me back years, to the last time I had heard it. The massacre of Inyae's village. An action as senseless and brutal as what was taking place now.

But this time it was different. The Calydrae had sheltered us, protected us. Cinaed had been our friend in very truth, although at one time we had feared him. And now we moved to conquer. . .

Chapter XI: The Way of War

The journey back to the island was a hard one for me. Tancogeistla knew that. Perhaps that was the reason he left me to myself on the voyage. We were traveling in sturdier craft this time, but my heart was twice as unsettled as it had been on the rafts years earlier. Then we had been returning to our people, jubilant in our own survival. Now we went back, to carry flame and sword to those who had befriended us. There was no justice in this battle. Malac never intended any.

Our army was divided between the Gallic and Goidilic contingents. Most of the slingers were settlers from Emain-Macha, men who had answered Tancogiestla's call for an army. So far as I knew, they were loyal to Malac, but at times I had my doubts.

Berdic was in command of one of the detachments of *iaosatae*. He did not share in my misery, failed to understand it. Boyhood friends though we were, fellow villagers—we were so different. I could never understand his carefree ways, no more than he could understand my silence, my reticence to speak on matters he talked so easily about.

Many of the Goidils were from the south, the area around Ivernis. Except for Lugort and his unit of *ordmalica*. The Goidilic noble had come aboard on the boat I sailed on. Apparently he and Tancogeistla knew each other.

He and his men set up a practice area on the stern of our small ship. I watched them at work from day to day, swinging their great hammers, the hammers I had forged.

After four days of sailing, we touched the shores of the island of tin. Malac chose one of the slingers who had been with Tancogeistla in the beginning to guide the column. And we set out, on our mission of death.

Ogrosan was coming, a terrible time of the year to war, but Malac did not seem to care.

I rode beside Tancogeistla near the head of our column. Malac's men were watching constantly.

It seemed to amuse the general, as though he knew something I didn't. "We are nearing Attuaca," he stated calmly the second day after our landing.

I nodded. "You know of no way to stop him?" I asked, glancing across at him as I rode at his side.

Tancogeistla shook his head, chuckling grimly. "If I had, I would not have permitted him to come this far. No, my son. We are in too deep to back out now. The die is cast. We win, or we die."

"And we win by killing those who saved our lives!" I snapped, anger boiling over inside me. He nodded slowly, acknowledging the truth of my words.

"There is no way to prevent it. Even now, I doubt not that the Calydrae know of our advance. They will be preparing their defenses." Tancogeistla looked back over the marching warbands. "Many will die. On both sides."

"Senselessly!" I hissed back at him, overwhelmed by the absurdity of it all. His gaze met mine.

"Such is the way of war. . ."

We rode on, through fields of now-snowy heather, the flower that had blanketed the fields in purple when I had wandered these hills with the Belgae maiden, Diedre. She hadn't entered my thoughts in all the years since my departure from Attuaca, but as each hoofbeat carried us closer, my thoughts turned toward her. Was she still in the city? Was she still a slave of the Calydrae? They were unanswerable questions, and in very truth, she meant nothing to me. Just another friend I was about to betray.

Toward nightfall, one of our scouts came riding back in, his horse lathered with sweat. "My lord," he began, reining up before Malac, "the town is ahead of us."

"Attuaca?" Malac demanded. Even from my position twenty feet away, I could see the glitter in his eyes, watch the expression on his face change. The face of a conniving old man.

The scout nodded.

"Good," Malac replied, turning in his saddle to face his warbands. "Tonight we camp outside the walls. Tomorrow—we avenge Cocolitanos!"

"Rabo! Rabo!"

I could not sleep that night. Instead I paced back and forth through the camp, endeavoring to find a way to slip through the sentries. There was none. Malac intended that no one be able to reach Attuaca. Several parties of the Goidils had been set to work fashioning crude battering rams. They worked long into the night.

Fires were burning in the town, reminding me of the signal fires that had summoned the host of the Dumnones to our destruction. Perhaps Cinaed needed no warning from me. A savvy warrior, he doubtless suspected Malac's treachery. Or so I tried to console myself.

I sat down on the stump of a tree that had been cut down for the ram, my javelins in my hand, my eyes gazing toward Attuaca. The night was long. . .

I awoke to the sound of shouting. Shaking my head to clear the fog of sleep from my brain, I raised myself up from the ground. Apparently I had gone to sleep at some time during the night and fallen from my perch on the stump.

A small group of men was advancing from behind the palisade of Attuaca, coming toward our camp. I recognized Cinaed almost instantly, although he had grown a beard and his hair was duller than I had remembered it. Still, he walked tall and proud toward our lines, accompanied by his retainers. A noble man.

He stopped in front of our camp and cried with a loud voice, "Where is the leader of this army and wherefore have you come?"

Malac appeared, a coat of chainmail over his shoulders. His sword was strapped to his side. He appeared to have thrown on his armor hurriedly. Tancogeistla was right behind him.

"From the land of the Aedui are we come," Malac replied, drawing himself up in front of the Calydrae chieftain. "We have come to demand the surrender of your people."

Unbidden, I walked toward the little group. There was so much I wanted to say to Cinaed, words I knew I would never have the chance to utter. He ignored Malac's speech, but rather was staring at Tancogeistla. "My people sheltered and fed you through the dark months many years ago, when you and your men were starving in the wilderness. And this is how you repay that kindness?"

"Malac is my ruler. I obey his commands," Tancogeistla shrugged piously, deceiving no one, much less Malac. He raised his eyes to meet Cinaed. "This was not my wish."

The chieftain shook his head. "When you left, you told me that you sailed to take the throne of your people. Was that too a lie?"

"I was deceived," was Tancogeistla's simple reply. Cinaed looked toward my approach.

"Cadwalador," he said slowly. "My men saved you from the snows."

I nodded in painful acknowledgement of his words. His face twisted into anger. "I wish to the gods we had let you all *die!*"

"I'm sorry," I whispered, looking into his eyes. He turned his attention back to Malac, who was speaking again.

". . .what is your answer? Will you lay down your arms and surrender the town?"

Cinaed glared into the face of the Vergobret. "The Calydrae have never known the meaning of surrender. As for our arms—come and take them."

Malac nodded. "We will do just that."

I watched as the delegation of the Calydrae turned and walked back, disappearing behind their palisade. A dark certainty overcame me. Many that I called friend would die.

On both sides. I knew the Calydrae too well to think that their defense would collapse easily.

Our Vergobret turned, facing the troops that were now pouring from our camp. "Bring forward the rams! We attack as soon as they are in place!"

Despite Malac's intentions, we were not formed up for an attack until almost noon. The Calydrae did not let the time go to waste. That much I knew. I dressed myself in a suit of mail I had forged in the gobacrado, took my javelins in hand and mounted up, beside Tancogeistla and the rest of the *brihentin*. The tension in our ranks was palpable.

Many of us felt the fight was unjust. Even more were breathless in their anticipation of plunder. Tancogeistla was right. We were past the point of no return.

Malac rode forward on his mighty gray warhorse, and tossed a javelin toward the palisade of Attuaca. Despite his age, his arm still possessed incredible power and I watched as the javelin stuck quivering in the logs.

His gesture was greeted with defiant taunts from the Calydrae. He turned, waving to his men. "Forward, my people! Forward, to the walls!"

The men assigned to the battering rams moved forward to Malac's command, pushing the rams in front of them. Berdic's *iaosatae* followed, moving to cover them with their slings. He waved to me as he passed, grinning from ear to ear. He had yet to see the sorrows of war. The way I had.

In the distance, far ahead of where Tancogeistla and I sat astride our steeds, I could hear the thud of the rams being shoved into the palisade. They should make short work of it.

I could hear the screams of men dying as the Calydrae pelted the rams with their javelins. My stay in Attuaca had convinced me firsthand of their proficiency with that weapon. They were putting up a stiff resistance.

Malac's *brihentin* pranced a short distance behind the rams, just out of range. Minutes passed, dragging slowly. I could feel the impatience in our men. They were lusting for battle. Lugort's *ordmalica* stood in formation beside us, their battle hammers held easily at their sides.

The tall, sober Goidilic noble stood at their head. He acknowledged my glance with a silent nod. He did not

91

seem to share the exuberance of many of our warriors. Perhaps he, like myself, had seen too much of war. Or maybe fighting beneath an Aedui banner was what perturbed him. A distant crash turned our attention back to the front. Our rams had broken through the gate.

A horn sounded in front of us. Malac, sounding the charge. His *brihentin* galloped forward, nearly trampling several of the men pulling the ram back from the broken gate. The Goidils from Ivernis followed, making for the other two rams, which were just then smashing through the palisade to the right and left of the gate.

I looked at Tancogeistla, who was holding himself rigidly in place, as though waiting for something. What, I had no idea.

"Shall we go, my lord?" Through the gate ahead of us, I could see Malac's horsemen fiercely engaged with the warriors of the Calydrae. For the moment they were all alone.

He smiled, barking a quick order to Belerios, the *brihentin* who had been his guard over the years of his captivity. The swarthy Gaul spurred his horse forward, to the line of the *iaosatae*, where Berdic stood with the rest of the slingers.

He reined up beside Berdic and said something to him, which was quickly passed down the line. The slingers ceased their fire. The Goidils of Ivernis had disappeared inside through the breach of the wall.

Everyone was engaged, *except*, I noticed with a sudden sense of disquiet, the men of Emain-Macha. Every detachment, every warband that had followed Tancogeistla's call to war.

"What's going on?" I demanded sharply, sensing that there was something he was holding back, something he had kept from me. "Do we not ride to his aid?"

Tancogeistla chuckled. "This is the day, my son. The day the authority of the vergobret returns to me. Your faithfulness will be rewarded, after all these long years."

Just at the moment, I could have cared less. I merely wished to know what he meant, to have him deny the horrible sense of treachery that was rising within me.

"You intend that he falls by their hand, don't you?"

He turned in his saddle. "Far more honorable than if I should slay him, don't you think, Cadwalador? And far less divisive."

"You speak of honor?" I asked incredulously. "Malac is a treacherous dog, but those men—all the Aeduans who will die with him. What have they done?"

His countenance was calm, undisturbed by my anger. Indeed, if anything, he seemed vaguely amused by it. In that, he suddenly reminded me of Cavarillos.

"They have chosen their side. And their death. They will die as heroes of our people."

"Everyone will know how you abandoned them," I remonstrated fiercely. Part of me wanted to abandon Malac, to do what Tancogeistla had planned, but the other part wanted to go to the help of my people. Even if it meant lifting my hand against the Calydrae.

"We will charge," he stated, an irritating patience in his voice. "Wait."

We could see the fighting through the massive gaps in the palisade. Here and there dashed a figure on a horse, presumably one of Malac's *brihentin*. I had seen no horses among the Calydrae during our stay.

Tancogeistla sat silently on his horse, for perhaps another ten, fifteen minutes. What we could see of the carnage in the town was terrible. Our men were dying by the dozens. As were the Calydrae. My friends, all of them.

Tancogeistla leaned forward and spoke to Lugort. His voice was too low for me to hear, but we started forward, toward the walls of Attuaca.

My horse broke into a fast trot, his hooves a steady drumbeat against the snowy sod. We rode in the north breach, picking our way over and around the dead and dying. Just then a shout went up.

"He is fleeing! Gods preserve us, for he is fleeing!"

I looked back just in time to see Malac and two of the surviving nobles break from the mass of struggling men, riding toward the rear. Nay, not riding, but fleeing as the men had cried. Running from the enemy. I had never thought of such a thing.

Malac was a cruel and treacherous foe, but I had never doubted his courage. Until now.

Tancogeistla laughed with delight, drawing his sword from its scabbard. It was now left to him to rally the men, to turn the tide of battle. A role he was more than willing to accept. "Forward my brave warriors!" he screamed, his voice carrying above the din of battle. "Rally to my banner! Follow on!"

I rode behind him, struck with the realization that he had deceived me in more ways than one. He was more than willing to destroy the Calydrae—in fact he was eager to do so. He had manipulated the whole situation from the beginning—everyone, including me. In a mad attempt to regain the judgment seat of the Aedui.

We rode forward, into the thick of the fighting.

I glimpsed Cinaed's figure almost immediately—a bear-like figure in the middle of the struggle, fighting bravely with his thrusting spear. Apparently either his javelins were expended, or else our men had come too close. In my heart, I prayed that he might be spared, that somehow he could survive this madness. Prayer to whom, I had no idea. Perhaps to the ancient God Motios had spoken of. Certainly not to any of the triad of my forefathers, the gods which had abandoned me so many years ago on this desolate isle.

I rode behind Tancogeistla, into the sea of struggling men, trying to remain out of it. I had no wish to strike down those who had befriended me and saved my life in the dark months so many years ago.

My horse let out a shrill, pitiful whinny and I glanced down, broken from my trance. A young warrior stabbed his spear upwards into my mount's belly, clearly attempting to unhorse me. His eyes full of hate and rage. I tossed one of my javelins at him, but the range was too short and the blow merely knocked him back, the tip not piercing his chest.

His comrades seemed to materialize out of the earth, surrounding me. My horse fell, flinging me to the side, to the ground. One of the Calydrae came rushing toward me, screaming his battle-cry, his spear leveled.

I rolled to one side and grabbed the shaft with both hands, twisting with all my strength. The muscles I had developed at the forge were aiding me now, but the chainmail taxed my efforts to rise. With one final effort, I ripped the spear from his hands, swinging the blunt end toward his head.

He went down as though pole-axed. I reversed the spear quickly, throwing up my free arm to block the blow descending toward my head from another of the Calydrae. His effort had taken him off-balance and I counterattacked, thrusting the spear into his belly. He screamed, his eyes glazing with death as blood flowed from his body. He went down into the street, taking the spear with him.

Once again I was weaponless. The conflict ebbed and flowed around me. Men were dying on every hand. I moved forward, dazed by the carnage. The *brihentin*, the champions of Tancogeistla, dashed to and fro, almost trampling some of our own men.

A javelin hissed past my ear, burying itself in the doorpost of a nearby house. I looked up to find an enemy warrior rushing toward me. His face was familiar to me, one of the young men I had played at javelins with, testing our skill and accuracy. One of my friends among the Calydrae.

There was no friendship in his eyes now, only a lust for blood. I stooped down, as though guided by instinct, my hands closing around one of the war-hammers used by the *ordmalica*. The corpse of its owner lay scarce a foot from it.

I parried his thrust with the haft of the hammer, and then swung back at him, putting all my strength into the swing. I was entering the zone now, detached from myself, issuing commands to a body I no longer inhabited. I seemed to see myself, as though I watched in a dream, fighting against the army of the Calydrae. The army of my preservers.

I heard the sickening crunch of bone breaking, a twisted cry erupting from his throat as my hammer slammed into his breastbone, collapsing the chest cavity. He slumped to the ground, frothy blood escaping from between his lips. Death was knocking at his heart's door.

I looked down into his eyes, eyes once vibrant with the joy of living, now harboring only the vacancy of death. "I'm sorry," I whispered. And yet to survive, I had to keep moving, keep killing. And I did.

A sudden blow from the side stunned me, nearly spinning me around as fire raced up and down my back. I was bleeding.

Cinaed. "You should have stayed in your home," he hissed, raising his spear for the final blow. "We did not seek this war."

"Nor did I," I whispered, lacking the strength to raise the hammer against him. His thrust had ripped open my side, letting the blood flow freely. "Nor did I."

He hesitated, one moment, as though confused by my words. But it wouldn't matter in the end. I knew that.

A sword descended from the air, smashing into Cinaed's bared neck, just above his cloak. A crimson spray erupted from severed veins as the chieftain collapsed to the ground, his life flowing from his body.

I looked up into the eyes of Tancogeistla. There was a fraction of my mind that knew I should thank him for saving my life, but a larger part of me wanted to curse him for his manipulations, for bringing us here in the first place. For I knew now that he had possessed the power to stop Malac, even before we came across the waters, before we had marched on Attuaca. And he had not used it.

I stumbled away through the carnage, moving as though in a dream. I collapsed in a doorway, weak from blood loss, my hammer slipping from between my fingers.

The skirmishers, the *imannae* of Ivernis, were putting up a stiff fight only a few yards from where I sat.

I lacked the strength to join them. Something warned me, a glimpse of motion out of the corner of my eye, a sound, what I don't know. I rolled weakly to the side just as knife plunged into the doorpost where my head had been resting.

"Dog!" A woman's voice cried, loud and shrill. And familiar. I reached up, grabbing at the knife hand, arresting its downward swing.

A young woman glared down into my face, her eyes red from weeping, rage on her countenance. Then her eyes changed. "Cadwalador?"

I shook my head to clear the cobwebs from my mind, attempting to place her. "Diedre?" I demanded incredulously.

She nodded, falling to one knee beside me. The knife fell from her hand, much to my relief. I could scarcely believe that the young woman now at my side was the same girl I had walked with over the heather-covered hills so many years ago. She had blossomed into the maturity of womanhood in the intervening years, leaving behind the gawkiness of her youth.

96

And she was very clearly with child. Tears flowed from her eyes, silent sobs wracking her body.

"Why did you come back?" She gasped out through her tears. "Why, like this?" I gazed past her, out the doorway. The ranks of the Calydrae were broken now, men running for the town square, disheartened at the death of their leader.

There was no answer to the question of her broken heart. "Had it been my decision, I would never have returned," I replied quietly, my own heart torn in two at the betrayal I had been an unwilling part of. "But some men's ambition knows no limit."

My words had no effect on her sorrow. I had hardly expected that they would. I wanted to reach out and comfort her, but I was acutely aware of the awkwardness of my position.

"Where is your husband?" I asked, my hand stealing surreptitiously toward the hilt of the knife. In my weakened condition, I hardly wanted to be caught in this compromising position with another man's wife.

She shook her head, some of her anger returning as she gestured out the doorway to the body-covered ground. "Somewhere out there."

I looked across the hard-packed sod, so thickly strewn with the dead and dying that it was impossible to walk without stepping on a corpse. Her husband, the father of her babe, was dead.

All at once, cheering seemed to erupt from the ground, rolling down from the hill in the center of town where the last of the Calydrae had taken refuge. Apparently, the day was ours. But none of that mattered. Not to me. Not to the young widow who grieved at my side. All that mattered was the loss—that could never be restored.

Oh, yes, this was a victory. . .

Chapter XII: Aneirin moc Cunobelin

The days which followed were filled with mourning, the women of the Calydrae weeping for their dead. Our troops rampaged through Attuaca, looting and burning, drinking themselves drunk. Diedre bandaged my wounds and together we went out to find the body of her husband.

The corpses were beginning to stink, bloating under the sun. Only the intense cold kept the town habitable. Some of the bodies were barely recognizable. Tancogeistla's sword-slash had nearly taken the head off Cinaed's body. The chieftain lay face-down in a frozen pool of his own blood.

We found her husband, lying in front of a nearby door. He was stretched out on his back, his spear still clutched tightly in hands now stiff with death. His torso was smashed in by a hammer, the entire rib cage collapsed inward.

He was the man I had killed. Diedre let out a small cry and fell to her knees beside the body, cradling his head in her lap. Clearly, she had loved him.

I saw no need to tell her that I had taken his life. It would only add to her grief, as it already had to mine. My friend. Her husband. Dead at my hand. War. . .

Malac came skulking back into town a week after the battle's conclusion, but we saw little of him. People avoided him in the streets, shunned him by their scornful silence. Vergobret though he still was, he was an outcast

Tancogeistla was leader in all but name. The people listened to him, respected him for the bravery he had shown in the battle. They called him *Kuaroas*, or champion. Men flocked to his banner.

But I did not. His deceitful ploy to reclaim his rightful place had cost many lives and wreaked havoc in many others. Mine included.

Rumor had it that he still sought Malac's life and the Vergobret fled from Attuaca, back to Erain, where he assumed the governorship of Emain-Macha. However, he had lost almost all his influence and for the moment Tancogeistla seemed to have other things on his mind. His rival could be dealt with later.

Tancogeistla quickly went about quartering his troops in every house in the settlement, thus securing at the least the overt loyalty of the inhabitants.

Almost three months to the day from the fall of Attuaca, Diedre brought forth a baby-girl, the child conceived of her and her husband's union.

Over the months, I had found the fondness I had once felt for the Belgae maiden growing steadily into love, and it seemed that the feeling was mutual as she bandaged my wounds and endeavored to make me at home there in the town in those early days. I made the necessary arrangements to take her as my wife once the time of her mourning was fulfilled.

My dreams of Inyae had finally ceased to haunt me, those visions of that dark night with Cavarillos. Instead, as I lay beside Diedre in our small chamber, Inyae's face was replaced by another.

Diedre's husband rose up before me on our first night as man and wife. I could see the look of agony on his face as my hammer smashed into his breastbone, hear his death cry as his broken body collapsed to the ground.

Then all that passed away and his face changed, a look of reproach crossing his countenance. I could almost hear his voice rebuking me for my action. I rolled onto my back, coming awake with a start, sweat rolling in beads down my face. Diedre still lay at my side, her slow, regular breathing assuring me that she was still asleep. There were three of us in the bed that night. . .

A year passed, then two. I saw nothing of Tancogeistla, save in public. Perhaps sensing my condemnation of his actions, he no longer visited the man who had saved his life. The rewards he had promised during the battle never came to pass. I had hardly expected that they would.

And yet, for all the fame and power that he had gained through his cunning, still one thing eluded him. An heir. Perhaps it is man's desire for immortality that causes him to crave a son, someone to continue his noble exploits, fulfill the dreams that are now beyond the grasp of his aged hands. Tancogeistla and his wife had never been able to have children.

Some spoke in hushed whispers that this was the curse of his usurpation of power from Malac, but the more sensible realized the truth. He and his wife were simply too old. His youth had been spent fighting the wars of the Aedui. Such things as siring an heir had been cast by the wayside until it was too late.

Friends of mine who came to the forge told me he had even employed a witch of the Calydrae to try to work her magic. Whatever she attempted, it failed to work.

Thus, the announcement in the city square nearly two and a half years after the fall of Attuaca came as no surprise.

Tancogeistla arrived in the square, standing tall and erect despite his years. If one improvement had been made to his character in the years since our migration together, it was that he had finally won his war with the bottle. Wine no longer had the same power over him that it once had. He was dressed in full battle regalia, chainmail and all, the helmet concealing his snow-white hair. But beside him stood another, a far younger man whom I did not recognize.

Tancogeistla raised his hands over the assembled crowd, calling for silence. "As all of you know," he began,

"I am old, and well stricken in years. And I have sacrificed my life in the service of my people. My days upon this earth are numbered."

His speech was interrupted by the cries of the people, earnest protestations against what he was saying. It was as though he had become a god to them, a champion who would continue to lead their forces through eternity. They did not know him as I did. Diedre stood at my side, cradling her daughter in her arms. She was with child once again. I too prayed for a son.

Our leader continued as soon as the crowd would allow him. "It is true, my people. And if I die, who will lead you? The old woman who ran from battle those years ago, the man some still recognize as vergobret? Or the fruit of his loins, those two young boys who have not yet grown to manhood? Might they not too run from the test of brave men?"

Shrill cries of approbation greeted his words.

"The man who stands beside me is one in whom I have the greatest confidence. A man I have decided to adopt as though he were my own son. A man from the tribe of the Cruithni, whose homes have been made in Erain for countless centuries."

My ears perked up. The Cruithni were an ancient race, but in the years since the invasion of Erain, they had hardly been known for their loyalty to their new Aeduan overlords. Perhaps this man was an exception.

The crowd went wild. A figure pushed through the mass of people to stand at my side. It was Berdic, an unusual sobriety on his typically carefree countenance. We exchanged greetings and he stood in silence for a moment before asking what I thought of the new heir.

I shrugged. "Only time will tell us. Until then I shall reserve my judgement."

He nodded slowly. "You know, old friend, that could have been you. . ."

Diedre suppressed a small gasp. I turned, staring him full in the face. "I have no idea what you mean."

"Of course you do. . ."

I shook my head, wondering if despite his sober countenance, my old playmate was drunken. "What are you trying to say?"

101

Berdic smiled grimly. "Tancogeistla had every intention of making you his heir, instead of this cursed Cruithni."

He was dead sober. I didn't know what to make of it. Perhaps it was the reward Tancogeistla had alluded to several times. Still, if so. . . "What kept him from it?"

"You," he replied. "Your rebuke of his actions at Attuaca. I feel he no longer trusts you as he once did, Cadwalador. You should watch your back."

"My loyalty to him is unquestioned," I retorted hotly. "I saved his life many years ago in this island, at great cost to myself."

"My statement to you still stands. In this time, loyalties are changing, as unstable as a brook of water. This day the people flock to Tancogeistla's banner. The next, they could just as easily turn back to a resurgent Malac. Tancogeistla knows this. And he will crush anyone who stands in his way."

"Or in the way of his heir, Aneirin moc Cunobelin."

"Exactly," Berdic warned, his tones dark with meaning. "You have a family now, Cadwalador. The daughter of a Calydrae warrior and a wife who will bear your child. Take care of them. Don't offend Tancogeistla again."

"I did only what I felt was right," I replied, feeling a need to defend myself from the accusation my friend had made. "There was no justice in this war."

"Does there need to be?" Berdic asked, laying a hand on my shoulder before disappearing into the crowd. "Take care, my friend."

I looked down into Diedre's worried eyes. "Are you in danger, my love?"

Wishing to reassure her, I shook my head. "Nothing that you should worry about," I replied, taking her into my arms. But even as I did so, I looked up to the platform where Tancogeistla and Aneirin still stood. There was danger there. Should Aneirin moc Cunobelin prove as ruthless and cunning as his patron, there was much danger. . .

Thus it was that Berdic's words were on my mind when a knock came on my door early one morning five weeks later and I opened it to find Belerios standing there. As always, a longsword nestled in the scabbard at his side.

102

The swarthy *brihentin* wasn't smiling as he bid me a good morning.

"Tancogeistla wishes to speak with you. Immediately."

I glanced back into the shadows of my home, saw the fear in Diedre's eyes as she held her daughter close. "What does my lord wish?" I asked, endeavoring to fathom Tancogeistla's intent.

"He wishes you to come with me," Belerios replied stolidly. "That is all you need to know."

"I will be with you in a moment," I responded. "Let me bid my wife good-bye."

"Very well."

I closed the door and turned back to Diedre, folding her into my arms. "Come back to me, my husband," she whispered, her tears falling against my chest. I could feel the child she bore kick against me from her womb and I smiled.

"Our child is strong," I stated, stroking her long hair with my fingers. She nodded, tears still streaming down her cheeks.

"A strong son. And he will need a father. Please, Cadwalador," she begged, gazing steadfastly into my eyes. "My first husband was taken from me by this man's lust for power. He will destroy you as well if he thinks you are a threat. Please return to me."

My heart was torn by the despair in her voice, by the earnestness of her plea. "Don't worry, love," I whispered, gently pulling myself from her embrace. "I will do everything I can. We will sup together tonight. I promise you that."

Belerios knocked again at the door. "Are you ready, Cadwalador?"

"Yes," I replied. "Goodbye, Diedre. Remember, I will be home before the night falls."

I left my house and walked through the streets of Attuaca with Belerios. Much had changed in the years since its fall to our army. More of the Aedui from Erain had moved to this new possession, thus securing their mastery of the place.

Tancogeistla's dwelling, more of a rude palace than anything, stood at the end of a long street. It was of new construction.

103

Guards stood at the entrance as we approached, the light of the early morning sun glittering off their bared weapons. I knew Tancogeistla to have been a light sleeper ever since the night with Cavarillos so many years earlier. Clearly his feud with Malac had not diminished his desire for security.

Together we were ushered into an inner courtyard, where several young men practiced at javelins. One of them was Aneirin moc Cunobelin. Tancogeistla stood watching them.

He turned at our entrance. "Welcome, Cadwalador. It's been some time."

"Yes, my lord," I nodded. "My forge keeps me busy."

"And your wife," he added, with a hint of a twinkle in his eye. "She carries your child, I hear."

"Yes."

"The gods have blessed you." I felt it was prudent to acknowledge that statement with a short nod, whether I believed it or not.

"You wished my presence, my lord?" I asked, but he seemed to be in no hurry to get to the root of the matter.

"I remember you were rather skilled with a javelin at one time yourself, weren't you, Cadwalador?" he asked, gazing past me to where the young men practiced.

I nodded. "Decently."

"Ah, yes, I remember you using them against that traitor Cavarillos. Too bad you didn't kill him," he said absently.

"I did everything within my power," I replied shortly. My failure to kill Cavarillos still haunted me. I didn't appreciate him bringing it back up.

"I know you did," he responded, looking into my eyes with the same strange magnetism he had always possessed. The charisma that drew men to his banner, that had seduced me into his service more than once in the past. I had enough of it. "I have never doubted your loyalty to me, Cadwalador. That is why I have called you to me today."

I remained silent. A reply was neither required nor expected. He went on after a moment. "I need you to go back to the mainland."

"Permanently?"

A shake of the head. "No. Merely to deliver a message. Aneirin!" he called, lifting his voice and summoning the young man who was his heir.

The javelin flew from Aneirin's hand just as Tancogeistla spoke, slamming into the logs several feet to the left of the target. It was a pitiful showing and I could see several of the soldiers covering their mouths to conceal their laughter. A bad sign, I observed. Tancogeistla had succeeded in his bloody path to the throne only because he commanded his men's absolute respect as a warrior. Aneirin moc Cunobelin did not.

He walked up to our small party, shaking his head as if well aware of his failings. "Aneirin," Tancogeistla began, "I wish to introduce you to an old bodyguard of mine, one of my *brihentin* when we first came to Attuaca. His name is Cadwalador."

The young man acknowledged the introduction with a careless nod. "My father has spoken much of you."

Alarms sounded in my head. What had been said? Aneirin was perhaps seven years my junior, shorter and not as muscular. My work at the forge had strengthened me beyond anything I could have dreamed of when I first left my homeland. His head was topped by a rough shock of red hair, similar to the color I remembered Tancogeistla's had been so many years ago. Looking at him now, it was hard to think it could have been so long.

Aneirin's posture was relaxed, almost languid. He had the look of a sedentary man, not a warrior. I didn't know what to think of Tancogeistla's choice.

"This message you speak of," I asked, focusing my attention back to Tancogeistla, "whom shall I deliver it to?"

His eyes had lost none of their fire as he turned, his gaze locking with mine. "Malac. . ."

Chapter XIII: Message for Malac

His words took my breath away. Apparently it showed on my face. "Is there a problem with that?" he asked sharply.

I shook my head. "No, my lord. I was just surprised." Honesty seemed like the wisest answer at the moment.

He snapped his fingers at a servant who stood nearby. The man disappeared into a nearby doorway and came back out with a leathern packet in his hand. Tancogeistla took it from him and handed it to me. "Give this to that dog of a vergobret," he growled, snarling out Malac's name.

"Right away?" I asked, remembering my promise to Diedre. If I did not return by nightfall. . .

"Immediately!" the old general snapped. "Or do you have commitments that take precedence over my orders, Cadwalador?"

I shook my head in the negative. "I had promised my wife that I would return to her by nightfall. That is all."

The expression on Tancogeistla's face never changed. He turned and barked at Belerios. The *brihentin* took a step forward to stand beside me. I watched him out of the corner of my eye, an imposing figure even in his street

106

clothes, the sword strapped to his side. There was a vest of mail beneath his cloak, I knew. I had made enough of them. "Belerios, inform this man's wife of the reasons for his absence. See that she is made comfortable."

"Yes, my lord." The *brihentin* turned and left the courtyard, his strides long and purposeful. He had his orders. As did I.

"I was glad to meet you, Cadwalador," Aneirin said, smiling at me as I started to leave. I nodded.

"Should I wait for an answer?" I asked, my attention still focused on Tancogeistla. No matter what his intentions for young Aneirin, my old general was still the man I had to deal with.

He smiled grimly. "No," he responded, shaking his head. "He will be coming back with you. The message will explain it all."

A regular ferry had been established for the use of men passing between Erain and the land of the Calydrae. I rode hard the rest of the day, reaching the ferry just before nightfall. The sun sank into the western sea, drowning its flames in a pool of molten blood. Reminding me of my promise to Diedre.

I encamped with the ferrymen that night, lying alone by the fire. I dreamed of Diedre, her face rising up before me. I fancied I could feel her, as if she lay there beside me on the sand of the beach.

The years of our marriage had been good ones, as I established my gobacrado there in Attuaca, attempting to provide for the family I had so suddenly taken upon myself. A wife, and a daughter. And soon, a son. . .

I smiled at the memory. The night before, when we had lain together on our small wooden pallet. Diedre had taken my hand and placed it against her swollen belly. "Feel him, my love," she had whispered, smiling into my eyes through the darkness. "Feel him move. A miracle—a miracle of our love, Cadwalador."

I had bent over and gently kissed her lips, whispering my love softly, as though afraid of waking her daughter. Her face was radiant with joy, glowing in the moonlight that shone through our window.

And at once it changed, her face wet with tears, her eyes red from crying, her voice calling out my name. Screaming. . .

I sat bolt upright, a fear gripping my heart. The sun was just beginning to peek over the hills behind me. It was a dream. Just a dream.

I went aboard the ferry with the boatmen and together we began the passage. I stood in the stern of the boat for a long time, gazing back at the land of my home, where I had left my beloved. I had never dreamed of anything half so powerful as the love I felt for Diedre. United in sorrow, our union had endured and become stronger because of it. She was a part of me, inseparable. As the bard said, two had become one.

But once again, I had a duty to fulfill. Perhaps this last obligation to Tancogeistla would quit me of him forever. I had lost too much following his banner.

It took me several days to find Malac. He had hidden himself away from the world, from everyone that had shunned him. When I reined my horse in outside his house, the only sign that it was the residence of the Vergobret were three guards standing outside. It was little more than a hovel.

"I need to speak with Malac," I demanded, swinging down from the back of my horse. "I have a message for him."

The *brihentin* seemed unimpressed. "From who?"

"Tancogeistla," I replied, watching their eyes for any sign of trouble. For there it was that it would come. Not in the tightening of a hand 'round the hilt of a sword, but rather in the flicker of an eye. Cavarillos had taught me that, drilled it into me in our mock sword-bouts back in the early days of our friendships. I could still hear his voice ringing down through the years.

My eyes, Cadwalador. Watch my eyes, not my blade. For my eyes will tell you where my blade will go. It is something no man, not even I, can help. The eyes hold no secrets. Watch my eyes.

But there was nothing to see. The oldest of the *brihentin* smiled at the mention of Tancogeistla's name. "The leader of our people," he intoned reverently. "Come inside."

108

I ducked my head to enter the hovel. Darkness filled the interior, but one of the guards went over and stirred the coals of the fire there in the center of the floor, fanning them into flame.

"Malac!" he called.

After a few moments, an aged figure shuffled from behind a partition towards the back of the dwelling.

I was shocked by the change two years had wrought. He looked old, far beyond his years. His white hair was long and unkempt, a full beard covering his face. His skin was white as paste, untouched by the sun. And yet I could see it in his eyes as he stepped into the firelight.

He was the same Malac. As crafty and cunning as ever. "Cadwalador," he greeted, surprising me with his remembrance of my name.

"Yes, my lord."

He sagged onto a rude bench carved by the side of the wall and motioned for me to sit across from him. "It has been a long time since anyone has called me that. No one feels I deserve the distinction. You may call me by my name, if you so wish. What is it you have for me?"

I handed over the leathern packet. "A message Tancogeistla wished me to deliver to you."

"That crafty devil," Malac whispered, almost chuckling. "He ruined me at last, you see that, do you not, Cadwalador?"

I nodded, watching as his thin fingers tore open the packet, unfolding the message inside. He spoke sharply to the *brihentin*, who stirred the embers into a brighter blaze, shadows dancing against the walls of the hovel.

He swore vociferously as he finished reading and I inquired the import of the message.

"As you undoubtedly know, your general is planning another campaign. Against the people of Yns-Mon."

I sat there in stunned silence. I knew nothing of such plans. And I told Malac so.

"Perhaps the general no longer takes you into his confidence as he used to," Malac suggested, the craftiness still there in his voice. "He wishes me to come and ride with him in this campaign. He challenges me to prove my bravery one last time."

My head came up. "You would be riding to your death!"

He nodded. "I know it. Yet, what is life here? A never-ending death of shame and disgrace." He stood, beckoning to the *brihentin*. "Bring me my sword."

"You were told to bring me back, were you not?" Malac asked, gazing into my eyes.

"Yes," I admitted.

"Then I will give you no trouble. You have stood unwavering with Tancogeistla for years. Would you mind if I asked you why?"

I shook my head. "I don't know, really. He was the rightful heir. . ." my voice trailed off.

"I will tell you why, if you so wish. It is because you are a man of principle, a man of loyalty. You cannot leave him now even should you wish to do so, even if you should wish it. Because you would feel that you were doing wrong. Tancogeistla should appreciate such loyalty. The gods know he cannot find it in half the fawning sycophants he gathers 'round himself. I will come with you."

"Very well. How soon can you leave?"

The *brihentin* returned, bearing Malac's sword. The old man took it and girded it to his body. "Immediately."

We rode back to the ferry together in silence, as I pondered the old Vergobret's words. There was something sad and something poignant about his calm acceptance of death.

Within two days, we rode into Attuaca. Malac smiled as our mounts trotted through the gate. "It has been years since I have seen this place, Cadwalador. It has grown." He paused. "And this could have all been mine had I not been so foolish as to run from the heat of the battle."

"Nay, my lord," I replied, surprising myself by my own words. "Tancogeistla would have killed you anyway."

He turned in his saddle, looking back into my face. "As he intends to do now?"

I nodded slowly.

"Be careful, my young friend. A man in Tancogeistla's position is not to be trusted. He will kill me, as he has every right to. But he will also eliminate anyone who he perceives as a threat. Tread wisely."

"I must leave you here," I said finally. "You will find Tancogeistla in the palace. I must go home to my wife."

"You are married?" Malac asked, raising his eyebrows. I acknowledged his question with a nod.

"Then tread twice as wisely. Fare thee well, young Cadwalador."

We parted ways, and I rode slowly down the muddy street toward my home, which was built beside the gobacrado. As I approached, I spied a figure slumped on my doorstep. It was Berdic, apparently sleeping off a drunken stupor.

But it was strange. Diedre knew he was my friend. We had given him hospitality before when the tavern had thrown him into the street. Why had she not taken him in now?

I dismounted, gazing down into my friend's face. He was clearly drunken, snoring loudly as he lay there on the step. I took him by the arm, but failed to waken him. Shaking my head in disgust, I stepped over his prostrate form and pushed open the door to my home.

Everything was quiet. Far too quiet. "Diedre!" I called, almost fancying in my imagination that I could hear her voice answering back, light and cheerful, as in days of old. Her beautiful face smiling around the curtains of cloth that partitioned our apartment.

There was nothing. Fear took my heart in its icy grip. I called again, for her, her daughter, anyone. The only sound was my own voice, and Berdic's snoring.

And then I saw. Food piled in a heap on the table, a mountain of it. I had seen it before. Gifts from neighbors and friends. The presents of death.

I raced from the room, grabbing Berdic by the shoulder and shaking him. He snored on, unfazed. Swearing viciously, I slapped him across the face.

"Berdic!" I screamed, fear in my voice. His eyes flickered awake. "Oh. It—it's you, Cadwalador," he said stupidly.

"Where is Diedre? Berdic! Tell me where she is!"

He gazed up at me through bloodshot eyes. My question didn't seem to make much sense to him. "Diedre? You don't know?"

"If I knew, I wouldn't be *asking*!" I exclaimed through clenched teeth. "What happened to her, you fool!"

"You don't know," he said, shaking his head as though to clear the cobwebs of drink from it. "Oh, Cadwalador. I'm sorry. You—you didn't know."

"Tell me!"

"She's dead," he whispered.

I stood there in shock, my lips moving but no words coming out. I had no power to form them. My entire world was crashing down around me. Malac's words flickered through my mind.

He will eliminate anyone he perceives as a threat. Tread wisely. . .

"Dead?" I asked, looking down into Berdic's face, begging him to tell me otherwise. That his words were a lie. That it wasn't true.

He nodded slowly. . .

Chapter XIV: Recompense

I turned and ran into the house, tears flowing freely down my cheeks. "Diedre!" I screamed, the echoes mocking me hollowly. I grasped the curtains and tore them from their hangings, casting the ripped fabric to the floor. "Diedre!"

The apartment was bare. I heard movement behind me and turned on heel, my heart twisting inside me. It was only Berdic, leaning staggeringly against the doorframe.

"What happened?" I demanded. He shook his head drunkenly. "A curse upon you, Berdic!" I cried, grabbing him by the shoulders and shaking him fiercely.

"What happened?"

Sadness was in his eyes. "She—she's dead, Cadwalador. That's all I know. Maybe—"

Another form flitted into the door behind him, a woman's figure. My eyes locked on her face. It was the neighbor woman. Clutching tightly to her hand was Diedre's daughter.

"I came as soon as I heard you were home," she whispered softly.

"Home?" I exclaimed in bitterness. "Is that what *this* is? That murderer has taken her away from me!"

Tancogeistla's face rose up before me and for a moment I could almost feel my fingers closing around his throat, strangling the life from the old drunkard's body. For him Inyae had been sacrificed. By his order, Diedre had been killed. Leader of my people or no, he had forfeited his life by this.

"The messenger came from Tancogeistla," the woman continued. "I do not know what he told her, but she took the news badly. Diedre was worried for you, Cadwalador. To the end, she called out your name."

I lowered my head, feeling the condemnation descend onto my shoulders. The woman was still talking. ". . .an hour later, her daughter came running for me. Her pains were upon her, that she might bring forth the child."

"But her time was not for months to come," I whispered, in shock at the news.

The neighbor woman nodded. "I know. It happens this way at times, often when the mother is under great stress. I sent my son to Tancogeistla to summon help."

"And he rejected you," I hissed, sure I knew now what had happened.

She shook her head. "No. He was concerned and sent back one of the druids in his retinue, a man skilled in herbs and surgery. There was nothing he could do for her."

"Tell me his name."

The woman looked up into my eyes. "Do not blame him for your wife's death. There was nothing—"

"Tell me his name!"

"Motios," she replied. I felt as though I had been slapped. Motios, the wise old druid I had communed with on Teamhaidh. No groveling pawn of Tancogeistla. I had seen him at work, curing the diseased in Emain-Macha.

"What happened?" I asked, swallowing the lump in my throat. I had to know the truth.

"He did the best he could, but when the child was delivered, there was no breath in him."

"Him? A son?"

She nodded. I turned away, covering my mouth with my hand as though to prevent the sobs from escaping. It was a futile effort.

"She was weak from the delivery, and could not bear the news. She died soon after."

"I should have been here," I whispered, condemning myself bitterly. If only. . .

My mind swirled with everything that filled it so suddenly. Had Tancogeistla intended my wife to die, he would never have sent Motios. He would have sent someone he could use, could twist to his own will. Or had I misjudged the druid?

I looked the woman in the eyes. "The neighbors brought food in her memory, did they not?"

"Yes."

"Take what you will of it," I answered brusquely. "Just take care of my daughter until I return."

I took my javelins down from the wall, brushing past Berdic to reach the door.

"Where are you going, Cadwalador?" he called after me, still slurring the words.

"To Tancogeistla!" I screamed back, my rage consuming me. I wasn't thinking clearly. I knew only one thing. My answers lay at the palace. . .

I remember nothing of my march through the streets that desolate afternoon, only my arrival at the palace gate just as the sun began its downward journey into the sea.

"Take me to Tancogeistla," I ordered the *brihentin* who stood in the entrance. They looked at me, at the javelins in my hand, and began to move towards me.

"Who sent you?" One of them called. "Malac? You were sent to fetch him and he has turned your heart away from our rightful vergobret!"

I raised a javelin in my hand, smiling in their faces. I outranged their swords. I could kill at least one of them, maybe both, before they could fall upon me. I could run before they could pursue me, encumbered as they were by their weapons and armor. But I had no intention of running.

"Stand away from him, my sons," a voice interrupted, coming from behind the gate. Tancogeistla.

The *brihentin* backed away, their hands still grasping the hilts of their swords. They looked at their leader in shock.

"I expected you, Cadwalador," Tancogeistla said calmly. "Diedre's death is a tragedy felt by all of us here."

"Liar!" I hissed. One of the *brihentin* started to draw his sword from its sheath.

Tancogeistla looked at me, and I could see something in his eyes. He seemed puzzled. "Why would you doubt that?"

"Belerios killed her! What message did you tell him to give to her?"

The old general shook his head. "I told him to tell her that you were safe, that you were undertaking a mission for me. He was to take whatever steps were necessary to ensure her comfort. Is that not what he said?"

"No."

"Then what?"

"I don't know. But it killed her. Where is he?"

"Follow me," Tancogeistla motioned. He barked an order to the *brihentin* and they grudgingly let their swords slip back into their scabbards. I lowered my javelin and followed Tancogeistla through the gates.

We found Belerios in the courtyard, exercising at swords with another of the *brihentin*. His helmet was fastened under his chin by a leathern strap, but no other armor was visible.

"Belerios!" I cried, a challenge, rage in my voice. He turned, and for a moment, I could see a smile light up his face.

"Cadwalador," he nodded, making no attempt to sheathe his sword. "You found your wife well, I trust?" He was mocking me.

"Put up your sword, Belerios," Tancogeistla ordered sharply. The *Brihentin* shook his head.

"Not with this rabid wolf in front of me," he smiled back. "What is wrong, Cadwalador?"

"This man has lost his wife, Belerios," Tancogeistla replied. "Now, I am ordering you, put up your sword."

"What concern is his wife of mine?" Belerios demanded, taunting me. I stepped around Tancogeistla, taking one of my javelins in my right hand.

"You meant for her to die, didn't you?" I challenged, my eyes fastened on the *brihentin*'s face.

"Perhaps," he replied, laughing in my face. At my grief. The javelin flew from my hand without conscious thought, as though propelled of its own power. I saw Belerios' eyes widen, then the javelin struck him in the center of his chest.

In my fury, I had forgotten the mail shirt he wore under his outer garments. The tip of my javelin struck the mail and glanced harmlessly aside.

"Stop this!" Tancogeistla cried, his voice a dull ringing in my ears, a far-away cry. Neither of us heeded him. We were beyond that.

"I knew you would come, Cadwalador," Belerios hissed, circling me with his sword. "To see what had happened to your woman. And the whelp she bore."

His hatred baffled me, but I was beyond caring. I was in the zone now, watching two fighters circle. One with sword, the other with javelins.

I threw my second javelin, ignoring Tancogeistla's shouted order. Belerios twisted away and I missed completely. My hands were shaking, my fury destroying my aim. I had to get hold of myself. If I was not to die.

"You have one left, Cadwalador. Throw it and I will kill you. As I did your wife."

I stared into his eyes, forcing myself to ignore the blade he brandished. The eyes. The eyes. It was there I needed to focus, if I was to survive this.

"Keep it and I will kill you anyway," he chuckled, mocking my hesitation. We continued to circle, looking for an opening.

He was becoming confident, my futile throws convincing him that the victory was in his grasp. And I saw my chance.

Reversing my grip on the javelin to hold it as I would a spear, I hurled myself across the open space, ducking low to avoid the slash of his sword.

The blade bit deep into my shoulder and I bit my tongue against the pain, throwing my weight against the *brihentin* in an effort to take him off-balance, stabbing deep into his thigh with my javelin, ignoring the splintering of wood that told me my weapon was broken.

Belerios screamed, falling backward to the earth with me atop him. His sword was gone. As was his advantage. He was mine. I whipped the knife from the waist of my trousers and jammed it against his chin, holding him against the ground. He struggled, but the weight of the mail hampered his efforts.

"Tell me," I hissed. "Why? Why did you cause my wife's death?"

He spat in my face. I barely felt it. My anger could be no greater. "I have never done anything against you or your house. Why did you do this?"

117

The knife-tip pricked the skin of his throat, drawing blood. "You call it nothing?" he gasped. "That you should take my rightful place?"

I sensed that he was looking behind me and I looked up to see Tancogeistla standing over both of us.

"What do you mean?"

"He speaks of nothing but you. Cadwalador, son of the Wolf. Cadwalador, his bodyguard. Cadwalador, the man who saved his life on the Isle of Tin. Cadwalador, the man he wanted to succeed him. He ignored the years I spent with him, building an army against Malac, spying on his rival. I have put my life in danger countless times for his sake. All for nothing."

"You speak lies," Tancogeistla interrupted, his face flashing with anger. "I have promoted you to great honor, given you wealth and station! And you forget all of this? Let him up, Cadwalador."

I hesitated, looking down into the eyes of the man who had been the cause of Diedre's death. I wanted to kill him, to feel his blood run over my hands, to drown my sorrows in his life's current. Revenge.

"I *said*, Cadwalador," he repeated. "Let him up." I looked up and saw the naked blade in the old man's hands, the fire in his eyes. And I obeyed.

"You are a dog, Belerios," Tancogeistla hissed, stepping closer as the *brihentin* got to his feet. "An ungrateful dog! That you should spurn all the blessings of my court. It is an offense of the highest order."

Both Belerios and I saw the blade coming and I saw terror fill his eyes for a split-second. The slash decapitated the *brihentin*'s body and the head spun off to one side, the torso crumpling to the dirt of the courtyard, blood flowing freely from the corpse. Tancogeistla looked over at me and I nodded silently. It was recompense. . .

Five months after the death of Belerios, Tancogeistla's army left Attuaca, moving south along the coastline, towards the land of the Cyremniu, Yns-Mon. I did not accompany him.

I could still remember his words to me as I had turned to leave the palace. *What he hath said is true, Cadwalador. Always had I looked upon you as my successor. Only at Attuaca did I question your loyalty to me.*

118

And in my anger, I made the foolish choice of Aneirin moc Cunobelin.

I had turned to gaze into his eyes and found nothing but sorrow there. *He is a fine lad, but he lacks the warrior's heart. The men fail to respect him, and he will not have the throne for long. Once again the Aedui will be torn apart. My throne can still be yours, Cadwalador. Everything I have amassed, in reward for your faithful service. All of it, yours.*

I shook my head slowly. *Your life is not mine, my lord*, I had replied. *As Aneirin moc Cunobelin will not survive, neither would I. One thing I ask from you. Give me back my* wife!

And I had left the palace, intending never to return. The months passed. Tancogeistla and Malac moved south together, at the head of the army. The old Vergobret smiled at me as they rode past, well aware he was going to his death. And that I was living mine.

Diedre's daughter was my lifeline, my one link to a happier past, and as time passed by, she reminded me more and more of her mother. Ofttimes, I would retreat to my forge and weep, that she might not see my tears and wonder why. Her childish innocence delighted me. I sought to bathe myself in it, that I too might return to that place. Before the knowledge of evil.

And then one day, a rider reined up beside the gobacrado, his horse dusty from the road. I watched from my window as he tethered the horse and walked toward me.

It was Motios. The first time I had seen him since Diedre's death. He had accompanied the army of Tancogeistla when they moved south. I went out to meet him.

"May I have a cup of cold water, my son?" he asked, throwing back the hood of his cloak.

"Of course," I replied with a smile, reaching for the dipper.

"Thank you. Tancogeistla is arriving in the city this evening."

"Then the assault on Yns-Mon—failed?"

The old druid shook his head. "No, my son. It succeeded, after a hard-fought battle against the Cyremniu. Many died, but the hill-fort was secured. Yns-Mon and the surrounding countryside are in our hands."

There was pride in his voice. "And Malac?" I asked.

"He is dead," Motios replied simply.

"Tell me what happened, please."

Motios glanced into the interior of the gobacrado. "Perhaps we should take a seat, Cadwalador. The story is a long one."

I nodded slowly and led him back into the cover of the building, where we could be shielded from the wind.

"We encamped around the city for many long weeks," he stated, beginning his tale. "Many of our young men wished to attack, but Tancogeistla advised caution. Malac threw in his lot with the young men and for a while nearly succeeded in splitting the army."

I shook my head in disbelief. The old man had not intended to die passively. Not by a long shot.

"However, Tancogeistla rallied the men to his banner and reminded them that his decisions had carried the day in the past, and that they should be careful of Malac. That it was Malac's foolishness and cowardice that had cost us so many lives in the assault on Attuaca. Should we chance another reckless assault based on his advice?"

"Finally, on a snowy day just over a week ago, the Cyremniu, weakened and desperate from the siege, burst forth from behind their palisade to attack us."

"Malac's bodyguards were the first into the saddle and they almost immediately charged the enemy, scattering skirmishers left and right, trampling men underfoot."

"Tancogeistla soon followed, and the vanguard of the enemy was chased back in the town. However, a brave contingent of the *cladaca* followed so hot on the heels of the enemy skirmishers that they entered the gates before the enemy could close them, and fought boldly there until more troops arrived to bolster their line. It was then that Malac apparently spied the chariots of the enemy king, a chieftain by the name of Virsuccos, and wishing to engage him in single combat, he gave chase. I do not know whether Tancogeistla was unaware of Malac's departure, or whether he merely wished the vergobret to die fighting, for he sent no men to reinforce Malac. The vergobret galloped off after the enemy chariots with only seventeen of his bodyguards."

"It was intentional," I interrupted, fire flashing in my eyes. The old druid glanced over at me.

"There is a change in you, my son. You have developed a bold tongue. It is not a gift to men who wish to live long."

"I no longer desire long life," I snapped back in anger. "All reason for that has been taken from me."

His face softened. "I did everything I could for your wife, Cadwalador. Everything in my power. You must believe that."

"Go on with your story," was my only response. My grief was still too great to discuss Diedre. With anyone.

After a long pause, he went on. "All this I have told you, I witnessed with my own eyes. Of what follows after, I have only the word of one of the *brihentin* who escaped from Malac's retinue. Virsuccos, the Cyremniu chieftain, retreated rapidly, his bodyguards tossing javelins back at Malac as they rode away, their chariots bouncing over the rugged terrain."

"They led Malac far from the town, as he pursued in a fruitless effort to regain his reputation for bravery. It was at this time that Tancogeistla heard of Malac's gambit and left the infantry within the walls of Yns-Mon, riding with his horsemen and I to discover Malac's fate. When we reached the ridge to the south of the town, we discovered the Virsuccos' chariots had turned and were engaged in a fierce melee with Malac's *brihentin*."

"Malac's bodyguard told me that the chariots wheeled on them suddenly and dashed through the midst, their wheels breaking the legs of horses and grinding their riders into the snow. Many men died in the first charge, but Malac rallied the survivors bravely and threw them into the combat, cutting down many of the Cyremniu charioteers. The slaughter great on both sides."

"It was as though Malac had a death wish. He stayed in the melee with the charioteers for far too long. Finally only a few of his bodyguards were left, the rest killed or unhorsed by the vicious attack of the Cyremniu."

"Malac was engaged in hand-to-hand combat with one of the charioteers when a rider in Virsuccos' chariot raised himself up and cast his javelin at the Vergobret. The javelin smote Malac in the neck, just under the helmet, and he screamed, falling from his horse into the snow, dead."

"The last bodyguard of Malac cried with a loud voice at his lord's downfall and turned his horse to flee from the field of battle. Malac's body was trampled 'neath the wheels of the chariots."

"And where was Tancogeistla?" I asked, gazing earnestly into the face of the druid.

Motios held up a finger to silence me. "Let me continue, my son. I will tell you all."

"Seeing the death of Malac, Tancogeistla ordered his *brihentin* to charge down upon the charioteers from their position on the top of the ridge. Virsuccos was taken by surprise and Tancogeistla rode quickly to the side of his chariot. I followed, my own sword drawn. I could see the terror in the eyes of Cyremniu chieftain. He was facing his own death. Then Tancogeistla's sword descended upon him."

"Malac's death was avenged at the hand of Tancogeistla."

"After he had suffered him to be killed," I interjected sharply, rising and going over to the window of the gobacrado.

Motios' brow furrowed. "This man would have killed any of you he deemed a threat. Even at the last, he still tried to turn the army against Tancogeistla. As he would have done against you."

After a long moment, I nodded. "We spoke of Malac many years ago, Motios. And you told me that the enemy who faces you, sword drawn, is not the one you need to fear. Rather it is the man who greets you with a kiss. Is that not so?"

"Tancogeistla did only what he had to do. Malac was far from an honest enemy. You know that."

"Yes," I acknowledged. "I know. Tell me the rest."

"We rode slowly back to the town to find the *balroae* of Attuaca still engaged in fighting with one man in the square of Yns-Mon."

"He was a large man, a champion, skilled in the use of the sword. But at long last they overwhelmed him and thrust him through with their spears as he lay on the ground. The hill-fort was ours. We had overcome the Cyremniu."

Chapter XV: Honest Words

Tancogeistla returned to Attuaca a few months later, and was given a hero's welcome. His men had begun referring to him as Tancogeistla oi Neamha, or Tancogeistla the Berserker, a reference to what they viewed as his courageous sword-fight with the leader of the Cyremniu. I did not see him again until two years later, at the marriage feast of Aneirin moc Cunobelin. . .

I was working in my gobacrado when the messenger came from the palace. Diedre's little daughter, Faran, was in the care of a neighbor woman for the day. "Cadwalador?" he asked, striding toward my forge.

"I am he," I answered, looking around at him. "What do you want?"

"Aneirin moc Cunobelin desires your presence at the feast being given in honor of his marriage tonight."

I acknowledged the news with a nod. Indeed, I had heard of the girl who was to be his bride. A woman picked out for him by my old friend Berdic, or so I had been told. If that was so, then her beauty was assured. As for her purity. . .

"I will be there," I replied, taking the iron from the fire and placing it on my anvil. The messenger smiled and wished me good-day.

That evening, I made arrangements for the neighbor to continue taking care of Faran and put on my best clothes for the feast.

I felt a pang of sorrow as I prepared. The last feast of this nature which I had attended—had been my own, celebrating my marriage to Diedre. It seemed such a short time ago. Indeed, our happiness had been short-lived. All I had left was memories, how precious they were. I found myself regretting each moment I had spent at the forge, the nights I had spent in Berdic's company, everything that had taken the place of time I could have spent with her. A man never knows how precious something is until it is taken from him. . .

I heard wild laughter coming from the palace as I dismounted outside. Clearly, the feast had already begun.

I passed easily through the guards who stood outside. Who is Tancogeistla afraid of now? I asked myself silently. I looked from left to right as I entered the courtyard. A pavilion was set up at one end, with two mock thrones placed beneath its shelter. On one of them sat a very beautiful young woman in the bride's attire. The other was empty.

She caught me looking at her and smiled across the crowd, jewel-green eyes sparkling as they looked into my face. Clearly she was not unaccustomed to men staring at her. I turned away, unsettled by her gaze.

"Cadwalador!" a voice called loudly, a hand descending jovially on my shoulder. I turned, looking full into the face of Aneirin moc Cunobelin.

"It is good to see you, my brother," he declared, kissing me on both cheeks. "It has been too long."

"Ah, well, I have preferred to remain to myself these last few months."

He nodded, ignoring the import of my words in his own excitement. "But come, brother. I wish you to see my bride."

"I already have," I smiled, remembering the early days of my own marriage. The newness of it all.

"She is beautiful, is she not?"

"Indeed. May I congratulate you upon your marriage."

"Thank you. And thank our mutual friend."

"Oh?" I asked, unsure of what he meant.

"Berdic," he answered, smiling as he gazed upon his new wife. "He introduced me to her."

"Of course," I nodded. "It has been good to speak with you."

"And I am honored by your presence, Cadwalador," Aneirin stated earnestly, turning to look me in the eye. "I hold the man who saved my father's life in great esteem."

"Nay, but you honor me, my lord," I replied.

He shook his head, reaching out to grasp me by the arm. "I meant those words, Cadwalador," he remonstrated, gesturing to the mug of ale in his hand. "I am not drunken—not yet. Look over there and tell me what you see."

I looked in the direction of his gaze. "It is Tancogeistla."

"Oi Neamha," Aneirin added. "The berserker. It saddens me, Cadwalador, all his life he has striven for the throne of the Aedui, to become the vergobret of his people. And yet now that he has attained it, he is an old man. He cannot live for many more years."

"I pray you are wrong," I replied honestly.

"I know why you say that, Cadwalador," Aneirin said after a long moment of silence. "You do not believe I am prepared to follow in his footsteps."

"I have never said such a thing, my lord," I responded, startled by the suddenness of his statement.

"But don't deny that you haven't thought it, Cadwalador. You are too sharp of a man not to have. Because it's true. The Aedui must be led by a warrior. And I lack in skill at arms."

I didn't know how to answer him with the honesty he seemed to demand. "That is why I will need you at my side—I will need your advice in the days ahead."

I stared at him in disbelief. "As you are not a warrior, neither am I, my lord. There are many who could better advise you than I."

"But none whom I would trust," he replied fiercely. "You were with my father on this island in the early days of the migration. And you followed him and protected his life at great cost to yourself. I know this, as does he. The rest, they circle like wolves, hedging their loyalties and watching for the opportunity to vaunt themselves above the rest. Above me and the trust Tancogeistla has placed in my care."

"I will do my best to repay your trust, " I said quietly, numb with the impact of his words.

"I have faith," he responded, "enjoy your evening, brother." He moved off through the crowd, the ale in his hand, leaving me alone.

I made my way over to where Tancogeistla stood, surrounded closely by several of his *brihentin*. As I came closer, I saw what Aneirin had meant. The years had taken their toll on my old general.

"Welcome to the feast, my son," he greeted, extending his hand to me. I still did not share Aneirin's sentiments. The same strength was still there as he gripped my hand firmly.

"I am glad to be here, my lord."

"I regretted that you could not accompany me on the expedition to Yns-Mon, but I understood your reasons."

Did he? I doubted it, but my doubts were not those that should be voiced. Just as I opened my mouth to continue the small talk, a man entered the courtyard, breathless and shouting.

"Tancogeistla! Tancogeistla!" Someone pointed him in the right direction, and I saw him pushing through the crowd toward us.

The Vergobret frowned, a puzzled look crossing his aged face. "I come from Ivomagos moc Baeren," the man gasped out, falling at Tancogeistla's feet.

"Who?" I heard one of the nobles ask.

Tancogeistla waved his hand for silence. "What is it, man? What message do you bring?"

"My master is in Caern-Brigantae, carrying out your mission among the Casse. Three days ago, he was summoned before Mowg, the chieftain of that place."

"Yes? Go on!" Tancogeistla exclaimed impatiently.

"Mowg informed my master that he was canceling our alliance with his people, that our advance on Yns-Mon had displeased him and the High King and that they could no longer continue in fellowship as friends with us."

Tancogeistla turned to me, his tone grave, a dangerous fire glittering in his eyes. "Bring Aneirin to me. I must see him at once. . ."

126

Chapter XVI: War Upon the Wind

I was not privy to what passed between Tancogeistla and Aneirin moc Cunobelin that night. All I knew was that they left the marriage feast early, and together.

The Casse were a tribe in the south of the island. In the early days, when the migration had begun, their power had been centered in the southeast, all of their tribal territory centered around a hill-fort known as Camulosadae. However, in the fourteen years since, they had expanded their power, taking in almost the entire island. We had snatched Yns-Mon after they had attacked it three times, each time being repulsed with heavy losses. In the south, only Ictis held out against their armies.

Ictis. . . The name brought memories flooding back into my mind. The place where we had been routed so decidedly back when we had first landed on the island. The defeat which had condemned us to our wandering. Rumor in Attuaca was that Tancogeistla was setting his sights on it as the next target of our warbands, that he wished to avenge his defeat before he died.

I could understand why. However, I had the feeling that the new aggression of the Casse might change all that.

Two weeks after the night of the feast, two contingents of men arrived from Emain-Macha. The sight of them marching through the gate nearly took my breath away. These were no levies, drawn from the poor of Erain. These were the finest warriors I had ever seen.

In front marched the chieftains of the Goidils, the *eiras*, now rallying to Tancogeistla's banner.

And right behind them came warriors from the Ebherni, one of the most powerful tribes in all Erain. They were cloaked in armor from their heads to their thighs, armor like the scale of a fish.

I had never seen anything like it, and from my position beside the street, marveled at the craftsmanship. I could barely dream of the level of skill needed to create such masterpieces. They were beautiful.

But their arrival boded something far darker. Tancogeistla was once again bracing for war. Whether it was his preparations to advance upon Ictis, or whether he planned to strike our former allies, the Casse, I knew not. But war was upon the wind. . .

And then one day a runner came from Yns-Mon, with a message from the military commander there, a captain named Piso.

His news was undoubtedly intended for Tancogeistla's ears only, but within hours of his arrival it had spread all over Attuaca like a wind-fanned fire.

A man had been caught spying on the defenses of Yns-Mon. Placed under guard and tortured by Piso, at long last he had given up the name of the man who had ordered him on his mission. It was Massorias, a chieftain of the Casse, brother of Mowg, the chieftain who had given Tancogeistla's emissary their ultimatum.

And once again, as he had after the messenger from Ivomagos, Tancogeistla went into council with several of the nobles of the Aedui, as well as Aneirin moc Cunobelin.

What they decided was none of my affair. I went back to my forge, in hopes that if hostilities commenced, I would be left out of them. I wanted nothing further to do with war. It had taken too much from me. However, Aneirin's words at the feast left me very much in doubt as to whether I would be permitted to stay away.

A year passed, a year of tension and preparations. Troubling news came also from Erain.

Praesutagos, the eldest son of Malac, had come of age and had assumed the governorship of Ivernis, without Tancogeistla's leave or assent.

Yea, in the same year, his sister Keyne was given in marriage to a Caledone by the name of Erbin moc Dumnacos.

His loyalties at the present were uncertain, but the familial bond between him and Praesutagos was troubling. I looked toward Tancogeistla's death with a distinct sense of unease. It seemed forces across the waters were gathering against him and Aneirin.

Praesutagos was a Carnute, as had been his father. Harking back to the days of the Gallic Council at Cenabum, the majority of the druids had supported Malac's usurpation of the throne. And they had become increasingly disenchanted with Tancogeistla. . .

Ogrosan descended upon us, the tall trees around Attuaca bearing snow upon their eternally green branches. And with the snow came the end of campaign season. Armies did not go forth to war in the dark months. To do so was to tempt fate.

Apparently, the Casse had other notions, or perhaps they had decided to make their own fate. Either way, I was walking with Faran one sunny wintry day, just outside the kran, or palisade, which protected Attuaca. Aeduan carpenters had repaired the damage caused by Tancogeistla's rams so long ago. Faran was nearly six years old now, and was reminding me more of her mother with each passing day. She had no memories of Diedre, something which saddened me far more than words will permit me to express. Her mother had been taken from her far too soon.

As we walked, I heard a cry and turned to see a man floundering in the snow. I let go of Faran's hand and rushed through the knee-deep snow to his side. A scraggly beard heavy with snow and ice covered his face. He looked like he was starving, weak from his exertions. Too weak to rise.

I put my arm around his waist and pulled him to his feet, carefully guiding him toward the gate. He was shivering uncontrollably, his teeth gnashing against each other. "Let me help you inside, my friend," I said cheerfully. "I'll fix up a bed and you can warm yourself by my fire."

A light came suddenly into his eyes and he gripped my arm with the power of a madman. "No," he whispered insistently, the words coming from between cracked and bleeding lips. "Take me to the palace."

"Why?" I asked, surprised by his request. "Do you have business there?"

"Yea," he replied, "with Tancogeistla. I come from Yns-Mon."

"All this way," I exclaimed in surprise. "In the middle of *ogrosan*? You must have been mad!"

"They sent me to bring word," he gasped out. "We are besieged."

"By whom?" I asked, knowing the answer before he even breathed.

"The Casse. . ."

Chapter XVII: Relief of the Oppidum

We set out for Yns-Mon four days from the arrival of the runner. I rode with Aneirin in the vanguard, accompanying some ninety-one *brihentin* and nobles of the Aedui. Taken together, the army consisted of five hundred and twenty-eight footsoldiers, comprising *lugoae, vellinica, balroae, ordmalica*, Briton champions recruited in Yns-Mon itself, as well as the contingents of Erain which I had seen arrive in Attuaca.

The *brihentin* were the only cavalry accompanying the army, while my old friend Berdic led a force of one hundred and twenty of the *iaosatae* to screen our advance.

The news of the Casse's attack did not entirely take me by surprise. Still, their attack in the midst of *ogrosan* was unexpected, to say the least.

Aneirin's nerves were at a fever pitch as we rode southward. I could see it in his eyes, hear the uneasy excitement in his voice when he spoke. In his manner, I saw myself reflected as though in a glass, the way I had been when we had first come to this isle, before the defeat at Ictis, the brutal massacre of Inyae's village, the flight north into the snows. And in that moment, I realized how much I had changed. It was unsettling.

I could sense that he wished to speak of his feelings, but was unsure how to do so, embarrassed at the presence of the *brihentin*, hardened warriors all.

He looked at me one night as we encamped, building a fire to ward off the chill. "Let me take that, my lord," I asked quietly, taking a bundle of sticks from his arms and placing them gently on the embers, so as not to extinguish the struggling flame.

When I straightened, I found him looking at me. "We will be heading into battle soon," he said nervously, rubbing his hands together in an effort to warm himself.

"Yes, my lord," I responded. "Only four days journey, if Tancogeistla's geographer knows what he's talking about."

"What is it like?"

"What?" I asked. "Battle?"

He nodded, looking around as if to see if anyone else had heard his question. We were alone. "I remained with the baggage train during the assault on Attuaca. Everyone deemed me too young to be of any use. I have never actually seen the fray."

I waved my hand to the many fires that flickered through the trees, where our army was encamped. "There are many warriors here, men who enjoy the battle, to whom the cries of our enemies are music to their ears. I ask nothing more of life than that I be permitted to return to my gobacrado, my forge. Why do you not ask them?"

He sat down beside me on a fallen log, gazing earnestly into the flames. And for a long time he did not answer. Finally, "Because I trust you not to despise me, Cadwalador. Not to despise me as all these men do. They know I am not one of them. I am a Cruithni, an outlander. I must gain their respect if I am to lead them. Yet I know not how to accomplish that."

"What is the advice of Tancogeistla?"

"That I win their respect by my deeds in battle. That is why I asked you the question. What is battle like?"

I was silent for a long time, staring into the fire in my turn, watching as the sparks danced into the night sky, shooting ever upward, their light illuminating the forest. His question turned over and over in my mind. Unanswerable. . .

"It is chaos," I said at long last, my voice a mere whisper to the trees. "Chaos and confusion. Men sent screaming into eternity. It is the knowledge that you must kill to live, keep moving, keep killing even if the carnage sickens you. Men are turned unto the beasts of the forest as though seized by a lust for the blood of their fellow man."

"And what decides the victor?" Aneirin asked, looking into my eyes.

"The victor. . ." I whispered, calling to my remembrance the words of Cavarillos those many years earlier, " the victor is the man who is able to keep his head in the chaos, who can forget that he is butchering men just like himself, who can fight with both the ferocity of a beast and the mind of a man. Such a man will emerge victorious."

"An incredible task," he said slowly, his eyes on the ground. He kicked aimlessly at the snow with his foot, watching as the flakes melted from the heat of the fire. His teeth clenched. "But I must do it."

I could see the pain on his face as he glanced sideways at me. "I will prove myself worthy of the Aedui. I have no other choice. . ."

We continued to advance, southward on the dirt road Tancogeistla had ordered built a few years earlier. If not for it, we could never have traversed the snows. Even with it, we struggled. Several men froze to death in the night. A horse wandered away from the camp and was found six hours later, as stiff as wood.

To our west we could occasionally glimpse the great sea. The oppida of Yns-Mon was built on what could be called a large peninsula jutting out into the waters. We were getting closer. Now our only fear was whether we had arrived in time.

Then one morning several of Berdic's scouts came running back into camp, breathless and gasping with excitement.

"We have glimpsed the kran of Yns-Mon!" one of them cried, calling out to Tancogeistla. "The gate is smashed open and one of the walls has been broken down."

I saw the fire catch in the old general's eyes. "And have the Casse taken the town?"

The scout shook his head. "None of the enemy are in evidence, my lord. Yet we could see mounds of bodies piled near the gate, as though a great slaughter had taken place."

Tancogeistla turned in his saddle, looking back over the column. "This may be a trap of the Casse. We must send a scouting party to ride in and scout out the oppida, lest our enemies lurk inside to ambush us."

"I will go, father," Aneirin said quietly. Tancogeistla glanced sharply at his adopted son and heir and shook his head. "No."

"Is there a man who will go and espy out the enemy for me? Who follows the banner of Tancogeistla oi Neamha?" the old king cried, his sword brandished high to the heavens.

Aneirin glanced at me and nodded slowly, kicking his mount into a trot, riding out to the front of the column, right past his father.

I clucked gently to my horse and he moved forward, bearing me toward Tancogeistla.

The general clasped at my arm as I rode by. "Take care of my son, Cadwalador. His life. . .I will require it at your hand."

"Yes, my lord," I replied, staring him full in the face. Then I was past, following Aneirin moc Cunobelin out into the open plain before the oppida of Yns-Mon. Behind me, I could hear the hoofbeats of the rest of Aneirin's bodyguard following us. Almost forty horsemen, riding slowly onto the plain. . .

The town was silent. It was as the scouts had said. I came abreast of Aneirin as we rode toward the walls. Sweat was running down his forehead, icy streaks of perspiration criss-crossing his brow. He was afraid, I could see it in his eyes. As was I. But in that moment, I admired him. Despite his fear, despite his innate disposition toward the easy side of life, he was placing his life in jeopardy. And I admired him for it, even if in my heart I knew he was merely desperate to prove his manhood.

We were within bow-shot of the kran. And yet nothing as we continued our slow advance.

Bodies in various stages of decay were heaped around the gate, which swung loosely on its broken hinges. Only the cold kept the flies away.

A shout went up from within the palisade, a cry of warning. Our presence had been detected.

A man stepped from between the broken gates, a spear clutched tightly in his hands. His neck and right shoulder were swathed in bloody, dirty bandages. "Who are you?" he asked defiantly, more men emerging from the palisade behind him.

"I am Aneirin moc Cunobelin, the heir of Tancogeistla," Aneirin cried, bringing his horse up sharply.

For a moment, the man just stared at him, at us, then his shoulders sagged in relief. "We had begun to think you would never come. I am Piso, the commander of the garrison. What remains of it."

"And the Casse?" Aneirin asked. "Are they still in the area?"

Piso kicked savagely at a severed head lying near his foot. "All that remain," he sneered, " are like unto him. The rest ran like dogs."

His eyes scanned the horizon nervously. "I know not when they may return. Howbeit, as long as your army is here, that does not matter. The army *is* with you, is it not?"

Aneirin nodded. "Tell us of your story."

Piso laid his spear to the side. "Come inside and I will. . ."

Chapter XVIII: The Winding of the Road

"For three months, they waited, constructing two mighty battering rams from the wood of the forest," Captain Piso began, sitting down in front of a half-burned hovel. "And then early one morning about a week ago, they attacked."

"They outnumbered us heavily, possessing well over three hundred men more than my small garrison. Therefore they came forward without fear, pushing before them the rams. I ordered my slingers to bombard the enemy as they came close, then positioned the rest of my men close behind the walls. Nothing we did succeeded in stopping the rams, and by the time the sun had risen high into the sky of *ogrosan*, the gates were destroyed."

"Yea, mere moments later, the second ram broke open the wall alongside the gate and the Casse poured into the breach."

"My men fought with courage," Piso stated proudly, looking around into their tired faces. "But the Casse steadily pushed us back. Their chieftain rode into battle in a chariot, surrounded by his retainers, and when he charged the gate, the *cladaca* broke, running for the center of town, followed by a few of the *teceitos*."

"The chieftain rode through the midst of our men and pursued the *cladaca*, coming upon them as they rallied near the foot of the hill."

"Summoning up their remaining courage, my men threw their javelins into his bodyguard and then charged, surrounding the chariots and hemming them in. The chieftain fought bravely, but it would do him no good. They hamstrung his horses and brought him to the ground, where they pulled off his armor and killed him."

"Word of his death spread through the army of the Casse like a flame, disheartening their warbands. I was standing with the slingers away from the carnage at the breach, and, sensing the panic beginning, I ordered the *iaosatae* into the fray with their knives. One by one, the Casse warbands broke before us, streaming back over the plain toward where you approached just now. The day was ours."

I looked over at Aneirin, who was drinking in the man's words as a thirsty man drinks water. And indeed, the bodies still strewn over the ground indicated nothing less than a heroic fight. Tancogeistla would be sure to hear of this. . .

We stayed in Yns-Mon for the next three months, biding our time and repairing the palisade. Though officially Tancogeistla was angry at Aneirin moc Cunobelin for his insubordination, I could tell the truth every time I met with the old general. He was proud of his heir's performance, and it showed.

He wasn't fooling Aneirin either. The young man had carried himself differently ever since that day. Gone was at least a part of the languor that had characterized his bearing ever since the first day that I had known him. He supervised the rebuilding of the kran, acting like the second-in-command of Tancogeistla he was.

And then one day, a week after the finishing of the kran, a messenger came to us as Aneirin and I stood together on a sharp bluff overlooking the sea.

"Tancogeistla wishes to see both of you. At once!"

Without speaking, both Aneirin and I swung onto the backs of our horses and rode quickly back to the oppida.

Tancogeistla was standing in the courtyard of Piso's house, sketching something in the dirt with the pointed end of a stick. Several of the nobles of the Aedui were gathered round them. With a flash of alarm, I saw one of them, a man by the name of Eporedoros moc Estes, scowl at Aneirin as we entered. Clearly, there was trouble gathering.

The old general looked up and smiled at our entrance. "Welcome, my son, Cadwalador. We are discussing preparations for a march."

"Against the Casse?" Aneirin, walking 'round the sketch to stand beside his adoptive father.

Tancogeistla smiled again, placing a hand on the shoulder of his young heir. "Nay, my son. Rather we march against the Dumnones, against the oppida of Ictis." He didn't wait for Aneirin's reaction.

"It has been many years," he continued. "They attacked us without provocation, slaughtering many of the Aedui. You remember, Cadwalador. You were there."

I nodded. The battle was seared into my memory as though with a hot iron. The hopeless stand outside Ictis, the ambush later on. I remembered Tancogeistla's drunken fury at the time, remembered that the Dumnones had not been *entirely* without provocation. Still, it would be a just fight.

"We have recently received information from our spy in the south that the Dumnones have just repulsed a heavy attack by the Casse. They will be weakened. It is now time to strike."

One by one, the nobles nodded their assent. Tancogeistla looked round and smiled with satisfaction. "Then it is settled. By the time of the full moon, we will march on Ictis. . ."

It was as he said. Within one month, our army had set out once again. With few exceptions, it was the same army that had marched to the relief of Yns-Mon. Apparently, Tancogeistla deemed Piso's garrison sufficient to hold the oppida against any further attacks.

And so we marched on as the days grew longer, the sun rising ever higher into the sky. Often, our route of march took us within sight of the sea. Tancogeistla still rode at the head of the column, but he seemed more tired with each passing day. Clearly, the journey was wearing on him. He reacted by forcing the men to march harder, seemingly angered at his own weakness.

And then the rain started, pouring down upon the fertile valleys of the island in torrents. The paths we were following quickly turned into a quagmire, churned by hundreds of marching feet. It made lighting fires at night nearly impossible, and only the warmth of the season saved us.

It was at the end of one of those long days of the march, after our meager rations had been consumed and our men had started to turn in for the night, that I stood under the shelter of a tree near the edge of camp, ducking my head against the relentless rain. And then I heard it.

Hoofbeats. The rhythmic pounding of a horse's hooves against hard ground. Coming ever closer. We had sent out no scouts.

Whoever was coming was not of our army. I reached under my cloak and tugged a dagger from my girdle, crouching there by the roadway.

The form of a galloping horse loomed out of the rain and fog and I sprang from my covert, waving my hands and screaming. Startled, the horse reared up, its hooves pawing the air dangerously close to my face.

"Halt!" I cried, clutching the dagger tightly in my hand.

The cloaked rider struggled to calm his horse, cursing it and me bitterly as he fought the animal to a standstill. Taking the reins in one hand, he slid to the ground, tossing back his cowl and staring into my eyes. A man about my own age, his hair red-orange and matted with rain. "What do you think you are doing?" he hissed.

I stared right back, never loosening my grip on the dagger. "Who are you?"

"Galligos," he replied proudly, as though the name would mean something to me. "Galligos moc Nammeios."

I had never heard it before. "I will take you into the camp," I said finally.

The warning was there, in his eyes, one moment before he struck. His left hand reached out with the rapidity of lightning and struck my wrist, sending the dagger spinning into the darkness. He stepped in close, under my guard, his blows knocking the breath from my body.

I slipped on the muddy ground and fell, striking something hard on my way down. Lights seemed to flash inside my head and then everything faded, leaving only the dim sound of footsteps slogging through the mud on into the heart of camp. Then that too disappeared as I slipped into the realm of the unknown. . .

Chapter XIX: Faces

When I awoke, my head was aching, images swirling frantically through my brain. What had happened?

And it all came rushing suddenly back. The cowled figure dismounting, pronouncing his name with the air of royalty, then disarming me and leaving me stretched senseless on the wet earth.

Where had he gone? I rose, rubbing my jawbone. It still ached from his blows. I stared down at the ground, still cloaked in the blinding rain and dark of night.

I could feel the outline of a footprint in the mud, the toe pointed toward the camp. He had gone in. Visitor or assassin, I knew not.

There was nothing to do but go in and find out. I ran swiftly down the muddy road, pell-mell into the camp.

One tent was pitched in the center of the camp, in the middle of hundreds of sleeping men wrapped in their cloaks on the rain-soaked ground. It was the tent of Tancogeistla and Aneirin moc Cunobelin. The most likely target for the shadowy rider, as well as the first place I had to go to organize a search.

I knelt by one of my sleeping comrades in the darkness, plucking a spear from his armaments. My own weapons were too far away. Speed was of the essence.

A single light burned from within the large tent, the flickering flame of an oil lamp. I could see men moving inside, their movements reflected by giant shadows against the wet fabric. Undoubtedly, our two leaders were still planning our next movements.

Grasping my spear firmly in my right hand, I moved swiftly to the side of the tent, straining to hear voices over the thunder of the storm. Tancogeistla's guards were nowhere to be seen.

An involuntary shudder ran through me, and it wasn't from the chill of the rain. Had Tancogeistla's ever-loyal *brihentin* been taken out with the same dispatch as myself?

And the assassin, where had he come from? Who was paying his hire? The Dumnones, the Casse, yea, even Praesutagos. My old general had made many enemies in his lifetime.

Moving stealthily, I slipped to the door of the tent, throwing back the flap suddenly.

Three figures were disclosed to my eyes, standing there around a small map drawn in the dirt, turning at my abrupt entrance. Three figures, where there should have been two.

Tancogeistla, Aneirin—and my friend from the road. Galligos, I thought, the name flashing back through my memory. He stood shoulder to shoulder with the leaders of the Aedui as they looked down at the map in the earth.

"Cadwalador!" Tancogeistla cried, looking with alarm at my uplifted spear. "What is the meaning of this?"

"Who is he?" I demanded, glaring at the stranger. I didn't lower my weapon. To my surprise, Tancogeistla's face split into a wide smile, then he began chuckling. He glanced over at the stranger. "Tell me, Galligos, is this the man you disarmed and shoved into the mud out there?"

The stranger nodded, smiling as though something was humorous. I looked from one to the other in confusion, then slowly lowered my spear.

"Galligos," Tancogiestla stated with a low chuckle, "you should not have done that. Cadwalador is one of my most trusted retainers—and an able warrior in his own right. Next time you trifle with him, he might have the incredible bad fortune to kill you."

He turned next to me. "This man," he said, pointing to the stranger, "is Galligos moc Nammeios, the spy who has spent the last five years searching out the lands of the Casse for our forces."

"He has served me well, and gathered much useful information in the service of our cause."

The tall spy reached forward, extending his hand to me. I grasped it awkwardly, slow to accept this sinister figure as a friend. "Where are the *brihentin*?" I asked, shooting a sharp glance at Tancogeistla.

"Galligos is a spy, Cadwalador. It is best that as few know his identity as possible. I ordered them away."

The spy looked over at me, an easy smile flitting across his face. "I regret that I had to hit you so hard," he said, gesturing to my sore jaw. "But I dared not brook delay, or chance that you might not believe my story."

"Galligos," Tancogeistla interrupted, "has brought us important news. It appears an army of the Casse is marching to intercept us."

"Indeed?" I heard myself asking.

"Yes," the general replied. "Tell us once again of your information, my friend."

Galligos looked uneasily in my direction, but Tancogeistla reprimanded him. "Anything you say to me, the same can be shared with Cadwalador. He has proved himself in my service, defending my life more times than I can remember to count."

"Very well," the spy said with evident reluctance. "I have come just this night from the camp of a sub-chieftain of the Casse, a man by the name of Orgetoros. He marches with nigh eighteen score of men."

"A mere handful," Aneirin asserted confidently.

" 'Tis true," Galligos stated, "you outnumber him heavily. However, do not let overconfidence be your doom. He is not a day's journey from this camp. And he intends to strike. Do not let him catch you by surprise."

The spy moved quickly past me and lifted the tent flap, disappearing into the storm, into the tomb-like black of night. And he was gone. . .

What Galligos had told us was true. With his information in hand, we stayed where we were, drawing up in defensive positions on the edge of the forest. The sun rose

143

the next morning and continued on its journey ever higher into the sky. Towards noontime, one of Berdic's scouts came running back into camp, out of breath. "The Casse!" he cried. "The Casse are approaching. They advance to meet our line!"

We were deployed in what amounted to a single line, the Ebherni elite anchoring the left flank, with the *lugoae* standing to arms beside them, the *cwmyr* of Yns-Mon to their right, then Lugort's small contingent of *ordmalica*, the levy spearmen of the Goidils, and the nobles of Erain holding the position of honor on the right. Berdic's two contingents of *iaosatae* provided a missile screen to the right flank.

Tancogeistla's *brihentin* were positioned directly behind the main line, while I hid in the woods with Aneirin and his bodyguards.

The plan, as Tancogeistla had explained to us earlier, was to use our shock cavalry to its best limited effect in the woods, essentially as a surprise for the enemy. An enemy that would not be long in coming.

Our line stood just on top of a low knoll that swelled suddenly from the ground behind us. The forest made it difficult to see the enemy, but we could hear the sound of marching feet and defiantly chanted warcries as they advanced.

The *lugoae* were the first to be struck, a thin line of Britonic warriors sweeping down through the brush and trees. The *dubosaverlicica* rose from the grass and tossed their javelins into the Casse line, causing great confusion.

Then they too were struck, a fierce contingent of *botroas* sweeping down upon the Ebherni.

Aneirin spoke to me quickly and our column swung into motion, sweeping from our covert around the back to the left flank of the line, where the battle was at its hottest.

We rode around the end of our line and turned, riding down into the rear of the Casse warbands. We were unable to build much momentum in the woods, and I was continually forced to duck low in my saddle lest a low-hanging branch dismount me. We smashed into the backs of a unit of spearmen, knocking them to the ground.

I saw a man disappear beneath the hooves of my steed, his eyes wide with fear, a scream dying on his lips.

Blood flecked the bright blue woad that adorned his bare chest. I saw Aneirin not five paces away, cheerfully hacking at the sea of warriors with his sword.

Another warrior went down, his neck pierced by my spear. Howbeit, his fall jerked the weapon from my hand.

I reached down and pulled a small war hammer from my belt, a smaller copy of the hammers the *ordmalica* used—one which I had crafted in the gobacrado back in Attuaca.

As Lugort had testified so many years ago, it was a useful weapon in melee. I brought it down upon many a shoulder, many a head, breaking bone and fracturing skull, bodies falling beneath my horse.

It was the chaos I had told Aneirin of. Kill or be killed. Shed the blood of your fellow man, or have your own blood drench the grass in an offering.

The Casse began to break, pressed in front and behind. Turning to meet our charge, they were in turn charged by the Cwmyr, the midlander champions from Yns-Mon. They started running.

'Neath the spreading shadow of a mighty oak stood the remnant of the Casse *botroas*, surrounded and fighting to the death. Similar to the mercenaries who had once marched with Cavarillos, these men's chests were painted with sacred patterns of woad. I rode closer, together with Aneirin and the *brihentin*, into their midst. They were the last. I saw the fierce determination, the defiance in their eyes.

And something else. With a cry, I sprang from the back of my horse, into the sea of struggling men, into the melee. A face, something familiar. A man rose up to my left and I clubbed him down with the war hammer. Aneirin's voice sounded behind me, a cry of warning, but I was heedless of it.

It was him, it had to be. Older now, of a surety, but the same. Another instant and we were face-to-face in the heaving mass of men. His mouth opened in recognition and he raised his spear to block me, but I smashed it down, splintering the wood with a single blow of my hammer, forcing him back against the trunk of the great tree.

I was looking full into the face of one of the mercenaries that had fought with Cavarillos that dark night, that had escaped at his side.

"Where is Cavarillos?" I screamed, my weapon lost in the confusion, my hands around his throat as I pinned him to the bark of the tree. "Where is he?"

I felt a blade pass through my garments from one of the other *botroas* and he spat in my face. I squeezed harder, watching as his eyes bulged from their sockets. "Tell *me!*"

"He is with the Casse. In—" A spear came flying through the air, piercing through his side. Blood poured over my garments as he slumped against me, the life draining from his body. I looked up into the eyes of Tancogeistla as he looked down from his horse. *Brihentin* were all around us, running down the rest of the fleeing Casse.

"Why?" I cried, gazing at the general with ill-disguised fury in my eyes. "*Why?*"

He looked surprised. "I feared for your life, my son. You seemed to have gone mad."

I didn't answer, rather looked down at the lifeless body of my last link to Cavarillos. Maybe I had. If so, so had the rest of the world. Gone mad. . .

Chapter XX: Return to Ictis

We stripped the dead of their weapons and provisions and then moved quickly south, continuing toward Ictis on roads that were considerably the worse for the heavy rains we had received.

And with each mile traveled, I found my sleep to be more troubled. I had not dreamed of Inyae in years, but with the reappearance of the *botroas* I found myself thinking more of the old days. Cavarillos. I was surprised to find how much hatred still lurked inside my spirit for my old friend, for the friendship he had betrayed.

I hungered for a meeting with him.

Arriving at Ictis, we quickly encamped around the oppida, cutting it off from all outside aid. Years of war with the Casse had taken their toll upon the standing forces of the Dumnones, and according to the intelligence of Galligos moc Nammeios, they could muster less than four hundred warriors in all of Ictis.

I prayed he was right.

We besieged Ictis for a year and a half, hoping to starve the defenders into submission. Tancogeistla looked worse with each passing day, old wounds taking their toll upon his aged body. Motios, the druid, did his best to attend to his master, but there were things even beyond his power.

And Tancogeistla would not rest. Ictis was his obsession, and each day he rode out before the palisade to taunt the defenders with their impotence, to taunt those who had humiliated him so many years before. He had returned. . .

And then, one day early in the month of Equos, a rider came pounding into the camp from the north, bearing word for Tancogeistla. Though his message was for the general only, we could see by the way he carried himself, the urgency of his steps, that the news he carried was anything but good.

An hour later, I was summoned to Tancogeistla's tent. A council of war had been called.

The general looked haggard, old even beyond his years. Aneirin moc Cunobelin stood at his side, surrounded by several of the highest-ranking nobles of the Aedui. I had a sense that all of them were waiting.

"My trusted friends," Tancogeistla began, coughing violently. He covered his mouth with his hand and when it came away, I saw that it was flecked with blood. He cleared his throat and started again. "This will be brief. I have just received word from Yns-Mon."

A murmur ran through the nobles.

"The garrison there has betrayed us. Three weeks ago, an emissary from the Casse approached, conferring with Captain Piso. And for a price, Piso agreed to turn over the oppida to our enemies."

"What he had so nobly defended from Casse swords, he turned over readily enough for a sum of Casse gold," Tancogeistla hissed, his lip curling upward in a sneer of disgust.

"The town and surrounding countryside belong to our enemies. Apparently most of the garrison went along with Piso's betrayal. Those that did not were slain."

I saw the shock in Aneirin's eyes. He had spent long hours with Piso, talking with the sub-chieftain about the defense of the oppida, the heroic battle fought there. Clearly he struggled to credit the news.

"Do we march north, then?" One of the nobles asked, laying a hand upon his sword's hilt.

"No!" Tancogeistla cried furiously, slamming his fist into the wood of the rude wooden table in front of him. "We will carry our revenge to the Dumnones first. Then we deal with the traitors. Drustan and his warbands think themselves proud that they humbled an Aeduan army seventeen years ago. They must be taught a lesson. They must die."

He looked across the table into my eyes, his fierce, charismatic gaze seeming to hold me in its spell. "We will prepare for an assault. Cadwalador, you will ride with my son."

"Yes, my lord."

Months earlier, two mighty battering rams had been prepared, and now men formed around them, preparing to push them against the kran of the Dumnones.

According to the plan Tancogeistla had outlined during the council of war, he was to lead the assault, at the head of over fifty *brihentin*, the flower of the Aeduan nobility. Following him through the gate would be the *ordmalica* of Lugort, and the *eiras*, the nobles of Emain-Macha. The rest of the army would follow.

Aneirin seemed nervous as we mounted for the battle, and I noticed his gaze constantly flickered to the other contingent of *brihentin*, his father's bodyguard.

"What is wrong?" I asked him.

He shook his head. "My father—he has. . ." his voice drifted off as though he hesitated to continue.

"He has been coughing up blood?" I asked.

He glanced over at me sharply. "How did you know?"

"I have seen it. How long?"

"Weeks. Ictis possesses him, consumes his body and spirit. He is not fit to lead this assault."

I shook my head. "He *will* lead the assault. He can do no other. And we must succeed. I was with your father the last time we came before these walls. And we were defeated. He will not survive another defeat here."

And so we rode slowly forward, approaching the kran and the starving men who stood behind it, ready to

149

defend their homes to the death. And scenes from the past came flashing back through my mind.

Cavarillos and I standing side by side, waiting for the Dumnone army to crash down upon us. The frenzied melee that followed, the men I had killed. Cavarillos had saved my life that day. If it had not been for him, I would never have lived to see another sunrise. Yet, for the friendship we knew, Ictis was the beginning of the end. An end that had been as violent and bloody as battle itself. Only it wasn't over yet.

The rams moved forward, and in the distance we could hear their steady, rhythmic pounding, battering at the palisade surrounding Ictis. A death knell.

Lugort's men smashed open the gate and we could see Tancogeistla's *brihentin* pouring through the breach to fall upon the levies on the other side.

I could see Aneirin was restless. But our time was not yet come.

The *eiras* moved forward, through the breach on the right side of the gate, following upon the Dumnones from the flank. They began to pull back from the gate and I nodded to Aneirin. It was time to move.

As one our horsemen moved forward, in column, a signal for the rest of the army to follow.

We reached the gate and poured through it. The *lugoae* of the Dumnones had pulled back a short distance and were now putting up a stiff fight. But Tancogeistla was nowhere to be seen.

Of a sudden, Aneirin cried out and clutched at my arm, pointing. I glanced up at the hill in the center of Ictis, and I could dimly descry the *brihentin* of Tancogeistla on the crest of the hill, engaged in vicious melee with Drustan's chariots. I knew what had happened. In his lust for revenge, Tancogeistla had singled out the enemy chieftain, intent on killing him with his own hand.

Our column swung forward, moving up the hill at a gallop. The fight on the rise continued, chieftain against chieftain, bodyguard against bodyguard. And silhouetted against the sky I could see the form of Tancogeistla, his blood-wet sword brandished high toward the heavens.

But his companions were dying, one by one, crushed 'neath the chariots of Drustan. The fate of Malac, come once again.

Kuroas. Champion. *Neamha.* Berserker. Tancogeistla was all these things, and never more so than on this bright day, slashing furiously at the enemies which surrounded him, slaying Dumnone charioteers by the dozen. None of his bodyguards could equal him, and they died because of it, killed by better warriors than themselves.

Then he was alone, yet the enemy chieftain dared not to close with his sword-arm. Instead, Drustan pulled back to the center of the town, where nigh a hundred warriors waited, the reserve of the Dumnone warbands.

And Tancogeistla followed, riding into their midst, scattering them left and right. Cernunnos reincarnate. It was as though he had a death wish. Perhaps he did.

Saddened by the perfidy of Piso and the garrison of Yns-Mon, obsessed with the killing of his old adversary, Drustan, he rode direct into the midst of the mob, his armor washed in the blood of his enemies, his sword dripping red. Calling out taunts at the cowardice of the Dumnone chieftain, he struck down his enemies like a man possessed.

Our horses blown from the gallop up the hill, we could do nothing. We were too far away. The *eiras* surged up the knoll behind us, driving enemy *lugoae* before them like cattle. Yet it was all too late. Far too late.

The lone horseman emerged from the ranks of the Dumnones, cutting a path with his sword, then the mob swallowed him up again. A fierce cry rang out across the hill, over the sound of battle. And then he disappeared, overcome.

I could scarcely believe my own eyes, a lump rising in my throat that threatened to choke me. I heard the sound of sobbing from someplace beside me, and turned to find tears running down the cheeks of Aneirin moc Cunobelin. Tears of grief—and rage. Word of Tancogeistla's death spread through the army like a fire and as one man we surged forward, up the hill, heedless of danger. Avengers.

Horsemen fell around Aneirin and me as we galloped forward, challenging the last chariots of Drustan. Two of them fell beneath the ferocity of our charge. Then we were face to face with Drustan. The screams of dying men surrounded us as the *eiras* and *ordmalica* charged onto the square, slamming into the warbands of the Dumnones, but it was all distant, far-off. All that mattered was Drustan. I rode beside his chariot, careful to avoid the wheels, my eyes focused on his face.

My first javelin missed the chieftain, lancing into the shoulder of his bodyguard. The wounded man let out a cry, toppling from the chariot. A moment later, the wheels rolled over him, breaking his bones with a sickening crunch.

Aneirin's form materialized out of the whirling melee, his mount's coat flecked with blood. "Leave him to me, Cadwalador!" he screamed, his voice full of rage as he rode straight at the Dumnone chieftain, intent only on taking his revenge.

I saw a smile cross Drustan's face as he saw the inexperienced heir ride to the side of his chariot, a sword in his hand.

Aneirin was going to die. I could see that from the moment their swords crossed. His rage was not commensurate with his skill, and he would die because of it.

I stabbed my second javelin into the flank of one of Drustan's horses, causing him to rear and paw at the air with his hooves, straining at the harness. The charioteer glanced at me and I saw the fear in his eyes as he struggled to restrain the horses. Fear replaced a moment later by the agony of death as the javelin pierced his throat.

Freed of restraint, the horses bounded forward, the sudden uncontrolled motion catching Drustan off balance.

With a scream, he fell backward, off the chariot, his body disappearing beneath the heaving mass of horses and men. To his death.

Our men let out a frenzied cheer at the sight of his death, hacking into the enemy warband of *botroas* with renewed fury. Within the hour, every last Dumnone warrior lay dead. Ictis was ours. But at what cost. . .

We found Tancogeistla after pulling several enemy corpses away from his body. His flesh was scored with countless wounds, his long white hair stained crimson, his armor and garments soaked in blood. Yet the breath was still in him.

At the sound of Aneirin's voice, his eyes flickered open for a brief moment. "Aneirin, my son," he whispered, his voice a fragile shell of the eloquence we had so long known of him.

I glanced over at Aneirin, motioning him to come to the side of Tancogeistla. The young heir came and knelt down at his adoptive father's side. "My father," he gasped out, the tears flowing freely as he removed his battle-scarred helmet. "I—"

Tancogeistla lifted one feeble hand to stay his words, before it collapsed weakly to his side. "Tell me, my son. How goes the day?"

"Victory belongs to us, father. Ictis is in our hands."

"And Drustan?" the dying Vergobret asked, a strange fire flickering in his eyes.

"He is dead, my father. As all those who lift sword against thee."

"It is enough," Tancogeistla breathed slowly, those charismatic eyes closing for the last time. "It is enough. . ."

I turned away to hide my own tears, unable to comprehend my emotions. Tancogeistla was dead. The strange, crafty old general whose banner I had followed for all of my adult life. The man I had defended with my life and yet stood against at Attuaca.

I can write no fitting eulogy for his death. I am a man of the forge and the spear, not the pen. I know not how to take the sum of his life. Therefore, these are the words of Motios, the old druid. His lamentation over Tancogeistla.

Tell it not in Caern-Brigantae, whisper it not in the streets of Camulosadae, lest the daughters of our enemies triumph, lest they take joy in our sorrow. For the pride of the Aedui wast slain in the high places, the mighty are fallen in battle. Valiant was he in his youth, and in his age, bravery did not depart from him. Neamha was his name and as his name, so were his deeds. From the blood of the slain, from the fat of the mighty, his sword returned not empty to its scabbard. Yea, even the sword of Tancogeistla.

He scattered his enemies with his voice and they fled, as the sheep in the highlands. They came against him in a host, and he laughed. Three score of the enemy were as nothing unto him. They came and he slew them, leaving their bodies in the field.

Cursed be thou, Ictis, and the people thereof. For on thy oppida was he slain, on thy heights was his life taken. The sword of the mighty is vilely cast away, it lieth in the dust of the streets, as though it ran not red in the blood of his enemies.

Dieth Tancogeistla as a brave man dieth? Nay, not as a brave man, but as a kuroas falleth, so fellest he. Weep, ye daughters of the Aedui, yea, weep ye for the mighty art fallen. . .

Thus endeth the reign of Tancogeistla. . .

Chapter XXI: Succession

It was a victory. Oh, yes, Ictis was a victory, but it felt hollow, as empty as the defeat we had experienced on these same plains seventeen years earlier. And now, as then, the situation was grave.

As we stood there around the body, Lugort came up to us, his clothes torn and clotted with blood. Only a few of his *ordmalica* had survived the assault on the square. "My lord," he began humbly, addressing our new Vergobret. "What is to be done with the population of Ictis?"

I almost thought Aneirin hadn't heard him. He kept gazing at the body of his adoptive father for a long moment. Then he slowly turned, glancing first at Lugort and then down the hill where the women and innocents of Ictis were being gathered at spear-point. "Kill them," he ordered, his face like a flint. "Kill them all."

Old soldier that he was, Lugort turned to obey, his expression showing no disquiet at the job he had just been tasked with.

Aneirin turned away toward the chieftain's palace, and I followed behind him. "Is this necessary, my lord?" I asked quietly.

He turned, anger in his eyes. "They killed my father, Cadwalador. A lesson needs to be taught here. It is what oi Neamha would have wished."

That I could not argue with. And indeed, I felt his anger surging through my own body. Yet I shuddered at the screams I heard floating up from the foot of the hill. The screams of women and children. Women like Diedre and Inyae. Children like Faran. There was no difference. We were all one.

"Come inside with me, Cadwalador. There are things which we need to discuss."

I turned, catching the eye of several nobles who stood behind us. Aneirin sensed my hesitation and spoke sharply to them. "Give us a few moments."

They obeyed grudgingly, and we went into the palace grounds. Aneirin's sword was still unsheathed in his hand, my javelins at my side. We knew not where enemies might still lurk.

"Much blood will be shed before I can take the throne Tancogeistla bequeathed to me, Cadwalador. You know that full well as I. And I need your advice."

I hesitated, unsure what to say. "My lord," I began slowly. "You ask for something I cannot give. There are many men in the Aeduan state far more experienced than I, men who would—"

"Betray me at the turning of the wind," Aneirin interrupted angrily, his eyes flashing. "You saved my life, Cadwalador. There in the battle."

"My lord, I—"

"Do not diminish it," he said, interrupting me once again. "My rage blinded me to my inability. If not for your intervention, Drustan would have killed me. And the adversaries of my father would have danced upon our graves. I owe you much, Cadwalador."

"It has been my honor, my lord."

"*Bah!*" Aneirin cried, spitting upon the sod. "You talk like one of the groveling courtiers of my father. Tell me the truth, Cadwalador. Forces are gathering, even as we speak. If you were in my place, what would you do?"

It was a long moment before I answered, "You need time, my lord. Time to consolidate your rule over the state. Time you will not have if we continue at war with the Casse."

"What are you suggesting?"

"That you send Ivomagos moc Baeren to them once again, to try to make peace with Barae, the High King of the Casse."

Silence. "Do you know what you are asking me to do?" Aneirin asked finally, looking over into my eyes. "You are asking me to go to our sworn enemies and beg for peace. You are asking me to pardon the garrison of Yns-Mon, to forgive their betrayal of my father. You are asking me to forget all that they have done to us!"

"Nay, my lord," I replied, shaking my head. "Not forget. Never could I ask you to do that. I only tell you that we must buy time. Else the Aeduan state will be torn apart from within while we are distracted by the warbands of the Casse. In Erain, Malac's son Praesutagos has already taken the governorship of Ivernis. His brother-in-law leads the garrison of Emain-Macha. We must make peace."

"And then what?"

"You must go to Attuaca without delay, establish the government there. Make Attuaca the center of power, the capital of the Aedui. Should Erain rebel against you, you dare not risk losing your capital as well."

He seemed to consider my proposition for a few moments, then he lifted his eyes to the western sky, where the sun was setting, a blood-red ball of fire slowly sinking into the sea. "It shall be as you say," he acknowledged slowly. "In three days, we will ride for Attuaca."

We set out at the appointed time, riding north with thirty-five hand-picked men. Ictis was left under the command of a sub-chieftain, a man Aneirin trusted to look after his interests there. Of course, so too had Piso been trusted, by both Aneirin and Tancogiestla.

However, there was an added surety with this man. His wife and children resided Attuaca. Should he betray us, he would never see them again. And that would have to be good enough.

Snow began to fall as we rode on, the chill winds of *ogrosan* whipping over the low hills and meadows of the southern half of the island. At one of the villages in which we stopped, we hired a guide to direct us to the northern road.

The village held many people loyal to us. It belonged to the territory of which Yns-Mon was the capital. Apparently the Casse had not yet completely subjugated the people, though they held the oppida.

Aneirin was quiet as we rode, a silent intensity transforming his person. Tancogeistla's death had changed him, I knew not how, but he was different.

We lit no fires at night, instead eating our rations raw. We were thirty-five men in a country that could muster hundreds hostile to us.

As we moved deeper into the territory of the Casse, we changed the pattern of our riding. No longer would we ride in the daytime. Rather we hid in the woods at dawn and saddled our horses again after dark.

It was on one early morning, as we continued to ride northward, that I heard voices through the fog in front of us.

I grasped Aneirin by the arm. "Listen!" I whispered fiercely. He pulled his horse up sharply, motioning for our column to halt.

"What did you hear, Cadwalador?" he asked after a moment.

"Voices, my lord. Directly ahead of us."

"Probably the wind in the trees, lord," our guide put in obsequiously, glancing at me from his position at Aneirin's right hand.

"No!" I exclaimed, returning the look. There was something wrong here. Something I couldn't quite place my finger upon. . .

A light breeze rustled the bushes near us and Aneirin smiled. "He is probably right, Cadwalador. With the sleep we've gotten the last few nights, it will be little wonder if we all don't start imagining the Casse behind every tree. Let us proceed."

I was looking at the guide when Aneirin spoke, and a smile flickered across his face at the decision. Not a smile at the words, or at the predicament we all found ourselves in, but something else. Something only he knew.

I placed my hand on Aneirin's arm to keep him from moving forward, looking him in the eye. "No," I said firmly, surprising myself with my boldness. "There's something wrong here."

I rode around in front of him. A worried look furrowed the guide's brow at my approach, a look which turned to defiance as I rode up to him. "What is ahead of us?" I demanded through clenched teeth.

"Nothing, my lord," he replied, in the same groveling tone he had used ever since I had first met him. "This is the shortest way to the road you wished to find."

Then, from the fog ahead of us, I heard a shout of alarm. We had been led into a trap, the nature of which I knew not, but his treachery was clear.

"Liar!" I hissed, grasping his horse's bridle to keep him from escaping. To my surprise, he launched himself suddenly upon me, a knife appearing in his hand.

I fell from the back of my horse, falling into the snow with him on top of me. I grabbed his wrist with all my strength, forcing the knife away from my face. Feral rage filled his eyes as he struggled to free his knife hand, sink it deep into my throat.

Around us I heard shouts, the sounds of hoofbeats pounding into the snow. Then it all faded away, all my senses focused on that glittering knife. The only sound surviving was the sound of our ragged breathing, puffing in the chill morning air. The only sight that of his face, his knife.

Do not wait for an opportunity, I thought, Cavarillos' words of years gone by flickering through my mind. *Make one.*

I spat in the guide's face and he flinched involuntarily. The opportunity made, I took it, heaving my body up in one mighty effort and throwing him off me. The knife fell into the snow.

He rolled over and retrieved it, started to rise, but my boot caught him just beneath the point of the chin in a savage kick. I heard a sickening crunch as his neck snapped. He fell helplessly back into the snow, dying.

I ignored him, realizing my own situation. The breeze was lifting the fog, revealing the scene around us. We had nearly ridden into a camp of the Casse.

One of the young *brihentin* rode up, looking at me with wide-eyed awe as he handed me the bridle to my runaway horse.

"Quickly, Cadwalador!" I heard Aneirin's voice call. Looking behind me, I saw the reason for his urgency.

Hundreds of Casse warriors rushing from their encampment and forming in line on the plain directly in front of us.

Indeed, there was the road, just as the guide had said. But, there also were the Casse on the other side of it. The voices I had heard.

I vaulted into the saddle with all my remaining strength and threw myself low over my horse's neck, kicking it into a gallop.

Satisfied with my safety, Aneirin kicked his own horse in the flanks and together we galloped across the plain, away from the pursuing warbands.

I could see the fear in Aneirin's eyes as we rode, fear mingled with disgust and fury at how nearly we had been tricked.

Had any of our enemies possessed horses, I fear that we would have been doomed, for the Casse possessed very fleet ponies, but no cavalry accompanied the warbands.

We rode hard until we reached the cover of the woods, then perforce we slowed our steeds, lest a low-hanging branch crush one of us from the saddle. Clearly, we would need to find another way north.

Four days later, as we saddled our horses at dusk, one of the young *brihentin* who had been posted at guard came running back into our small camp.

"Horsemen approach from the north, my lord!" he cried breathlessly, halting before Aneirin. "A small band."

"How small?" Aneirin demanded, anxiety clearly showing on his face as he reached for his sword-belt.

"No larger than our own, lord," the young warrior replied. " Perhaps slightly smaller. We should be able to take them easily."

His voice betrayed the confidence of youth. A confidence I myself had once felt. Aneirin glanced over at me, a question on his face.

"Stand or flee, Cadwalador?"

I looked up the narrow forest road. Whatever decision was made, it had to be reached quickly. "Perhaps first, my lord, we should find out the identity of these mysterious horsemen. They come from the north, perhaps they are messengers from Attuaca."

"And if they are an advance guard for the Casse?" he asked, uncertainty in his tones.

"Their horsemanship will do them little good in these forest glades," I replied, reaching for the war hammer that lay across my saddle bags. "Give me two men and I will go out to meet them. The rest of you saddle your horses to be ready for flight."

"I will go with you," Aneirin said quietly, drawing his longsword from its scabbard and hefting it in his hand.

"Nay, my lord," I replied. "Get you up and mounted, ready to ride should this be the enemy. We cannot afford that you should lose your life in these forests."

My words might as well not have been uttered for all the attention the Vergobret paid them. Seeing the example of their leader, the rest of the *brihentin* drew their weapons and moved out behind us. Instead of the two men I had requested, I had thirty-three. That would suffice just as well.

Hammer in my hands, I stepped out onto the forest trail, in the path of the oncoming horsemen. I saw them the moment I stepped from cover, a scant sixty feet away.

"Halt and declare yourselves in the name of Aneirin moc Cunobelin!" I demanded, planting myself firmly in their way. Aneirin came to stand beside me, the naked sword glittering in his hand. A faint sense of disquiet rippled through me. The horsemen were dressed in the manner of the Aedui. *Brihentin*, no less. But whose?

My question was answered a moment later when a stripling cantered his horse to the front of their body, taking off his helmet to reveal a smooth, hairless face. "I am Periadoc, son of Malac. . ."

Chapter XXII: Son of Malac

I stiffed instinctively at the mention of our foe's name, my hammer held more tightly in my grasp. Aneirin straightened perceptibly at my side, fire flickering in his dark eyes.

"Where are you bound?" I demanded, the first of our party to recover his voice. The youth looked at me sharply, apparently surprised at the hostility in my tones.

"I know not who you pretend to be, but I am on my way south, to join the army of Tancogeistla oi Neamha." He pronounced the name with audible pride, as though he expected its utterance to open all doors for him. A strange attitude for a son of Malac.

Aneirin stepped in front of me, his sword still unsheathed in his hand. "Tancogeistla is dead," he announced flatly. "Fallen in the taking of Ictis."

Periadoc's face changed in a moment, genuine sorrow in those youthful eyes. It shocked me, I must admit. He swung down from his horse to stand before Aneirin.

"Then who leads the Aeduan state?" he asked, looking from one to another of us with the air of expectation.

Aneirin nodded slowly. "I do. I, Aneirin moc Cunobelin, have succeeded my father as Vergobret."

Periadoc turned, staring into our leader's face for a moment. Then he extended his hand. "Then it is to you that I must offer the use of my sword. I have heard many things of you."

"All bad, I assume," Aneirin stated, his voice full of suspicion. I could scarcely blame him. Malac had been a shadow over all our lives. And this young man's older brother and brother-in-law had usurped Aneirin's authority in Erain.

Periadoc flushed red-hot, looking down at the ground. "You do me an injustice, my lord. I come to you, as I would have come before Tancogeistla oi Neamha, as a beggar, with nothing to my name save these men who have sworn their loyalty to me. And is not loyalty the greatest treasure of all?"

"What would a son of Malac know of loyalty?" Aneirin hissed, bent on provoking the young man.

"Were you to ask that of my brother," Periadoc replied calmly, "I know not how he would answer you with honesty. It is because of his lust for power that I find myself before you today. I fled Erain pursued by his *brihentin*. Only these companions follow my banner."

My eyebrows shot up instinctively. If what he said was true. . .

"Why does Praesutagos fear you?" Aneirin asked, still skeptical.

"He swore a false allegiance to Tancogeistla out of nothing more than fear. He knew he could do nothing against the charisma and power of oi Neamha. He dreams of nothing more than reestablishing the line of my father. He feared that I might become a rival. I knew I could find refuge with Tancogeistla's army. That is why I was riding south."

Aneirin seemed to consider his words for a moment, his eyes searching the young man's face for any signs of duplicity.

"We were on our way back to Attuaca," he said finally. "You are welcome in our camp."

Periadoc nodded respectfully. "It is an honor, my lord."

We rode north the next few nights, now in the company of the young Carnute and his companions.

He was a remarkably unselfish young man, willing to endure without complaint the same lot as his companions, despite his noble birth. He was nothing like his father. Indeed, there were times when I found myself wondering about the faithfulness of Malac's wife.

The snow continued to fall as we moved into the highlands. Aneirin seemed impatient at the delay. I found out why as we huddled together near the small fire one night.

"It has been over a year, Cadwalador," Aneirin said, rubbing his arms to restore their circulation. He went on before I could ask his meaning. "Over a year since I have seen Margeria, since I've held her in my arms." He blushed. "I'm prattling on like a stripling. You must find it amusing."

"No, my lord," I replied, gazing into the fire as the sparks pranced into the dusk-dark sky. I knew exactly how he felt, the yearning which seemed to come from deep inside a man, from the depths of his very soul. A yearning for nothing more than the sight of one's wife, one's love. Aneirin's marriage to Margeria had been a fruitful one. She had born him two fine sons, future heirs to the throne of the Aedui, perhaps. And he seemed to truly love her. Remembering her glance at the marriage-feast, and rumors I had heard since, I wondered if his love was completely reciprocated. But that was none of my affair, and I was glad of it.

Periadoc seemed to sink lower into the depths of despondency at Aneirin's words. The spirit seemed to have been taken out of him at the news of Tancogeistla's death and he had grown increasingly gloomy as the journey continued.

"I too, have a wife in Attuaca," he said soberly. Both Aneirin and I glanced his way in astonishment. He was young. . .

"That is yet another part of the reason for my flight. My brother wished her for his own."

164

I looked over at Aneirin, watching as the light dawned in his eyes. Perhaps we were getting at the truth at long last.

Aneirin forced a smile to his face. "Well, then. We have a double reason for haste. Let us ride."

Two weeks of hard riding later, we neared Attuaca. We rode single file through dark forest paths made slippery with snow. But something was wrong. I could feel it in my bones, as though the long years of campaign I had spent with Tancogeistla had given me another sense, a warning of danger.

Taking Periadoc and three hand-picked *brihentin* with me, I gained permission of Aneirin to ride forward and reconnoiter the ground ahead of us. Clear the road to Attuaca.

A feeling of danger gripped my chest as we rode forward, toward a narrow bluff which I knew offered a good view of the town. Below us, in the gathering twilight, between us and Attuaca, was an encampment of the Casse.

The town was under siege. . .

I felt my heart sink at the sight of the encampment, saw the despair in the eyes of Periadoc. But though my feelings were the same as his, I dared not express them. Despite his noble birth, I was the leader here. Mine was the decision to be made.

"I will stay here and keep an eye on the Casse," I whispered, well aware of how far a voice could carry in the chill night air. "Depart and warn Aneirin."

"What should we tell him?" Periadoc asked, obedience implicit in his tones. It was clear he wanted none of the responsibility of the next few hours. That was just as well.

"Tell him to bring his men on as quickly as possible. Smite the Casse by the light of the moon."

Periadoc stared down at the encampment and I could see the reluctance, the fear in his eyes. Another moment and his resolve might break. It was the critical moment. "If you confess defeat," I whispered harshly, "if you confess fear, the battle is already lost. Now go on and bring Aneirin moc Cunobelin back to me. Hurry!"

Without another word, he and his three bodyguards scrambled back down the trail, to where they had picketed their horses. And I was all alone, exposed upon the chilly bluff, looking down upon the encampment of my enemies.

It would take at least three hours for Periadoc to go and bring Aneirin, and that was if things progressed smoothly. I had no way of knowing whether other patrols of Casse roamed through the woods.

The moon was already coming out, rising into the night sky. One by one, the campfires of the Casse flickered out, their ashes growing cold as sparkling embers fell to the chilly sod. If I was to execute the plans forming in my mind, I would have to move quickly.

I guessed there were well nigh three hundred of the enemy below me. I would be going in all alone. For a brief moment, I contemplated slipping through to Attuaca and summoning help, but I dismissed that idea from my mind. The risks of being killed by a nervous Aeduan sentry were too great. Not to mention the Casse.

By the second watch of the night, I left my post upon the bluff and slowly slipped down the backside of the hill, careful not to dislodge any rocks or debris on my way down. I could scarce credit the plan I had formed, the madness that had seized my mind. I knew one thing, and one thing only. We could never hope to beat such a host in a fair fight. Thus craft and guile were our only allies. . .

Many of the Casse slept in the open, wrapped only in their cloaks. Others had taken shelter under trees, stunty conifers which dotted the highlands of Attuaca. Still others, I suspected the richest of the warriors, had brought some rude form of tent with them and set them up above their heads.

It was a motley collection, I thought as I moved stealthily, quietly, among them. Beardless boys and men in their prime, gray-haired champions and young men who had not yet drawn blood in anger.

Two hours had gone by. I could tell by the position of the moon. One more hour I guessed until Periadoc would return. Perhaps my last hour on earth.

My javelins were in my hand as I crawled slowly toward one of the last-burning fires, my knife thrust in the waistband of my trousers. Instruments of destruction. Death.

A few smoldering faggots still lay at the edge of the fire, along with several half-empty jugs of liquor. They had been drinking to keep off the cold.

I extended my hand toward one of the burning pieces of wood, seeking to seize it. The next moment, I withdrew my hand, hearing one of the sleepers stirring nearby.

Pressed flat against the ground, I held my breath, the night still as death around me. I could hear the sleeper throw off his blankets and rise, footsteps against the earth. Coming toward me.

I quickly reached out and grasped one of the jugs, jerking it toward me. The liquor splashed over my mouth and cheeks, staining my tunic. Then I sagged against the earth, the jug clasped in one hand as I lay on top of my javelins, apparently asleep. The footsteps came closer, then stopped directly above me. I nearly stopped breathing.

The next thing I heard was a low chuckle, as if he was mocking my drunkenness. Then he moved off. I watched him go, walking off to the edge of camp as if seeking to relieve himself.

The flame was dying on the piece of wood I had seized, dark coals flickering ever more slowly. I glanced toward the bluff again, then at the moon. Perhaps another twenty minutes. I breathed slowly upon the faggot, seeking to fan it into fuller flame.

I could wait no longer. I must be about my business. I pulled myself up onto my hands and knees, clutching the fiery brand in one hand, my javelins in the other. The little cluster of Britonic tents was only a few yards away. Undoubtedly their chieftain was within.

Silently, I whirled the brand round my head once, then twice, the air forcing the embers into full-blown flame. Perhaps the warrior who had passed me at the fire saw me. I thought I heard a shout. Perhaps it was nothing, but none of that mattered. I was past the point of no return. No one could stop what I was about to do.

I ran, stooping low, to the first tent and shoved the brand against the thin fabric, waiting until it smoldered and caught, then running on to the next one. At the third tent, I heard a shout from within. A light breeze came rolling down from the north, aiding my efforts.

I saw the fire leap from one tent to the next, fanned by the breeze as men came running out of the first tent. One of the men shouted and pointed in my direction. My javelin caught him in the hollow of his exposed throat and the words died on his lips. I tossed the faggot away, into the doorway of another tent. Now I was just another warrior. Nothing more. Nothing less.

The sower of confusion. The bringer of death. Another warrior, indeed. . .

Men rose from their resting places all around me, confused by the fire, panicked by the sudden attack from their midst. Screams, confusion, death wrought everywhere.

I tossed my second javelin at a tall, noble-looking figure who emerged half-clad from his tent, still struggling to pull on his armor. He fell, pierced through the chest. A spear swished through the air near my head and I turned to confront a young lad, an enemy *lugoae*. Whipping my dagger from my belt, I thrust it into his flesh, his scream filling my ears as he crumpled forward. His agony meant nothing to me, I was deaf to his cries.

All that mattered was the mission I had set for myself to accomplish. Faran sheltered behind yonder palisade, Diedre's little daughter. My tribesmen. They were all that filled my mind. This bloodshed was necessary.

Men were falling everywhere about me, as Casse killed Casse in their panic and confusion. And then I heard it, the sound of a horn sounding loud above the chaos. Looking to the south, to the hills above Attuaca, I saw a dark mass of horsemen.

They swept into the camp, the sound of their hoofbeats dark thunder against the frozen sod. A few tried to resist, I saw several horsemen fall. But the slaughter had already been too great.

One of the *brihentin* swung my way, his blood-flecked spear extending before him like a lance, seeking to skewer me.

I stepped nimbly to the side at the last moment, shouting at him over the noise and chaos of battle.

He pulled his horse up sharply, his steed rearing into the air at the suddenness of the halt.

"Is that you, Cadwalador?"

"Yes!" I cried. "Give me a hand!"

The young bodyguard extended his arm and I swung up behind him on his horse, my eyes scanning the encampment from the vantage point as we rode out of danger.

A dark mass of men was pouring from behind the walls of Attuaca, the garrison come to aid us.

It was the final blow. The Casse broke, running from the field with our horsemen pursuing hotly. The battle was over, if the night's slaughter could be called a battle. . .

I did not see Aneirin moc Cunobelin until the next morning, when his horsemen came streaming back into the palisade along with the rays of the dawning sun.

He dismounted, taking off his blood-stained helmet to reveal a tired face sweaty even in the cold morning air of *ogrosan*.

"I owed you much before this last night, Cadwalador. Now I owe you more than I can ever repay. The lives of my wife, my sons, for all this am I indebted unto you."

He grasped my hand fiercely, tears shining in his dark eyes, his words embarrassing me. "I did not do it for your sake, my lord," I replied with honesty. "I did it for my daughter's sake, for the sake of my last link to the wife I lost those years ago."

"*Why* you did it matters not, Cadwalador. The deed itself is all that concerns me. Thank you."

I looked across the square at Faran. It had been nearly a year since I had seen her, and the changes in her saddened me, at the thought of what I had missed. She was well past her seventh birthday now, maturing more with every passing day. And she still remembered my face. That was enough.

"Have you seen Margeria?" Aneirin asked, glancing once again in my direction.

"Nay, my lord," I replied. "Has she not come down to welcome you home?"

He shook his head soberly. "No. I must go assure myself of her safety. Fare thee well, my friend."

It was two weeks after our slaughter of the Casse in the plains before Attuaca, that a lone horseman came riding into the town. I recognized him immediately as he reined up his horse in the square. It was Ivomagos moc Baeren, the emissary Aneirin had sent to Barae, High King of the Casse.

He looked at me as he dismounted. "Take me to Aneirin," he said soberly. I nodded, leading him into the palace of Attuaca. The Vergobret met us there.

"What news do you bring?" Aneirin demanded, his voice anxious.

Ivomagos remained silent, stripping off his cloak and casting it onto the stone floor. He turned away from us wordlessly, revealing a back that had been flogged with a whip, the flesh scored into fiery welts and blisters of clotted blood.

"He ordered me whipped," he whispered, his voice a low hiss.

"What?" I heard Aneirin gasp.

"I was scourged by order of Barae!" Ivomagos hissed out. "He said that there could never be peace between us."

He reached into his baggage and pulled out a long, finely-crafted sword. "Barae told me also to give you this, my lord. He said to be sure and keep it sharp, for the day when he comes to meet you draweth nigh. . ."

Chapter XXIII: A Faithful Man

Spring came and with it news from the south. The oppida at Ictis had been assailed by a large force of the Casse, and the garrison nearly overwhelmed. My old friend and compatriot Lugort was among the slain, his *ordmalica* butchered by enemy slingers before the rams had even breached the walls.

Had it not been for the stalwart defense of the *dubosaverlicica* and the *eiras*, who alone slew nearly a third of the enemy force, the hill-fort would have surely been lost.

The words of Barae were not forgotten, and Aneirin went to work with a vigor, calling more warriors to his banner from among the Calydrae. He dispatched messengers to Erain to order levies to be sent from the Goidilic tribes, but his messages went unheeded. Erain was firmly in the hands of Praesutagos and Erbin moc Dumnacos, his brother-in-law and the governor of Emain-Macha, flatly refused Aneirin's call for warriors.

Dark times were upon the Aedui. I followed Aneirin wherever he went, my sword at his disposal, to guard his person from dangers without—and within. . .

Aneirin's young sons were fast growing toward manhood, and with them his hopes for a lineage. They were his pride and joy and he doted upon them, like any father. And perhaps more so.

A granary inside Attuaca was torched one dark night in Fidnanos, apparently by Casse saboteurs. Aneirin grew steadfastly more suspicious of all who trafficked within the city, to the point of evicting several strangers who were ostensibly on their way to visit kinsmen in the north.

Diedre's daughter Faran spent most of her time in the palace now, playing with Aneirin's young sons and looking out for their safety. It was an incredible responsibility, but she was no longer the little girl I had left when I had followed oi Neamha to the south, to Yns-Mon and Ictis. I had to remember that.

Galligos moc Nammeios rode into Attuaca a few months after the sabotage of the granary, with two pretty young women riding behind him.

He reined up his horse outside the tavern and went inside. I laid my tools aside and entered behind him, wondering what could bring Tancogeistla's spy to the environs of the capital.

"Cadwalador!" he exclaimed, slapping me on the back. "It's been too long. Another ale, if you please!" he shouted at the innkeeper.

I shook my head. "I don't drink." The example of Tancogeistla had been enough for me.

Galligos shrugged. "So, what brings you to Attuaca?" I asked, when we had sat down in one corner of the tavern. His women didn't sit with us. Instead they circulated around the room, singing with the other visitors to the tavern and laughing at bawdy jokes. At length one disappeared. Clearly about her master's business.

"Business, Cadwalador. As usual." His black eyes narrowed, fire glinting within them like dark coals. "I heard about the granary."

"Ah, yes. An unfortunate business."

"You haven't caught the miscreant." His words were more of a statement than a question. I shook my head in the negative.

"Nor are you likely to." His words spoke the obvious truth, but the certainty with which he uttered them

172

was sufficient to put me upon my guard. There was something behind the statement.

"Where have you been all this time?" I asked, endeavoring to change the subject. I could come back to the topic later, when he would not be expecting it.

"Camulosadae," he replied coolly. "In the court of Barae, gathering information of his operations against the Aeduan state. They are preparing to march against us, Cadwalador."

"Then why did you not go to Aneirin moc Cunobelin upon the moment of your arrival? He needs all the help he can obtain at this time."

"Barae is known for his spies, Cadwalador. I learned much about him during the months I spent in his court." A smile flickered across the spy's face. "One of those young women you saw ride in with me—she shared his bed for three months, until he tired of her."

"He is a formidable enemy. And his weapons are not those of the field of battle. Not when he can avoid it. Rather he prefers to move in the darkness, striking unexpectedly and without warning."

"What does all this have to do with your reluctance to report to your master?" I asked sharply, annoyed by his manner. I had the sense that he was toying with me.

"Everything, Cadwalador. Barae has a spy in the very household of Aneirin moc Cunobelin."

His words struck me like a blow to the face and I could do nothing but sit there, gazing into his eyes. "How can you be sure?"

"An unimpeachable source," he replied, seeming almost amused. "The High King himself, Barae."

"He told you this?"

Galligos shook his head. "Not me. The whore. And she relayed his words to me, as she was bidden. He was given to bragging with his women. Of his conquests, *to* his conquests." He chuckled as though he had just made a particularly funny joke.

There was nothing funny in the whole situation— not to me. "Why do you tell me this?" I asked, glancing sharply at his face.

"Who is better placed to find out the identity of the spy than you, Cadwalador? Trusted retainer of Tancogeistla.

Friend and companion of Aneirin moc Cunobelin. You can move unquestioned in the palace."

I shook my head. "I can't do that."

I glanced across the tavern to where one of the young women sat on the lap of an Aeduan warrior, laughing merrily as he whispered something in her ear.

"Why don't you use her?"

"You seem to have forgotten the king's fear of strangers," Galligos reminded me grimly. "He would be reluctant to accept a new maid. And with his legendary devotion to his young wife, her beauty would not be of aid to us." He looked pensive. "A faithful man, Cadwalador, is one of the greatest obstacles to my work that I know. Fortunately for my profession, it is a quality few men possess. A few men like yourself."

He rose from his seat, tossing a coin upon the table to pay for his drink. "Let me know what you can discover," he stated unequivocally, looking down at me. And then he was gone.

I sat there for hours, seeming frozen in my place, his words running over and over through my mind as I thought through my friends within the palace, considering and rejecting them all in turn. The idea of spying upon them was repulsive to me, yet Galligos' words held the ring of truth. And if he were right. . .

I went to the palace.

Months passed and *ogrosan* approached once more. I had discovered nothing. The spy had left Attuaca without ever speaking to Aneirin. To my knowledge, I was the only one who even knew he had visited. The only one who had seen him and known his identity.

His words tormented me, rolling through my tortured brain in the darkness of night. Who was the spy? Who was the spy? Who was the spy. . .

Fate plays perverse tricks upon the lives of men. For it was not by stealth and by guile that I finally received the answer to my question. Nay, rather, it was by the mistake of a child.

I went to the palace late one night to retrieve Faran. She was late and with Galligos' warning ever in the back of my mind, I was worried about her.

174

Faran was in the gardens behind the palace, chasing a small hare that belonged to one of Aneirin's sons. She greeted me dirty and tired, with a huge smile on her face. Yes, there was still an element of the child within her.

"You have worried me, my darling," I whispered, clasping her to me in the darkness. She looked more like her mother with every passing year. She returned my embrace uneasily, as though sensing the tension in my body.

"I had to find the rabbit," she replied boldly, showing me the furry little animal. "He got lost."

I smiled. "Let's go home."

It was then I heard voices from within the gardens, voices from out of the night. I pulled away from Faran and bade her go on. "Return the animal and go home," I whispered.

A sixth sense seemed to warn me, as though this was what I had looked for, had sought for so many months.

I moved stealthily through the hedges and trees that Aneirin had ordered planted for his wife's enjoyment. Margeria was scarce twenty years old, but I rarely saw her in the palace. She seemed to keep to herself.

Soon I was close enough to distinguish the voices. A man's voice, hoarse and deep, and a woman's, softer and harder to understand. For a moment I thought I had merely chanced upon a tryst between the servants, but the same impulse that had separated me from Faran drove me onward, to discover the truth of the matter.

There was something familiar—as though I had heard the woman's voice before, long ago.

Moving from my position behind the hedges, I descried the couple, the man standing with his form silhouetted against the bright moonlight, the woman with her back turned upon me. Her next words were clear, distinct.

". . .do not stop until you hasten unto Ivernis. Tell Praesutagos that the Casse look kindly upon his overtures to them."

My heart nearly stopped beating. The woman, the unknown woman before me, she was the spy I had sought in the long months since Galligos' strange visit.

"How do you know this?" the man asked gruffly.

"A emissary from Barae, he came to me last night," she replied. "Bearing a message from the High King."

"It is enough," the stranger assented at last, seeming satisfied by her reply. He reached forth his hand and took the packet from her hand. "I will deliver this to Praesutagos."

I parted the bushes with one hand, drawing my dagger from my belt. He looked up to me, startled and took to his heels. I caught only a fleeting glimpse of his face as he turned, a hawk-like face dark as the night.

And then he was gone. I turned, grasping the woman firmly by the wrist, to prevent her escape.

"Cadwalador," she stated coolly.

I looked down into the face of Margeria, the wife of Aneirin moc Cunobelin. The dagger nearly dropped from my grasp in my astonishment. Never, in all my dreams, had I suspected. . .

"You?" I asked. Her dark eyes stared back at me, full of defiance. She pulled her hand away from my grasp.

"Forget what you saw and heard tonight, Cadwalador. Forget all of it," she whispered, intensity in her voice. "You were never here. I was inside the palace. None of it ever happened."

"You were spying for Praesutagos—for the *Casse*!" I hissed, spitting out their name as though it were a curse. "How can I forget that?"

"Easily, Cadwalador," Margeria whispered, looking up into my face. "As many another man in your position has."

Her hand traced its way up my arm to the shoulder, her eyes locking with mine with a seductive boldness. "Come lie with me, Cadwalador. Here in the gardens."

Taking hold of my cloak, she drew me down to her until her lips were only inches from my own. "Lie with me, Cadwalador," she whispered. "Lie with me and forget. . ."

I looked down into her face, disgust rising within me at the emptiness of her invitation, at the perfidy I saw in those dark eyes. Treachery lurked within their depths.

"How long?" I whispered, glaring into her face. "How long have you been a spy for the enemies of my master?"

Her chin tilted upward, the look of defiance returning to her face. "Your master was Tancogeistla, and you aided Aneirin in slaying him at Ictis."

176

I recoiled from her, my mind reeling in horror at her accusation. "What do you mean?"

"You left him to be slain, you and Aneirin. It was all part of the plan, wasn't it?"

I shook my head. "No," I whispered. "It was a tragedy. Our men were unable to reach him in time."

"A tragedy, Cadwalador? Then why did my husband poison him, slowly but surely, robbing him of his strength before he faced the battle? No, Cadwalador," she replied, laying a soft hand on my arm, "it was no mistake. Aneirin wished for the death of oi Neamha—more than for anything else in the world. And you helped him achieve that goal. So you see, we are all traitors here—you, I, Aneirin. We have all betrayed something within ourselves, to possess that which we desire. Just as you desire me this night."

I pulled away from her touch as though from a hot brand. "You are lying," I retorted, certain of her object.

She smiled briefly, her eyes never leaving my own. "You say that with confidence, Cadwalador, but your voice bewrayeth you. It is a confidence you do not feel. In your heart you know that what I speak is very truth. A truth you refuse to see. Come and lie here beside me. Take that which you desire."

I looked across at her, into the emptiness of those dark eyes. Diedre had been the only woman I had ever known, and she had given herself to me with all the love a wife should feel for her husband. And I had given her my love in return, as any husband. But there was nothing here— only the fragile shell of an alluring and treacherous young woman, a woman who would betray me as surely as she had already betrayed her own husband.

"How many men, Margeria? How many men have shared your bed? How many times," I demanded, my voice rising, "have you betrayed your husband?"

Her pretty face twisted into a sneer, an ugly caricature of its former self as she laughed in my face. "And for what would you know? That you might tell Aneirin? I will tell you this. I have born two sons unto Aneirin moc Cunobelin. One of them is not his."

My mouth dropped open. Nothing had prepared me for the words she had just uttered. She laughed at my astonishment. "One day, Cadwalador. Oh, yes. One day a bastard will sit upon the throne of the Aedui."

I stared at her, hearing the ring of truth in her words. In this, indeed, in this she was not deceiving me. "So, come in unto me, Cadwalador," she replied, a mocking smile dancing on those ruby lips. "And perchance your son will reign some day."

I turned away from her, my contempt too great for words. And as I did, my foot hit something there in the garden. I stooped, picking up a small leathern packet. The same one which I had witnessed Margeria hand to the messenger.

The realization flashed through me like a fire. Surprised by my sudden intrusion, he had dropped the packet in his flight. The message—it was the only thing which I knew of that could convince Aneirin of his wife's betrayal. I had to get it to him, quickly.

Margeria came up behind me, her soft hands on my shoulders. "Stay with me, I beseech you. You will never regret it." She paused suggestively. "How long has it been, Cadwalador, how long since—" Her voice broke off suddenly as she saw the packet in my hand.

"Where did you find that?" She demanded, her voice a low hiss. I looked into her eyes, saw the traitoress unmasked. All her beauty, every last shred of seduction gone in an instant as she gazed upon the packet, her eyes blazing with fire.

"You know what it contains, Margeria?" I asked, taunting her as I tucked it within my cloak. "As do I. As will Aneirin in a few moments."

Without warning, she threw herself upon me, catching me off-balance. I went down to the earth with her on top of me, her fingers clawing for the packet. I grabbed for her wrists, pinning them against my chest. She bit down upon my hand, her teeth raking the knuckles.

Her hand moved down to my waist and within a twinkling, my dagger was in her grasp, the blade glistening in the moonlight as it descended toward my throat.

The dagger sliced across my forearm, thrown up to protect my face. The pain seemed to awaken me to my peril and I responded with a blow such I had ne'er before dealt a woman. She reeled backward, falling upon her back on the earth. But in her hand I glimpsed the packet.

I rolled to my knees, clutching my wrist to staunch the flow of blood. Determination was written boldly upon her countenance and I reached out as she lifted herself upon her hands, raising up to toss the packet into the hedges.

She was out of my reach and I lunged forward, slamming into her as the packet went flying, sailing through the night air, into oblivion. My time was short. I knew I would never find it again.

My dagger was still clutched tightly in Margeria's fist and I grappled with her for a moment, sensing the ferocity coursing through her young body. Her robes tore in my grasp and she rolled away, leaving the strips of fabric in my hands.

The look of the devil was in her eye as she threw back her head, her voice uplifted for the first time that dark night, a wild, quavering scream piercing the air. A cry for help.

I confess for a moment I sat there, blood still trickling down my forearm, utterly confused by her sudden change of attitude. She huddled in a tight ball, sobs shaking her slender frame as she screamed, again and again. It was then I glimpsed her torn robes and it all fell in place. Her scheme, her plan to cloak her betrayal.

I rose to my feet, adrenalin flowing swiftly through my veins. My pain was forgotten as I ran, my feet drumming a loud tattoo against the hard-packed earth. I knew one thing and one thing only. I must flee. Without the packet, without the proof of her treachery, my story would never be believed. Flight was my only recourse.

At the edge of the garden, I met a young *brihentin*, his sword drawn. "What is going on?" he demanded harshly, moving to block my path.

"I was coming to get you," I whispered, my voice filled with intensity.

"Cadwalador!" He exclaimed, lowering his weapon with a smile of relief. "What is it?"

"Margeria. You must go to her. A sickness, something, has come upon her. Help her into the palace. And put up that *sword*!"

"Of course."

I watched him go, my mind harking back to the days of my own youth. Before I had known the darkness of our present world. Before my innocence had been ripped away by the perfidy of man. And woman. . .

Despite my successful deception of the young noble, my time was limited. I knew that. I went quickly unto the palace stables to secure my horse, the strong gray steed that had carried me through countless battles, that had saved my life more times than I could count.

Saddling him, I rode through the night to my house, near the palisade of Attuaca. Returning held its dangers, this I knew. But deserting Faran was more than I could bring myself to do. She was not of my blood, rather the daughter of a strange man, a warrior whom I had slain in battle with my own hands. But she was the blood of Diedre, and that bound me to her with bonds far tighter than words can describe.

I reined up at the door of my small dwelling, the roof of which had sheltered the dreams Diedre and I had once shared. All that was gone now, ripped away from me with the force of a mountain storm.

The house was dark. Probably Faran had let the fire die as she went to bed. I walked quickly to the door, extending my hand to the latch-string.

Figures rushed from the darkness, they were upon me before I could raise my weapon to defend myself. Something heavy crashed into the back of my head and I collapsed forward, slumping down on the step. Stars flashed, a galaxy exploding within my brain. Then everything faded away. . .

I awoke spluttering, spitting out the water which had just been splashed in my face. Torches burned brightly above me, their guttering flame casting strange shadows across my body. The back of my head throbbed with pain, and it took me a few moments to remember my situation. Then it all came back. Margeria, the messenger, the packet, the fight in the garden. But where was I?

Aneirin stepped from behind one of the torch-bearers, gazing down upon my supine form. I started to rise and then realized hands were holding me down, pinning me to the ground.

"Why, Cadwalador?" Aneirin asked softly, his voice full of sadness. "Why did you do this thing?" His voice rose as he continued, trembling with emotion. "Why, when I have given you everything, rank and station, a place in my court? Was it not enough for you? Had I known you were in need of a companion, I could have commanded a score of Aeduan maids for you to choose from among. There was no need that it should ever come to this."

I remained silent, aware that nothing I could say would alter my fate. Any attempt to warn him of Margeria's treachery would only further incense him. He went on.

"Yet you attempted to force my wife, in my very palace! Had she not succeeded in defending herself with your dagger, you would assuredly had your way with her."

I gazed up at him, unblinking. "Your wife tells me that you poisoned Tancogeistla. Is this true, my lord?"

Aneirin looked stricken. He shook his head slowly. "No. Why would she have told you this?"

"He is lying to you," Margeria said softly, her voice tremulous. She came to the side of her husband, burying her face in his chest at the sight of me.

"I—I never—want to see him again," she whispered, her body shaking with sobs. He placed his arm around her, staring down into my face, sorrow mixed with contempt.

"I never dreamed you would betray me, Cadwalador. Never dreamed after all your years with my father, the steadfastness of your loyalty to his banner—that it would come to this. I could have you executed for what you have tried to do this night."

Once again, I kept my silence. The only words I could have spoken in my defense had been washed away by Margeria's tears. My fate was sealed.

My mind flickered back over the life which had led to this point. My boyhood in northern Gaul, the wars with the Arverni. The beginning of our migration, our flight across the waters. The disaster before the oppida of Ictis. Cavarillos and his designs upon our drunken leader. Upon Tancogeistla.

Had I not stood in his way on that dark night, Inyae would have been spared and Tancogeistla would have died, helpless in a frozen pool of his own blood. How my life would have been different.

I that night, as every man at some point in his life, had come to a dividing of the ways. And I had chosen my way based not upon expediency, but upon loyalty. And it had led me here, to this place with oi Neamha's heir looking sorrowfully down upon me, pronouncing the words that would lead to my death. A bitter irony—that loyalty had led to the perception of treachery, that allegiance could be construed as betrayal.

"And if you were any other man, Cadwalador, that is the death you would surely die. Yet, with you, I cannot. You spent your youth in the service of my father, oi Neamha. In your age, you have been the most trusted of my advisors. As much as your deeds of this night anger me, I cannot bring myself to order your death."

Margeria lifted her face from Aneirin's chest, whispering something to him. Asking him to kill me, I had no doubt. Whatever it was, he shook his head and bade her leave. He watched her go, her body still wracked with sobs, then turned his attention back to me.

"Let him up," he ordered brusquely. The hands left my arms and freed from their restraint, I slowly rose to my feet, facing Aneirin moc Cunobelin in the torchlight. My head held high, I stared defiantly into his eyes. I had done nothing wrong, there were no regrets.

"Yet I cannot let this night pass without notice. I am forced to order your imprisonment."

I opened my lips to say something, but thought better of it. Words could do nothing to change my fate. He turned unto my guards, uttering words that would ring in my memory for the rest of my days. "Take him away. . ."

Chapter XXIV:
Confrontation

The price of loyalty. It was this that haunted me through the long months. I had remained true to first the standard of Tancogeistla, then that of Aneirin moc Cunobelin. I had sacrificed much for the Aedui, for these men who had desired the kingdom for themselves. Treachery was the way of the world. And a man like Aneirin had been trained to see it everywhere. Yet he was blind to the serpent which he cherished to his bosom, the betrayal of the woman he loved. Folly, yea folly threefold. . .

Three years passed. From the darkness of my cell, I knew little of what transpired in that time. The war against the Casse began to gradually worsen, helped undoubtedly by Margeria's information. I heard from another prisoner that Motios had died in the fighting. The news brought me sadness, somehow. The old druid's honesty had been something I cherished unto myself through the long years. A man without guile.

Ogrosan of the third year found me still imprisoned. The long months had worn away my garments till they were little more than scant rags. I woke one morning shaking uncontrollably, the cold wind whipping through the cracks of the fragile prison. I stood, the manacles dragging upon my weakened arms, rubbing myself with all the vigor I could muster. I was more than cold, I was sick. And nothing could help.

Two days thereafter, I awoke to the sound of my cell door being thrown open. "Up with you and out!" the guard ordered gruffly. I thought I detected a glint of sympathy in his eye, despite his tones. Perhaps he remembered the days of my service, when I had been the confidant of Aneirin moc Cunobelin. How the mighty have fallen. . .

I emerged into the bright sun for the first time in months, blinking like an owl caught in the light of day. Other prisoners were gathered around me, kept under guard at spearpoint. Most of them were thieves or other malcontents. Early in my imprisonment, there had been many of the Casse with us, but none within the last two years. I wondered at the significance of this. Perhaps nothing. And perhaps everything.

We stood there in a long formation, shivering in the chill morning air. A noble rode up, wearing the insignia of Aneirin's court. "Listen, ye rabble!" he called out, looking proud and strong upon his warhorse. As once I had been.

"The Vergobret has assigned me, Eporedoros moc Estes, to build a harbor upon the northern coastline. First, however, we must clear an area of brush and trees. You," he stated, smiling upon us with the gleam of a conqueror, "will accomplish this work."

It was a three-day march to the place, and we were under escort the whole way, guarded constantly by warbands of the Calydrae, now under the banner of Aneirin moc Cunobelin. I found it ironic that these were now the only warriors whose loyalty Aneirin could trust, these whom his father had labored so hard to destroy. The tribes of Erain were firmly in the hands of his enemies. He could count upon no aid from that quarter.

The march was hard, but it felt good to be out in the open air again. Arriving upon the coastline, each man was handed a rude axe. The ground where we were intended to work was covered with thick brush and we immediately fell to work clearing it. I had once been a strong man, but the

184

years of enforced inactivity had taken its toll upon my strength and I now found myself exhausted by a few mere swings of the axe. My hands were bleeding and covered with blisters by the end of the first day.

Berdic was in the camp, in command of a contingent of the *balroae*. He refused to look upon me as we passed each morning. Apparently he believed the lie of my betrayal. Ah, friends. . .

Margeria's face rose up before me each night as I lay on my threadbare cloak upon the cold ground, mocking me with the impotence of my actions. I had failed to unmask her deceit and was now suffering the penalty for failure. If only there was something. Yet nothing could be done upon this desolate cape, so many miles from the palace at Attuaca. Or so I thought.

A month after our arrival upon the cape, a man came riding into camp. His horse trotted directly past the point where I stood, wearily swinging my axe a few last strokes before the close of day. I glanced up at his approach, and in that brief second of time I glimpsed the same aquiline nose, the hawk-like features.

I looked away quickly, fearing his own recognition. For brief as it was, I knew. It was the same messenger that had come unto Margeria on that fateful night. There was no mistaking the face that had been seared upon my memory. But what was he doing in this camp? I turned as he rode past, going boldly to the tent of the Eporedoros moc Estes. After a brief exchange with the *balroae* posted at the entrance, he was admitted. As a friend.

I dropped my axe and hurried away from my work, unsure of what I had just seen. Berdic was a few steps in front of me and I ran to him.

"Berdic!" I cried breathlessly. "Who is that man?"

Berdic kept walking, ignoring my words. Frustrated, I laid my hands upon his shoulders, gripping them fiercely. He turned, his hand moving to the hilt of his sword. "Let go of me," he hissed between his teeth. "I could slay you for that."

"Berdic," I whispered, my hands falling to my sides, "just tell me. Who is the man who just rode in?"

He looked at me for a moment, as though wondering at the impertinence of my question. Then, as though he could see no harm in the matter, he answered, "His name is Sucellyn moc Eporedoros. He is the cousin of our commander here."

I recoiled as though struck in the face, my mind swirling with a thousand thoughts, a thousand images. Could I have been mistaken? There was no doubt. "Berdic, that man is a spy for the Casse!"

Berdic looked upon me for a moment, then turned away as though disgusted by the audacity of my statement. "Of course," he replied dismissively.

I reached forward, seizing his cloak in my hands, turning him back to me, heedless of the danger. "Please, Berdic, listen to me! For the sake of our friendship, listen to me!"

His eyes locked with mine, scorn radiating from their ice-blue depths. "I have no friendship with traitors. What proof do you have of this man's treachery?"

"He was in the garden that night," I whispered desperately. "With Margeria. She was giving him a packet to take to Praesutagos from the Casse."

He stopped, turning once again to look upon my face. "And you would spare yourself by your denunciation of another?"

"Berdic, if I am lying unto you, slay me! But investigate Sucellyn's doings. There is a plot afoot here!"

He looked toward the tent, a look of indecision on his face. I knew the moment had come. I had to push him over that ledge in his imaginations. "Berdic," I cried hoarsely, "if I have deceived you, let not only my life be forfeit, but that of my daughter. But search out the truth!"

"Faran?" he asked. When I nodded, he continued, "She is dead already. Dead of the fever two years ago."

My world was swirling around me. I sunk down upon the snowy ground, no strength left in my legs. Tears coursed their icy way down my dirt-encrusted face.

Faran dead.

My last link to Diedre severed. In my heart I cursed all those months spent away from her. Diedre's death had taught me nothing. I had allowed the kingdom to come between my family and myself, Aneirin moc Cunobelin and his court. And in the end, all that had faded away, leaving me holding only the ashes of the past. Of what might have been.

I looked up at Berdic through tear-filled eyes. "Please, Berdic," I whispered, praying that he would not continue to be deaf to my entreaties. "Search out the truth."

He reached down and took me by the shoulder, helping me to stand to my feet. "I will take you to the tent of Eporedoros moc Estes. There you can make your accusation. It would not surprise me if he slays you where you stand. But you were once my friend, and I can no longer refuse your wish."

I followed Berdic numbly, moving like a man lost in his dreams. Or rather his nightmares. I heard his voice as he inquired at the entrance to Eporedoros' tent, distant and far away. The guards replied and then we moved inside. The cousins looked up, startled by our entrance. Sucellyn's face went white as he glimpsed sight of me behind Berdic. "You!" he gasped, realizing a moment later that his admission could cost him everything.

"You recognize me, don't you, Sucellyn?" I demanded grimly, advancing haltingly toward him. "The man who caught you in the gardens with the wife of Aneirin moc Cunobelin. The Casse spy!"

"What is the meaning of this?" Eporedoros bellowed, looking from my angry face to Berdic's puzzled countenance. His hand was upon the hilt of his sword.

"This man, Cadwalador, believes that he once saw your cousin spying for the Casse," Berdic said, his tone almost apologetic.

"That is absurd, Berdic!" Eporedoros retorted, his voice trembling with fury. And something else. Something uneasily akin to fear.

But none of that mattered. I was a prisoner and Berdic believed not my story. I could do nothing against these men—unless. . .

My eyes left Sucellyn's face and traveled around the narrow confines of the tent. I had to find something. My gaze lit briefly upon Sucellyn's cloak, which lay across a rude bench. Peeking out from 'neath the folds of the cloak, as though someone endeavored to hide it in haste, was the edge of a packet. A packet much like the one I had taken from Margeria in the gardens.

I sprang for it, stumbling forward on shaky feet, falling to my knees upon the frozen sod as I grasped the packet in my hand. I heard Eporedoros' cry of anger behind me, felt rough hands seize hold upon my shoulder. Sucellyn.

I swung 'round, backhanding the spy across the face, surprising myself with the strength still left in my arms. He toppled backward, blood spurting from a broken nose. I stood erect, the packet in my hand.

Eporedoros stood before me, his sword drawn. His eyes glittered with hate as I moved to open the incriminating packet. "Give me the packet!"

I smiled, intending to infuriate him. "Why should not I open it, my *lord*? Tell me."

"Because you are nothing more than a deceitful, treacherous dog!" Eporedoros hissed, his fury growing. "Don't dare!"

"Then, perhaps," Berdic interjected coolly, "you would not object to a representative of Aneirin moc Cunobelin opening it."

The traitor and I both turned to find Berdic standing there, a naked sword in his hand, his eyes glinting with suspicion. "Give me the packet," he repeated calmly, gazing steadfastly into Eporedoros' eyes.

We stood there for a moment, the three of us, as Sucellyn rose from his recumbent posture, still clutching his bleeding nose. Then Eporedoros relented, glancing over at me. "Give him the packet," he assented grudgingly.

I turned, handing the packet over to Berdic. I saw the eyes of Eporedoros as Berdic took the small leathern package, eyes glinting with treachery. Berdic's sword-arm fell to his side as he moved to open the packet.

Eporedoros struck without warning, his sword lashing out in a fiery blur. I saw Berdic recoil backward, his left hand severed, blood spurting from the stump. He screamed in agony.

I threw myself upon Eporedoros without thinking, without hesitation, bearing him down under my frail weight. We collapsed to the hard earth, him striking his head against the edge of the bench. He lay motionless. I looked up, glimpsing Sucellyn with a javelin in his hand. "Berdic!" I screamed, warning of his danger. "Ride! Ride for your life! Ride unto Aneirin moc Cunobelin!"

Sucellyn turned upon me, casting the javelin in my direction. I rolled across the sod, dodging easily. His effort had been a clumsy one and the javelin stuck in the wood of the bench. Out of the corner of my eye, I saw Berdic rise and dart from the tent, holding his bleeding arm close to his body. "Run!" I cried after him.

Sucellyn drew his dagger and advanced upon me as two guards entered the tent, their weapons drawn.

I jerked the javelin from the bench and pressed the sharp tip against Eporedoros' throat, pressing in until a small trickle of blood flowed from the wound. "Take another step," I whispered, "and I plunge this into his body."

The trio stopped in their tracks, glowering at me, but remaining where they were. I rose, holding the noble's unconscious body tightly against my own. "Now," I declared, "lay your weapons upon the ground and allow me to depart in peace. . ."

For a long moment, I stared into Sucellyn's eyes, sensing his hesitation. I poised my exhausted body for one final break for freedom. It was my only hope. Then slowly he lowered his dagger and nodded.

I backed away from them toward the entrance of the tent, holding the body of Eporedoros in my arms. Out into the open, across the flat ground of the cape. I glimpsed several of my fellow prisoners glance up as I struggled by, saw one of the *balroae* pick up his javelin.

The forces in the camp were clearly in league with the noble I now held as a shield against me. A momentary flash of anxiety tore through me at the thought of Berdic. Had he been able to make it to his horse? Or had he been slain by the guards? My gaze flickered up to the heights overlooking the cape and saw a cloud of dust kicked up by a lone horseman at full gallop. It had to be Berdic.

I glanced behind me. Only a few more yards. The net was closing in upon me, Calydrae advancing, their spears held at the ready.

Without warning, I dropped Eporedoros' body, turning and darting for the cover of the scraggly undergrowth only a few feet away. Taken off guard by my actions, the *balroae* still reacted quickly and I felt a javelin rip through the air past my ear. Another moment and I was within cover, my feet pounding through the half-frozen, slushy turf of the salt marshes which covered a large part of the cape. I had to run, to hide. The life of a fugitive was a familiar one to me, I knew the tricks, the stratagems to be undertaken. I kept running, my feet soaked in icy brine, the snow cutting into my feet. Near a small brook of water I paused, throwing myself upon my belly in the snow.

Running footsteps filled the scrub near me, my pursuers searching like mad dogs for my blood. I heard voices at the stream, then feet splashing into the water as they crossed, in search of me on the other side.

A few more moments. Then I rose to my feet, coming face-to-face with a young *balroae*. His eyes mirrored the shock in my own and his mouth opened to scream a warning.

My javelin plunged into his belly, thrusting upward through his lungs as I bore him to the earth, my hand clasped firmly over his lips as his body thrashed beneath me, struggling in its death throes. I gazed into his eyes, watching their agony, watching as the glaze of merciful death entered into them.

We lay there for hours, I and the man I had slain, my ragged clothing soaked in his life-blood. He was little more than a boy—reminding me of myself years before, reminding me of the young man I had killed at Ictis in the early days of the migration. He, my first kill, this, my latest. I took pride in neither. Both equally senseless, the victims of other men's hatred and greed, the primary things which had sent men flying to each other's throats for thousands of years.

Several times I heard voices passing by, but no one entered the thicket. No one came in search of the boy. Yet that was only a matter of time. Another grief-stricken home, the wailing and lament in the streets. Because of me. What I had done.

There was no time to think of such things. The young man had been my enemy, and he had discovered me, and he had died for his discovery, and that was the end of it. My enemy.

What did such a word mean? Years before, he might have played 'round my anvil in the gobacrado, a carefree child. Many children of Attuaca had, the playmates of Faran. And now he was dead.

At nightfall I rose, wiping my javelin upon his clothes to clean it, and hastened west, my body chilled by the inactivity of the day. I could only hope that Berdic had not fainted from blood loss before arriving in Attuaca, before delivering his message to Aneirin. If he had, then the hunt would continue on the morrow. And I would be at the mercy of the hunters.

Sleep came but fitfully to me that night, stretched out neath the sheltering branches of a pine. Images of the young Calydrae, of the now-dead Faran, of Margeria, Diedre, Aneirin, all these flowing through my mind in an unending, tormenting stream. When I awoke to the rising sun thrusting its rays down through my shelter, I was more exhausted than when I had lain down.

I lay there for a moment, my ear pressed against the frozen sod, listening. Listening to a gathering thunder, a sound like unto the strength of waters. Hoofbeats. The hoofbeats of many horses, from up the mountainside.

I scrambled from my cover, javelin in hand. My ears had not deceived me. Nay, men blackened the heights far off to my south, the heights overlooking the work camp, overlooking that cape of sorrows.

I watched as the rebels assembled below them, forming up to defend their treachery, and I could dimly descry the figure of Eporedoros moc Estes in the van.

The *brihentin* of Aneirin moc Cunobelin swept impetuously down the slopes, crashing into moc Estes' hastily-formed line.

Rebels fell by the score, and I saw their line waver. I caught up my javelin and began to run toward the scene of battle, summoning up a last reserve of energy.

Balroae from Attuaca, Calydrae loyal to Aneirin, charged down the heights behind him, their javelins causing confusion and disorder among the rebels.

As I approached I saw Aneirin mounted upon his mighty war-horse, a blood-red sword in his outstretched hand. Many of the prisoners had joined with Eporedoros moc Estes, swelling their ranks. But it was of no use.

I heard another sound, swelling above the clash of battle. Something wet splashed against my hand and I looked up into the sky as rain began to fall.

191

Below me on the slopes, the rebels gave way at long last, turning to run as the *brihentin* chased them down, spearing them with their long lances. The rain started pouring down in torrents, as though the heavens were attempting to wash the earth of blood as fast as man could spill it.

Eporedoros was slain as he ran, butchered like the coward he was.

As I stood there, watching the carnage from a distance, I heard a voice calling my name. I turned to find Berdic sitting upon his horse a few feet distant. The stump of his left hand was wrapped in bloody bandages.

"You got through," I said, stating the obvious.

He nodded. "Margeria has been confined within the palace. Aneirin ordered her placed under guard until his return."

"It is good," I whispered, feeling as though a weight had been lifted from my shoulders. Still. . .

The *brihentin* started drifting back to where we stood, leaving the remnants of the rebellion fleeing from the battlefield. Aneirin moc Cunobelin rode up to us, slowly removing his battered helmet. He glanced from Berdic to myself, the awkwardness of the moment palpable.

A riderless horse cantered nearby, panicked by the clash of battle. Aneirin ordered one of the men to catch it and when the young *brihentin* came riding back, he looked down upon me.

"Cadwalador," he began slowly. "Come with me, my friend. We ride to Attuaca."

The words sounded so foreign, so alien coming from his lips. *Friend.* The man who had condemned me to prison now wished me to call him *friend.* The irony would have been amusing had it not been so serious. For a moment, I stared full into his face, my eyes hard and cold. "No," I whispered, turning on heel. Turning from all that had been my life for so many years. "Never again. . ."

192

Chapter XXV: End of all Dreams

I took up my javelins and my place with the *balroae* of
Attuaca, my people, as they had been Diedre's. For Aedui
was I no longer. Attuaca was my home. The Calydrae were
my people. A curse upon Aneirin moc Cunobelin. . .

And so it was upon the slow march back to Attuaca.
Back to my home. I forced myself to keep up the pace of the
march, exhausted though I was. We encamped that night
well nigh twenty miles from Attuaca, for the day was far
spent.

Sucellyn's form danced before me that night,
haunting my dreams. For his body lay not with the fallen.
The traitor, the spy of the Casse, had escaped from the
carnage of battle. And lurked somewhere out in the darkness
of the moorlands, biding his time. Waiting. To strike again.

Waking at dawn, we rose to take breakfast upon
fresh trout speared in the icy shallows by the Calydrae. I
gazed to the east as the rising sun cast its rays down upon
me, dawning upon a free man. For the first time in three

years. I closed my eyes, striving to black out the misery, the fear, the sheer horror of those years. Never again. . .

I had been born free, and so would I die.

A shout caught my attention and I turned to see a courier ride into camp, his mount's flanks lathered with sweat, steam billowing from the horse's nostrils into the crisp morning air. He swung down from his horse without preamble or ceremony and dashed toward Aneirin's tent. A moment's pause there, and then the guards permitted him to enter.

I stood for a moment, seemingly frozen to the earth, feeling the hairs on the back of my neck prickle and then stand erect. Danger was in the air, a familiar feeling, but something else also. Something beyond danger. Something tangible, yet unidentifiable.

Fear rose within me, fear of the unknown, fear of what had befallen us. I trotted slowly toward the center of camp, forcing down my rising panic, desperately clawing for the mastery of myself.

Aneirin moc Cunobelin stepped from within the tent, his helmet strapped firmly upon his head. Danger sign.

He raised a hand, calling for the attention of his men. "My people. I have just been given word. A large army of the Casse has advanced upon Attuaca. Periadoc and the garrison are surrounded. Our people are besieged."

Shouts filled the camp as Calydrae scrambled to gather their weapons. I followed, shocked into action by the news. My arms, though weakened through long disuse, could still hurl a javelin. My legs, though wasted by endless days, could still carry me into battle. I had sworn never to bear arms for Aneirin moc Cunobelin again, but this was different. This was for my homeland. This was for Attuaca and all we had left behind. This war was righteous. . .

Righteous or not, it would make no difference, I realized as we surmounted the heights above Attuaca, snow falling gently from the heavens, the foresign of an approaching squall. Including Aneirin's *brihentin* and the *iaosatae* of Berdic, we numbered scarce three hundred men. Not quite two hundred comprised the garrison of Attuaca.

The host of the Casse stretched out before us in the plain, like the sand upon the seashore in number.

194

I looked across the way, to where Aneirin moc Cunobelin sat upon his nervous steed, looking down upon the enemy army. Still, after all these years, after all the two of us had been through, he was no more a warrior than the day I had first met him. I remembered that day, something I had clutched firm hold of during my long imprisonment. Remembered his efforts on the javelin range. Remembered the warriors' ill-concealed laughter.

Nay, he was no warrior. Yet he it was who would lead us forth to battle this day. I watched as he turned his warhorse to face us, steel bared in his right hand. The order to advance burst from his lips. And our line swung into motion. Into battle. . .

We formed up in line of battle on the plain below, before the host of the Casse, waiting for them to come out of their encampment. A single ragged line of *balroae*, with the *iaosatae* sheltering behind our spears. Aneirin's *brihentin* took up positions behind us as well, a heavily-armored reserve.

The Casse advanced to meet us, moving across the plain like a cloud. There were so many of them.

I looked to my left, to my right, seeing the fear in the eyes of my brothers, the warriors of the Calydrae. Javelins were clutched nervously in sweat-soaked palms, wet despite the cold. Snow was falling, the harbinger of *ogrosan* upon us.

Yet the chill I felt had nothing to do with the weather. I raised my javelin over my head, poised to throw as the Casse line descended upon us like a storm.

Men went down under a lethal hail of javelins but more advanced to take their places, stepping into dead men's shoes. They crashed into our line and I grasped up my spear, thrusting it into the belly of a heavy-set man who appeared in front of me, his broad chest covered with designs in blue dye. He screamed and went down, his blood staining the snow. Magic or no magic, the woad had done him little good.

I saw a young warrior fall to my left and I jabbed with my spear toward his assailant. The tall spearman blocked it with his shield and thrust back at me. I felt the speartip graze my skin as I turned, plowing a fiery furrow

195

into my ribs. He went down, pierced through the back by a javelin.

Yet for all of our valor, it was of little use. For each we killed, five more rose up to fill his place. And our line was melting away.

A young warrior of the Calydrae dropped his spear and ran for the rear, screaming at the top of his lungs. I thrust him through, spearing him like a fish as he dropped to the snow, a death-cry on his lips.

Yet it was too late. His fear was infectious and within minutes our line broke, men running for their lives, running for the rear, for the deception of safety.

I stood for a moment, a lone island amidst a sea of the enemy, then I too found myself running. In shame. . .

I heard the *brihentin* thunder forward, catching a warband of the Casse in the flank and turning it. Berdic's *iaosatae* were also engaged, but they broke within moments, joining the rout.

We rallied in a grove of trees, their naked limbs stretched leaflessly toward the sky. A rag-tag, bloodied band of Calydrae gathered 'round me, their unused javelins still in their hands.

The Casse swept into the grove like a wave, their impetus irresistible, unstoppable.

More men fell, blood staining the pure white snow now falling all about us. More lives ripped away in the space of an heartbeat. Tragedy.

A young neighbor of mine fell beside me, pierced through by a javelin. He lay there in the drift of the snow, the light gradually leaving his eyes, replaced by the emptiness of death.

Our fragile line broke in two, men once again scrambling for the rear. The Casse cut them down as they ran.

A riderless horse galloped past, his sides heaving. I grasped hold of his bridle and swung myself up, into the saddle. All around me men fled, our lines in disarray.

In the distance, I could descry the garrison of Attuaca and Periadoc making a valiant effort to harass the enemy flank. But the son of Malac had nowhere near enough men. He too would be crushed.

But what of Aneirin? Despite his deeds, despite his distrust, I felt my concern grow as my eyes scanned the battlefield in vain. Then I saw him, on foot, surrounded by a few unhorsed bodyguards, in the midst of the Casse. Cut off.

Loyalty. The drumbeat of my life. Driving me on to bravery. To madness. It drove me now as I plunged my horse into their ranks, forging my way toward my leader. My chieftain. Toward the Vergobret.

He stood in the midst of the enemy, fighting desperately against a tall, muscular, sword-wielding foe. The warrior's hair was the color of flame, liberally streaked with grey. An older man. And there was something about him—familiar. I watched his blade, watched it slice the air, meeting against Aneirin's sword with a clang. Something from my past. All over again.

My horse reared up, nearly throwing me as he trampled several of the Casse 'neath his hooves. And in that moment of time, I saw the face. The face, though now lined by the years, which had haunted me through so many of the nights of my life.

Cavarillos.

With a cry of fury, I threw myself into the maelstrom, the fury of the melee, hacking my way to Aneirin's side. The look was there, the look of victory, of triumph which I had seen in the mercenary's eyes that dark night, so many years ago. Aneirin was losing the fight.

I poised my remaining javelin above my head, aiming it straight and true. "Cavarillos!" I screamed, anger in my tones. He looked up, momentarily distracted, as the javelin left my hand.

His eyes widened in surprise, then recognition. The crafty old warrior dodged, taking my javelin through the flesh of his upper arm. He reached over effortlessly and tore it out, breaking the shaft as though it were a straw. "Cadwalador!"

Another of Aneirin's bodyguards fell to the snow, entering in unto the sleep of death. I leapt from the saddle, taking the sword of the fallen. "Mount, my lord!" I cried, screaming at Aneirin. He heard me, and turned.

I saw Cavarillos smile, his sword twisting through the air to fall upon the Vergobret's mailed shoulder. A sickening crunch announced the breaking of bone and Aneirin cried out, his arm falling useless to his side.

As Cavarillos had wished to kill the father, now he desired to slay the son. It was happening, all over again. And once again, I was thrust into the role of protector. I parried his next slash with my own blade.

"How many years, Cadwalador?" He demanded, taunting me as of old, his voice rising above the battle like the bellow of an ox. "How many since I killed your woman?"

Twenty. Twenty long years, the figure burned into my memory as though with a brand. Yea, but those twenty years had wrought other changes as well. I was no longer the stripling he had once faced. He was no longer in the prime of his life.

Out of the corner of my eye, I saw one of the *brihentin* help Aneirin up onto the back of the horse. The Casse were surging forward. Another moment and all would be lost. And Cavarillos knew it.

"You stood in my path once before, Cadwalador!" he hissed, his sword grinding against my own. "In the days of oi Neamha. We were brethren and you betrayed me."

His reference to Tancogeistla took me off balance. For the old general had not received his surname until long years after Cavarillos' treachery. He had spied upon us—for how long?

"I swore that next time I should meet you, you would not live to see another night. And that day has come." I took a step backward, his blade pressing me hard. This was the day I would die.

I heard a shout and turned, one of the young *brihentin* appearing like a ghost out of the battle, out of the swirling snow. He extended his hand to me and I sprang onto the horse behind him, feeling the sword bite into the back of my leg, drawing blood.

All around us, our army fled, running for safety, running off the field of battle. As we rode through the midst, I glimpsed Aneirin moc Cunobelin ahead of us, desperately trying to rally his men, his sword brandished in his one good hand. I looked back to Attuaca, the place which had been my home for so many years, and realized what he did not.

We had failed. Nay, this was worse than failure. Worse than defeat. The end of all dreams. . .

Chapter XXVI: Sunset of an Empire

The work of years destroyed, torn apart by the hands of Fate. Lives extinguished in the space of a moment. We fled for the mountains on that dark day, the falling snow obscuring our retreat as the squall turned into a blizzard, icy wind lashing at our bleeding and worn bodies. We were scattered across the highlands of the north, scarce two men together. I joined myself unto Aneirin and his bodyguard Catuvolcos, a young Aeduan like myself. The last of the breed.

Over the weeks that followed, a few more survivors trickled in to join our banner. Casse pursuit had ceased for the moment, as they returned to their siegeworks around Attuaca. For indeed, the oppidum had not fallen. Periadoc had managed to pull his bloodied force back within the kran, and now held out in defiance of the Casse chieftain's threats.

The months passed by, and the days grew lighter. The month of *Lugonatos*, *fidnanos*, the time of light. The time of war. And the Casse launched their assault upon Attuaca.

199

We watched from the heights surrounding the plain of Attuaca, our numbers too few to effect any diversion, to do anything to help the beleauguered garrison. The last message from Periadoc, slipped out from behind the kran by a runner, had been a defiant one. *"Our defenses are strong and our hearts are true. Though the end of our lives draws near, the fear of our memory will burn in the hearts of our enemies for generations. Come and help us if you can. If that is impossible, then know that we will defend this our kran to the last breath. The enemy shall never raise their banners over this place while a one of us remains alive."*

Words of pride. Words of defiance. The words of a young man unschooled in the ways of man. In the ways of war.

The Casse attacked on the south of the town, using two huge battering rams pushed forward on crude wooden wheels.

Nearly nine hundred men against the handful of Periadoc. He never stood a chance. Only the gods could have saved him. The gods, the false gods which had deserted me so long ago on this forsaken isle.

The rams advanced, their wheels groaning ponderously over the rough terrain.

Two hours later, they succeeded in smashing open the gate and a portion of the southern wall of Attuaca, forcing an entrance. For a time, we saw a tangled mass of men as Periadoc's warriors met them in the breach, fighting toe-to-toe with the Casse.

Then silence fell over the town, the silence of death. A cheer swelled up the heights to where we stood, looking down upon the city which had once been the capital of the Aeduan state.

Aneirin turned away, tears of anger in his eyes, an angry impotence. There was nothing that could have been done. I knew that. Within his heart, he knew it as well. But he had stood by as his men died, an indelible stain upon his soul. Helplessness. . .

We retreated into the mountain fastness, gathering our followers unto us. Three weeks following the fall of Attuaca, a courier arrived from the south. From Ictis.

There, the oppidum had held out stalwartly against repeated attacks from the Casse. Yet at long last, the survivors had surrendered, exhausted by their long struggle and tempted by Barae's gold. Our last stronghold was torn away from us. Erain remained, but Ivernis and Emain-Macha lay in the hands of Malac's eldest son, the pretender. The man who had conspired with the Casse against us.

I saw it in Aneirin's eyes. The shadow of defeat. He had been handed a kingdom, an empire, only to have it ripped away from him. Forces beyond his control. Divisions within and without, conspiring against the young ruler. Tancogeistla had succeeded only because of the fear he had created in the hearts of his enemies. Fear engendered by his prowess, by his deeds as a warrior. Aneirin had come to the throne without that advantage, without those skills. And he had failed in the task left to him by Tancogiestla.

I had long forgiven him his distrust of my motives with Margeria. He had been taught to look for treachery everywhere—and in the end he had, in every place except where it truly lay. He had gambled all, and lost everything, including his family. A treacherous wife, and the sons of his love, one of which was not his. I had never told him of this. The truth, I knew, would destroy him.

Now even the place of oi Neamha's death had been torn from us, the hill upon which our leader had been slain.

And one morning, as the sun rose over the highlands, he gave the only order that could be given. We would march westward, to the ferry that would take us to Erain.

It was a tired, footsore, ragged group of men that marched from those hills.

Aneirin had been wounded in the leg during the battle, and the wound had never completely healed. Now the wound reopened and infection set in, prompted by the duress of the march. He was unable to keep to his horse and we had to bear him in a rude litter fashioned from the boughs of the trees.

I could see the pain in his eyes, discern that each step we took was agony for him, but he opened not his mouth. He was still trying, endeavoring, struggling to match the unmatchable, to live up to the legend oi Neamha had left to him. And he was failing, because it was just that—a legend.

It is the way of man—the past is ever better than the present, the leaders wiser, the truth truer. Let a man die, and he becomes what he never was. It was thus with oi Neamha.

The young warriors who marched with Aneirin moc Cunobelin were not those who had followed Tancogeistla through the early years of the migration, who had seen his drunken folly before Ictis. These only knew what their elders had told them—of the great deeds, of the Berserker, of the great deeds *they* had done with him.

Lies. Innocent, guileless falsehoods now combining to drive a man to the brink of himself, to the breaking point.

But we marched on, our heavy hearts growing gradually lighter with each step that took us closer to what remained of our homeland. And hope rose within, the impossible hope that there still remained in Erain those loyal to Aneirin moc Cunobelin, to the legend of oi Neamha. That they would rally 'round our banner and hail Aneirin as their rightful king.

He was delirious at times with fever brought on by the wound in his leg, crying out in the night. I took him by the shoulders one night and shook him awake. Sweat was running down his cheeks.

"What is the matter, my lord?" I asked, the bland, foolish question escaping my lips unbidden. What was the matter, indeed! Everything was the matter.

He gripped my arm, rabid, unreasoning fear in his eyes. "They were there, Cadwalador. All around! Every one of them!"

"Who, my lord?" I asked, puzzled by his outburst. Almost instinctively, I found myself glancing into the darkness that surrounded us, searching for danger.

"All of them," he whispered in his delirium. "Men, women, and children. All of them helpless. Mine—*mine*! I killed them!"

His flesh was clammy from the fever, rivulets of sweat trickling down his forehead. "The children of Ictis, their blood calls out to me from the earth. They haunt me, Cadwalador. Their *screams*. . ."

We resumed our march the next day. Aneirin showed no recollection of the night's events, but the pallor of death was upon his brow. I feared for him, but I knew not the solution to the difficulties which plagued us.

Three days later, we arrived on the heights looking down upon the ferry. I heard shouts of joy from the column as we pressed forward, the sight of open water invigorating the spirits of every man of us. For across the waters lay safety. Across the waters lay a new hope.

Good, faithful Berdic came riding back to the column, guiding his horse with the one hand he had left. He had learned to ride well in the only way he had left unto him. Truly I admired his courage—and his loyalty.

But despair was in his eyes, his countenance betraying the nature of his news even before he spoke. He rode up to the litter of Aneirin moc Cunobelin where I stood, looking down upon his recumbent king. "My lord, a force of the Casse have seized control of the ferry. "

Aneirin raised himself up suddenly, gazing earnestly at his trusted subordinate. He shook his head, unable or unwilling to believe Berdic's message. "What—why?"

"Our escape has been cut off. . ."

I saw it in Aneirin's eyes, the same crushing weight that fell upon all of us at Berdic's words. A growing sense of hopelessness that threatened to destroy us all.

"Is there no other way across?" I turned, finding Aneirin's young bodyguard, Catuvolcos, standing there.

Berdic shook his head. "The only ships on this side of the waters are below us—with Casse seamen aboard."

"And there is nothing else?"

"There is—at least there should still be, a light ponto two miles from here. I remember from the last time I came unto this area," I interjected, my mind working feverishly. "Two men could use that to cross over to Erain."

"But what good would that do?" Berdic snapped, the frustration clearly showing in his tones. "Had the oppida of Erain been upon our side, Attuaca would never have fallen!"

I saw Aneirin raise his hand for silence. "Cadwalador," he said softly, raising himself up on one elbow. "There is a man—who might be able to give you the help we so desperately need. He is a noble of the Goidils in Emain-Macha, a merchant, and a friend of oi Neamha's."

Again. The legend. It possessed him, as it possessed all of us. The very name was now something mystical.

"He has ships," Aneirin whispered, sinking back onto the litter. "You must go and find him, Cadwalador. For my sake."

I nodded slowly. "His name, my lord?"

"Cador. A merchant named Cador. You will find him in the courts of Erbin moc Dumnacos."

I shook my head, not understanding his words. "And what," I asked, "is a friend of Tancogeistla doing in Erbin's court?"

"Spying for me," was the simple reply. "He will aid you."

I straightened up, looking around at the little band of men that still stood with us. "I will need a man to go with me. Two men must row the ponto."

"I will go." It was Catuvolcos, an earnest look upon his young face and a longsword strapped to his side. I looked at him for a moment, gazing into his eyes. He was so young. As I had been once. He returned my gaze unwaveringly, conscious of my appraisal.

"Very well," I said after a moment. "We will move at dusk. In the meantime, my lord, we should withdraw our forces to the shelter of the trees. There is no need to expose ourselves to a Casse patrol."

The sun was low in the sky when Catuvolcos and I left the camp that night, a ball of fire sinking lower and lower until it was finally extinguished in the waters of the western sea. Darkness enveloped us as we slipped down the cliff path to the beach below us, swords drawn and in hand.

The only sound was our breathing, the water lapping against the rocks below. It was quiet, tranquil. Too quiet—and too tranquil. Unnaturally so.

The moon shone bright, pinpoints of light dancing upon the waves as we made our way along the rocks. I led the way, young Catuvolcos following behind me. I had not been to the spot in years, yet I could remember everything. Just around the next turn of the cliff, a jagged outcropping of rock jutting into the sea, was the ponto.

My foot splashed into the water. Oh, yes. My memory was not as good as I had thought. We had to enter into the sea to make our way to the boat. It was hidden just around—a voice broke upon my consciousness with the rapidity of thought.

I held up my hand for Catuvolcos to stop and he did so, both of us standing stock-still in thigh-deep water.

There was an explanation for the stillness, for the quiet. The presence of man. The presence of the Casse.

Moments passed, then the voice rang out again, a guttural challenge in the darkness.

I felt a presence move forward through the darkness, until I was able to descry a man standing upon the beach, his form silhouetted against the moon. A long spear was clutched in his right hand. He stood there for a moment, only a few feet from us, his eyes scanning the night. Then, apparently satisfied that his imagination was playing a joke upon him, he turned away, returning to his post.

I launched myself out of the water upon him, falling upon his back, driving the dagger between his shoulderblades repeatedly, a madness seeming to possess me. He must die.

When I arose from the corpse, my hands and knife stained with blood, I saw young Catuvolcos looking at me in wonder, his unused sword in his hand. I wiped the dagger on my trousers and moved forward, ignoring his gaze. There was no heroism in what I had done. No honor, no glory. The sentry had been alone.

The ponto lay a few feet beyond, its shape discernible in the moonlight. With the help of Catuvolcos, I pulled it out and floated it upon the waves.

The corpse of the man I had slain still lay there, his blood staining the sand. I forced him out of my mind. I had a mission, and for this moment, that mission lay across the waters. . .

Chapter XXVII: A Night Meeting

Catuvolcos and I arrived in Erain two days later, the light craft speeding smoothly over the waves. At night, we had sat side by side in the small boat, as he asked me of days gone by. Of the days of Tancogeistla.

"What was he like?" he asked me the second evening out, the waves lapping against the sides of our craft.

"Who?" I asked, his question breaking into my thoughts, my plans for action in Emain-Macha.

"Oi Neamha. You were his bodyguard, his friend. What was he like?"

I turned, gazing into his youthful face. When I answered him, my voice was hard and cold. "Tancogeistla was a drunkard and a fool, carried away by his lust for power. He would brook no interference and crush anyone who stood in his path. I should know—I was one of them."

There was shock in those young eyes, the disappointment of fantasies shattered, of illusions washed away. I turned away, disgusted with myself. He was but a child. It was unreasonable of me to expect him to understand. I had difficulty with the matter myself.

We hired a cart and horse from a small fishing village near the edge of the sea, hoping to pose as traders. It was a ploy I trusted to get us closer to the man Cador, himself a merchant. It should work—no, it *had* to work. Erbin moc Dumnacos would have no compunction at killing either one of us, should he discover our true mission.

The journey to Emain-Macha took five days, long, slow days of plodding along. In very truth, I doubted that our disguises would survive a careful inspection. Neither Catuvolcos or I possessed a merchant's skills. All our lives had been spent in other pursuits, namely those of war. For man must ever be at war.

At the outskirts of Emain-Macha, we enquired for the man, and were told we could find him at his shop in the danoch, or city market.

It had been years since I had been in the city, and I was amazed to see the changes time had wrought. Yet for all that had changed, still more remained the same. Above all, the hill of Teamhaidh glowered down, its slopes dark and forbidding. I thought back to my meditations upon its brow, the hours spent in the company of Motios, the old druid. So many years hence.

Upon reaching the danoch, I left the reins in the hands of Catuvolcos and jumped down from the cart. I strode into the row of shops, my sword girt to my waist. There was no inconsistency in my costume. These days, every man went armed. Ever since the beginning of the troubles. . .

"A man named Cador?" the first shop-owner asked, in answer to my question. "Of course! One of the most respected merchants in the city. His prices, now, they are higher that what a man like yourself would wish to pay. However, I have wares just as good as his, but much cheaper. If you would just honor me by—"

"Where is this man?" I demanded, cutting him off. He shot me an aggrieved look, but answered the question.

"Normally you could find him here in the market, but this is the third day of the week," he stated, as though this was self-explanatory.

I was in no mood for games. "Where?"

"At the palace, my lord," he said obsequiously, apparently glimpsing the danger in my eyes. "He is very good friends with Erbin oi Neamha."

"Oi Neamha?" I asked, puzzled. "The berserker?"

"Yes. It is what my lord governor Erbin prefers to be called. It is used all over town now, and the little ones know him by no other name. A reference to his bravery in battle, of course."

That made things little clearer. "What battle?" I asked, well aware I could be treading upon treacherous ground.

The shopkeeper winked and drew me closer, looking about as though to see if anyone was listening. "He has fought no battles, my lord. Not even against the bandits that plague the countryside. They whisper that his sword is rusted tight to its scabbard." His thin, pinched face spread out into a wide smile, a silent chuckle escaping from his lips.

I smiled in return, my eyes showing my appreciation for his joke. "Take this," I whispered, pressing a coin into his hand. It was old and battered, still bearing the likeness of Cocolitanos. Silver minted in the days before the migration. "Take this and give a message unto Cador when he returns to the market."

"Yes, my lord?" he asked, his eyes lighting up at the sight of the money. He popped the silver between his lips and bit deeply into it, assuring himself of its authenticity.

"There is a swift-flowing stream two miles to the north of the oppidum. Crossing it is a narrow footbridge. Tell Cador to meet me there tonight during the second watch of the night. Alone."

"Yes, my lord," he nodded eagerly. "I will tell him this."

"Do your duty well," I whispered, "and I will give Cador another piece of silver to reward you with."

His eyes glittered with greed, and I added quickly. "However, play me false. . ." My hand drifted toward the sheathed knife protruding from beneath my jerkin. He gulped audibly and turned away. "Of course, my lord. Cador shall receive your message."

"Thank you, good sir."

Catuvolcos and I were at the bridge that night, our wagon hidden away 'neath the shadow of a nearby grove of trees. I stationed the boy beneath the footbridge, his naked sword in hand, a safeguard against treachery. For I trusted no man. Not anymore. There was no safety in trust.

About the time of the second watch, I heard a low sound off to the southwest, toward Emain-Macha. Stooping down, I placed my ear against the earth, listening. The sound of a horse galloping swiftly toward our position.

Nervously, I checked my own sword, making sure it was girt firmly to my side. The moment of truth. A horseman appeared in the distance, his mount's hooves drumming against the hard-packed road.

Espying me by the footbridge, he reined up his horse and dismounted, tossing back the hood of his cloak.

"My name is Cador, of Emain-Macha," he announced, extending a hand to me. "The shop-keeper said you had a message for me?"

"Does anyone know of your coming here tonight?" I asked.

He shook his head in the negative. "These are hard times, and a man must take precautions for his life. But who are you?"

"My name is Cadwalador," I replied, watching his eyes. "Servant of the Vergobret, Aneirin moc Cunobelin."

His face broke into a smile. "I remember you! You rode with oi Neamha, as one of his *brihentin*, didn't you?"

I nodded good-naturedly. "Then, tell me," he continued, "how go things with our lord since the fall of Attuaca?"

"How did you know?" I demanded, taking a step closer to him.

"An emissary came from the Casse not three days hence, bearing word of the success of Erbin's alliance with him," Cador replied, his visage unruffled by my tone.

"An emissary?"

Cador snorted his disdain. "So he calls himself. He is no diplomat, nor is he even a Briton."

His statement startled me and I looked keenly into his eyes. "Describe him. . ."

He did so, the words driving a knife betwixt my ribs, the blade twisting deep into my soul. It had come to this.

I placed my hand on the merchant's shoulder. "I need to see this man. Can you arrange for me to appear in Erbin's court?"

"When?" Cador asked, appearing startled at my request.

"On the morrow. . ."

My gaze flickered from right to left as we approached the guards at the front gate of the palace of Erbin moc Dumnacos the next day. Despite Aneirin's assurances about Cador, it was not *his* life in danger in this place. It was mine—and that of the boy.

I could see the same unease in Catuvolcos, in his eyes, in the tight-lipped smile he flashed me just as we were passed on through. After the departure of Cador the previous night, I had explained my mission to him. His instructions were simple, and to the point. Guard my back.

I had never entered the palace of Emain-Macha. During my years in the city, Malac had been Vergobret, and Tancogeistla had never returned to the oppidum after his ascendancy.

But here I was. My hand slipped almost instinctively to the hilt of my sword, assuring myself of its presence. I need not have worried.

Cador turned to me as we entered. "Let me do the talking," he hissed between clenched teeth. "And remember! You are my brother and nephew from Ivernis, come north to seek employment in my service."

I nodded, my eyes fastening themselves on his face, a silent warning emanating from their depths. *Do not betray us. . .*

At the next guard, he inquired after the emissary from the Casse. "He holds court with the king."

Apparently Cador knew the guard, for he drew the man close to him and whispered into his ear. I stepped in close, just in time to catch his final words. ". . .is there a way inside?"

My instructions to him, followed to the letter. I hoped to make my entrance unobtrusively and escape just as quietly. Should there be another traitor in the inner circle of Aneirin moc Cunobelin, I had to know. Or so I told myself, reasoning away my madness in a futile attempt to justify my actions. For I knew perfectly well who Cador had described, those features burned on my memories for years. And I would not be content with escaping.

I watched as Cador slipped a few golden coins into the man's hand, once again bearing the timeless image of Cocolitanos upon them. I had been but a child like

Catuvolcos when he had been the Vergobret of the Aedui. The shrewd old leader who had made the decision to abandon our homes on the headlands of Gaul and migrate north—to Erain, to the isles of tin.

What would the old man have thought if he could have seen the chaos into which his decision had plunged the Aeduan state? I checked myself. The bloody power struggle between Malac and Tancogeistla could have happened anywhere.

Men's hearts are not changed nor influenced by geography. Men are still men, and crave power. In Gaul, Tancogeistla and Malac would still have flown to each other's throats, and the Arverni would have overcome us, just as the Casse were doing now. Everything the same, only different players. Caught in a web with no hope of escape. . .

The guard moved away from his post, leading us toward a large double door. "The throne room. . ." he whispered.

Catuvolcos and I each bore baskets of fish, presents for Erbin and the pretext for our entrance into his presence. Only Cador, in his prestige as our employer, was unencumbered.

"My lord Erbin oi Neamha!" The guard announced, stepping inside ahead of us. "The merchant Cador wishes an audience with you."

There was a muffled sound of assent from within, and the door swung back open, revealing the throne room to us. Erbin oi Neamha sat upon a rough wooden throne, its hard edges cushioned by furs from the north country, from Attuaca. From the lands he had abandoned to the people whose representative stood before him even as we entered. I stole a glance from beneath the hood of my cloak.

Older, yes. Once flame-red hair now slowly graying, the beard still as full as ever. A face now lined with age. The battle had been too frenzied for me to take a full glance at his features. But there was no denying.

Cavarillos.

His long sword was at his side, thrust carelessly into the folds of the sash he wore twisted around his waist. The battle outside Attuaca had convinced me that years had worn away none of his skill with it. I kept my eyes averted as we approached the throne, fighting the madness that seemed to suddenly posess me. The desire to reach out and kill the demon that now stood beside me.

I heard Erbin's voice in the distance, heard Cador's reply as though through a haze. It was all lost upon me, devoured by one all-consuming passion. *Kill Cavarillos.*

My mind flickered back over the years. I could see Inyae's face rising before me, the look of death in her eyes—the sword of Cavarillos protruding from her body. Feeling the life drain from her as I cradled her head in my arms, noiseless sobs wracking my body. The grief came back like a flood. Reason was gone.

Cavarillos spoke, his voice as gruff and coarse as I remembered it. "And who might these men be, Cador?"

Something snapped within me and I turned, throwing the basket of fish at Cavarillos. He recoiled in surprise and confusion as my hand went for the dagger concealed in the folds of my cloak.

Chaos broke forth in the throneroom.

I whipped the dagger out and threw myself upon him, close, inside his guard, just as he had instructed so many years before, the master with his pupil. He had no room to draw his sword.

The blade gashed along his forearm, ripping open his jerkin, sliding toward his unprotected heart. And it stopped.

I swore in desperate frustration, the useless dagger clattering to the flagstones of the throneroom. The mercenary wore a shirt of mail beneath the outer garment, as protection against the very kind of attack I had just launched. If only I had known. . .

Cavarillos roared like a wounded bull, throwing me off him. Caught off-balance, I stumbled backward toward the throne. His sword materialized in his hand as though by some magician's device, glistening like polished silver. Catuvolcos grabbed my arm and pulled me away, bringing me momentarily to my senses.

The guard Cador had bribed moved to block our exit from the palace, his spear in hand.

Erbin oi Neamha stood behind his throne, bellowing orders to everyone and no one in particular, seeming only concerned with his own safety. Neamha, indeed. . .

Catuvolcos' sword was drawn and he brought it down in a smooth, slashing motion, breaking the guard's spear-shaft. Terrified, the man turned to flee.

The boy let him go.

My senses had returned to me and deep within I cursed the folly of my actions. Aneirin, the state, everything jeopardized through my foolishness. But it was too late for regrets. Now was a time for action.

And we ran, fleeing through the corridors of the palace, the sound of guards shouting to each other lending wings to our feet. Up one corridor and down another. It seemed to me countless times as if we must be losing ourselves hopelessly in the labyrinth of the palace, but each time Cador led us out.

Another door loomed large ahead and Cador shoved it open, knocking down the surprised guard with his fist. The street lay beyond and we hurried into the open.

"We must split up!" Cador hissed, anger flashing in his eyes. His opinion of my madness was evidenced within their depths and I silently agreed with him.

I hurried along, seeking refuge in a small alley not far from the palace. They would search far and near for the fugitives, but they would expect them to run as far and as fast as they could. Or so I hoped.

I could hear the chaos from the palace, orders shouted in a blind frenzy of confusion, every man doing his best to sound louder than his fellow, all of them with their own opinions and ideas. Pandemonium.

I closed my eyes, reliving that moment, the look in Cavarillos' eyes as he recognized me. I could feel the dagger sliding toward his heart. If only I had guided it a few inches above, it would have been enough. A lust for revenge had blinded me, robbing me of my senses at a time when I needed them most.

Running footsteps passed the alley, then hesitated. I crouched, my blade in my hand, cowering behind a stack of wine barrels, undoubtedly bound for Erbin's cellars. A pause, my ears pricked at the slightest sound.

I could sense the man standing there, deciding. A presence. Then slowly the steps turned and began coming down the alley toward me. He had sealed his doom.

I waited, crouched to pounce, waiting until he had passed the stack of barrels. Then I would kill him.

Heavy footsteps against the dirt of the alley. He passed my hiding place and I threw myself upon him, grabbing hold of his cloak with one hand and swinging him around, prepared to drive my sword into his heart.

He turned on heel and in that moment I saw his face.

Cavarillos.

Surprise was on his face, turned quickly to joy when he recognized me. "So, Cadwalador, you play the spy?"

I met his sword slash with my own, well aware now of his mailed shirt. We were all alone. The two of us. Just as it had been on that dark night. I saw the hatred in his cold eyes, hatred unmatched save by mine own.

"You never forgot her, did you, my brother?" he asked tauntingly. Evidently, he hadn't either.

I ignored his words, only too aware of their intent. Of their purpose. I retreated farther within myself, searching for the place he had taught me of. Street noises faded, leaving only the ringing of steel against steel, the instruments of death sounding its knell.

I was myself, and yet not in myself—looking down from above at this cloaked fighter, his sword slashing through the air.

The warrior's place, Cavarillos had called it. His taunts all melted away, falling from my shoulders like the droplets of rain. Sparks flew from our swords as blade ground against blade.

I was pressing him back, unsure of my supremacy, watching his eyes for the treachery I knew him so capable of.

He met my sword with his own and gave it a fearful wrench. I recognized the ploy instantly. The one I had never been able to meet on the headlands of Gaul. The one which had robbed me of my sword the night of Inyae's death. I cried out in fear.

But I was not the twenty-year-old lad that had fought him on the isle of tin. The years had matured and hardened me, while taking their toll upon his body. The advantage was there for me to sieze, if I only could.

The sword was nearly torn from my hand, but I kept hold of it and replied with a blow of my own. He dodged and my blade bit deep into the wood of one of the wine barrels.

He was upon me before I could pull it out, his sword gashing open my shoulder. His eyes danced with merriment. "I swore an oath that I would kill you, Cadwalador. You were taken from my grasp at Attuaca. This is the day. . ."

I heard a shout from behind him and Cavarillos turned, distracted. It was the boy, Catuvolcos, his longsword in hand.

Cavarillos' blood-wet blade flashed in the sun as he turned, beating down the child's guard as I screamed a warning.

Summoning up all of my remaining strength, I jerked my sword from the wine barrel, ignoring my now-useless left arm.

Catuvolcos went down as Cavarillos' sword cut deep into his thigh, his blade ringing uselessly against the stones.

Time itself seemed to slow down. I watched, helpless to intervene as Cavarillos ran the lad through the belly, transfixing him to the earth. Screaming an impotent cry of rage, I descended upon Cavarillos like an avenging angel, my longsword raised on high.

He started to turn back, facing me. It was too late, and in his eyes I saw the awareness of death as the sword bit into his neck, severing the blood vessels there.

His sword fell from his hand and he crumpled into the dust of the alley, clearly dying.

I knelt by the side of Catuvolcos, looking down into the lifeless hollows of his eyes. Aware that he had given his life for mine.

A faint voice penetrated my consciousness. Cavarillos.

"You have bested me, my brother." I turned to see him laying there, his life draining away, his voice still holding the faint hint of mockery. "Curse the day I ever taught you the use of the sword. . ."

He slumped back against the stones, dead.

Tears fell from my eyes as I turned back, looking down at the child that had rescued me, that had traded his life for my own. As I had fought for Tancogiestla, the chosen successor, in my youth, so he had fought for a man

215

he knew only as a follower of oi Neamha. Because of the legend.

I heard a rush of feet, rough hands seized hold of my arms. I bit deep into my lip to keep from crying out, pain flowing from my wounded shoulder. I lifted my head, looking around.

Palace guards surrounded me on every hand. I stood no chance. Their leader stooped low over the body of Cavarillos. "He is dead," he announced grimly. "The Casse will want to know what became of him."

He turned, looking me straight in the eye. I stared defiantly back, my gaze never wavering.

After a moment, he barked an order to the guards. "Take him away. Erbin will want him questioned. . ."

Chapter XXVIII: The Chosen Few

A blood-red sun sank into the hills beyond Teamhaidh, mirroring the blood I had spilt earlier in the day. The blood of Cavarillos and Catuvolcos mingled together in the sodden dust of the street. The life-flow of a warrior and a child, mixed in their death. Both dead at my hand.

The child had died because of me, giving his life as a wild sacrifice on the altar of the ideals he still cherished to his breast. In a strange way, as I had known him, he had probably felt honored to die in the service of the bodyguard of oi Neamha.

I stepped to the window of my cell, a narrow four-by-five room built on top of the oppidum. Three iron bars were strategically placed to bar my exit. I paced back to the door, remembering the two guards placed outside, and wondered if Cador had succeeded in making his escape. It was unlikely, in that of the three of us, he was the best-known and the most easily recognized.

And if he had been captured, the fate of Aneirin moc Cunobelin had been sealed. The dreams of empire we had cherished since the days of the migration dashed forever to the ground. For Erbin and Praesutagos loved their comforts too much to take the war to the Casse with whom they had conspired. They would hold on to their precious

217

little kingdom of Erain for as long as their perfidious allies permitted. And then they too would fall.

But if he were still alive. . . With life comes hope, not for me, but for the kingdom I had given my life for, the kingdom I had endangered by my foolishness.

I clenched my fists together, thinking of the morning. Of Cavarillos. Surprised, I realized that his death brought me no joy. Was it because of the slaughter of Catuvolcos, or was there something deeper?

The words of Motios the druid came drifting back to me through the mists of time. *Vengeance is like this pitcher, Cadwalador. Poured out, it leaves one empty. . .*

That was the only word to describe how I felt. Empty. For nigh twenty years I had lived with Cavarillos in the back of my mind, haunting my dreams, waking from my sleep with visions of Inyae's death. I had known I would kill him—one day. It was my destiny.

And now it was all over, a curious let-down from the feeling that possessed me over those long years. No matter. I would not live to see too many more sunsets. Erbin would make sure of that.

Hours later, or what seemed like it, I heard voices outside my cell. The gruff tones of the guards contrasted against a softer, almost feminine voice. I rose from my seat on the rough flagstones and went over to the door, pressing my ear against the solid wood.

"Give me a moment with my husband," the voice asked, quietly pleading. It was a woman, her youth indicated in her tones.

I could not make out the guard's reply, but the bar slid suddenly back. I turned quickly, my face once again to the window.

"My husband!" I turned to see a young woman perhaps twenty years old standing in the doorway, flanked by my two guards. With an exclamation of joy, she threw herself into my arms, two loaves of bread falling to the floor of the cell.

Her lips grazed my cheek, her eyes flashing with anger as she whispered, "Kiss me, you fool."

The realization hit me like a thunderbolt. There was no mistake here. This strange young woman was here because of me. I returned her kiss with all the warmth I

218

could muster, my hands sliding around her slender waist. But there was something there, something beneath her garments.

I heard the bar slide back into place and looked up to find the guards gone. They had left us to ourselves.

The young woman pulled away from my embrace with a toss of her head, fiery-red curls dropping to her waist. She turned from me, opening her robes and unraveling the thin cord that had been wrapped around her slim body. It was that which I had felt.

She handed me the rope, nearly a hundred feet long and breathtakingly woven. I pulled at it roughly, testing its strength. The fibers held.

"It will carry you to the bottom of the wall," she whispered, her gaze indicating the window.

Puzzled, I looked into her eyes. "The bars?" I asked.

"In the bread," was her cryptic reply, her voice urgent. "Hide the cord carefully. Men await you at the footbridge to the north."

And in a moment, she was gone, tears glistening in those sea-blue eyes as she passed the guards.

I waited a few cautious moments, then I tore open the loaves of bread with a vengeance. A file fell from within the one and I snatched it up before it could fall against the stones.

Within the other was a small bottle of oil, to lubricate the file. Placing a piece of the bread within my mouth, I sprang to the window, testing the strength of the bars. Filing through them would be long work, in order to produce an opening large enough to squeeze my body. And I must be out before the breaking of dawn.

I set to work, piling the rope in one corner of the cell while I pressed the file against the rightmost of the three bars, near the bottom so that the file nearly scraped the stone as I pressed it back and forth.

Back and forth. Back and forth. Sweat was trickling into my eyes by the end of the first hour and I anointed the file with oil to keep it from getting too hot.

The first bar was cut half-through.

I paused, putting another piece of the coarse, dark bread in my mouth, chewing on it for sustenance. Then back to work. Back and forth. . .

The first bar gave way readily enough. I was working in pitch darkness now, no torch to illuminate my cell. But my eyes had memorized my surroundings in the hours of daylight, so I worked unencumbered.

I laid the file carefully to the side, taking the loose bar in my hands and bending it outward. Frustrated, I nearly cried out as pain tore through my injured shoulder. The iron held.

The bar was cut, but it was still present, still blocking my way. The two hours had been wasted. The young woman, her dangerous mission, all in vain. It would take me another six hours to free both bars to a point where I could escape. By that time, daylight would once again be creeping over the hills of Erain.

My strength utterly spent, I sank down against the flagstones, my nerves frayed beyond the breaking point. There was no escape, and I would die for my efforts. Unless. . .

I leapt to my feet, suddenly renewed by the thought. My escape could still be effected, but two must die. I pushed it away, forcing myself to focus on escape. That was all that counted, *how* mattered not.

I struck the file against the bars with a sharp, ringing sound, looking down at the blood seeping from the reopened wound in my shoulder. That was the only weak point, the only flaw in my plan. The only thing that could cause me to fail.

Fail. I forced the thought from my mind. I could not, would not fail. And I struck the bars again, the sound like a bell.

The bolt securing the door slid back with a clatter and one of the guards hurried in, his spear held at the ready. I was upon him before he could present it, my hands clutching his throat, squeezing the life from his body. He let out a strangled scream, bringing his comrade running into the room.

I wrenched the spear from his hands with my remaining strength, sending him toppling backward into his fellow.

Neither wore a helmet or armor, and his head struck the flagstones with a dull *thud*, rolling listlessly to the side.

His comrade jumped to the side and I saw the fear in his eyes. He blocked my first pass with the shaft of his spear, but I pulled back and thrust beneath his guard, skewering him against the wall.

A soundless scream died on his lips, and I jerked the bloody spear-tip from his belly. Released, he crumpled forward, his face pressed against the cobblestones. Soft moans escaped from his mouth as he lay there, life draining away.

I forced myself to turn away, ignoring his plight. Thus to all the lackeys of Erbin. I crossed the room and scooped up the lengths of rope, pulling the door shut behind me. My heart beat fast as I crossed the narrow hall, pushing open the door that led to the outside.

I pushed it open cautiously, peering into the darkness. Ahead of me, by the light of the moon, I could see a guard pacing along the top of the wall. He was nearing the end of his beat. Another few moments and he would be coming back toward me.

Minutes passed, the steady footsteps of the guard ringing a knell in my ears. I crouched there by an embrasure, shrinking against its protection as he passed close enough to touch.

Another moment gone by and he turned, re-passing me as I knelt there upon the wall.

I rose from my crouch and in a trice had the thin rope twisted around the embrasure, anchoring it on the solid rock. I jerked hard on it, painfully aware that I was silhouetted against the moonlight. I had to be over the wall before he turned to come back.

Assuring myself of its hold, I swung over the wall, seizing hold of the cord with both of my hands. The pain flowed like fire through my veins as weight hung from my injured shoulder. I bit my lip to keep from crying out.

It felt as though my arms would be pulled from their sockets. I placed my feet against the wall, forcing myself outward as I began to slowly back down the wall. The thin fibers of cord cut into the palms of my hands, drawing blood.

My descent was painfully slow, my feet digging into the sod and stone that formed the oppidum of Emain-Macha. I dared not look down, aware that the height would shake whatever confidence I had left. My hands were slick with my own blood, jeopardizing my hold on the rope.

I hung there like a spider upon the oppidum, inching my way backward. My mind was focused upon one thing and one thing only. Getting down.

I had forgotten all about the guard.

I was perhaps two-thirds of the way down when I heard a shout above me, a shout of alarm and challenge.

"Halt!" he screamed, a sword in his hand. I watched the naked blade, entranced by its proximity to the rope I hung from. I looked down.

Perhaps thirty feet separated me from the ground. Enough to kill me, if he should cut the rope. I continued downward, swaying with each foothold.

The glistening sword moved ever closer to the thin cord separating me from eternity.

And in that instant, with my life hanging in fate's balances, I heard a faint *swish*, an arrow flying past me in the darkness.

The shaft buried itself in the guard's throat far above me. With a gurgling cry, he disappeared from view over the parapet.

I slid the rest of the way to the ground, the rope burning the skin from my palms. None of that mattered to me. My feet were upon firm ground once more.

A slender form materialized out of the darkness, leading a horse. The young woman from the tower, a strung bow in her hands. She cast a glance up at the tall, forbidding oppidum and bade me mount.

"We must hurry. My father awaits us."

We rode swiftly through the night, a cool breeze fanning the young woman's long hair back over my face as I rode behind her, keeping a tight grasp of the saddle. I closed my eyes, ignoring the pain in my hands and shoulder, the searing torment flowing through my veins.

I had escaped.

I nearly had to pinch my arm to convince myself of this truth. Just hours previous, I had been locked securely away in the guardhouse of the oppidum. Now I was free.

Or was I. I had asked my rescuer her name when we had mounted, asked her who had sent her on the perilous mission. She had answered with a shake of her head.

"All will be answered," she answered cryptically. "Soon."

The horse covered the ground with long, pounding strides, carrying us farther and farther away from Emain-Macha. Toward the north. Toward the footbridge where I had met with Cador, the merchant.

Catuvolcos and I.

The young woman serving as my conductress reminded me of him with a pang of sorrow. He would have enjoyed meeting her, of that I was sure, his tastes similar to that of most young men.

A dark mass of men were clustered around the footbridge when we rode up. Their leader stepped forward, a burning torch in his hand. "Uctia, my daughter," he exclaimed as the girl swung gracefully from the saddle. "You are well?"

It was Cador, a long, dirty bandage swathing his neck. His concern for his daughter satisfied, he turned to me. "Cadwalador, my brother. It is good to see you."

I limped painfully toward him. "As you, friend. Who are all these men?" I asked, waving a bloodied hand to the assembled company.

He looked me in the eye, his gaze sober. "All the nobles of Emain-Macha who still follow the banner of oi Neamha. Of Tancogiestla. Of his anointed."

Again. The legend. A pounding drumbeat filling the minds of men from all walks of life. Power. This was the secret that filled Tancogeistla's life, the power to motivate men to either hatred or devotion. One of the two.

Or those like me, who lingered somewhere in the deadly no man's land of indecision.

"How many?" I asked, pushing away the philosophy of oi Neamha for the cold reality of the present. This was all that mattered. Here. Now.

"Sixty," Cador replied with the same level of sobriety. "I called only those I could be sure of."

"I see," I said slowly, walking along the ranks of the *eiras*, the nobility of Goidilic Emain-Macha. Those whose fathers had been conquered by Cocolitanos, who now fought 'neath the Aeduan banner which had crushed them. Brave men, warriors all. I could see it in their eyes, in the hardened faces that stared back at me.

But only sixty. A scant few. Far less than I had hoped. Compared to the thousands the Casse had fielded at Attuaca.

"How do we reach the Vergobret?" I asked, going on to my next question.

"I own ships on the coast. They await my orders," Cador replied calmly, clearly having thought through his plan. "Howbeit, I do not know the location of Aneirin moc Cunobelin. Only you can lead us to him."

"I am willing."

It was then in the moonlight he glimpsed my bloody hands, stripped of their skin by the cord. "Uctia," he barked sharply.

His daughter materialized at his shoulder, a dark vision. "Yes, father?"

"See that our friend's hands are bandaged and he is given sustenance. We leave within the hour."

We arrived at the coast a full week and a half later, our journey hampered by the patrols from Emain-Macha out searching for us. We traveled only at night.

We slipped aboard one of Cador's merchantmen one dark night, the moon obscured by clouds. His master met us on the gangway, warned of our arrival by a noble Cador had sent ahead.

"A good journey, my lord Cador?" the master asked nervously, grasping his employer by the hand. "Erbin's men have been here."

The merchant halted. "What did they want?"

"They were seeking to impound your ships, to keep a watch aboard them until your capture had been effected."

Cador looked at me, alarm in his eyes. "And?" he demanded.

"I called together our sailors and threw them from the ship. We were too many for them. Have I done right, my lord?"

A nod was the only reply he received, Cador clearly lost in his own thoughts. "They'll be back," he announced grimly. "Let's get the men aboard."

I nodded, moving back to the main contingent, my eyes full of wonder as I took in the sights around. The ships were long and wide, clearly suited for the carrying of cargo and men. An entire *trevas* of pontomora lay in the harbor, far larger vessels than anything I had ever seen before.

Oh, would that we had owned such ships as these in the days of the migration! But none of that mattered now, either. The past was just that and only the future could still be changed.

Word spread among the *eiras* and they filed silently aboard, their weapons wrapped in cloth to keep them from making noise.

Our preparations took most of the night, but finally Cador was satisfied with what had been done, and he gave the master orders to cast off. A stiff breeze was blowing as the mainsail was unfurled and we began to slip out of the harbor.

Moving to the stern of the ship, I once again marveled at the beauty and sheer size of the vessel. My eyes flickered back over the harbor, the still-sleeping port. And caught sight of a large torch-lit procession making their way down to the waterfront.

I threw back my head and laughed aloud, for the first time in years. Erbin's men had arrived a few minutes too late. . .

Chapter XXIX: Oi Neamha

We found the encampment of Aneirin moc Cunobelin after two weeks of searching, poking the bow of the pontomora into every inlet and sending scouts ashore to search for him. A long, frustrating search rewarded at last.

His face lit up as we marched into the camp late one evening, having passed safely through the picket lines.

"Cadwalador, my brother," he whispered, hobbling over on his bad leg. He fell upon my neck and held me in a tight embrace. "I feared for your life. But you got through."

Cador stood by, keeping a respectful silence. I introduced them, the merchant to the king, warriors both.

"How many men could you bring?" he asked as soon as the greetings were over.

"Three score," I replied swiftly. I could see it in his mind. Combined, our force numbered barely two hundred warriors. And his were weakened from their exertions over the past months.

"We can begin moving the men down to the ships," Cador interjected.

To my surprise, Aneirin shook his head. "My men are wearied. If we embark in the middle of the night, someone might be forgotten. We will wait until morning."

"As you wish, my lord."

It was a fateful decision.

As we lay down that night, I taking my accustomed station near Aneirin, as his bodyguard, I realized that never had a fire been lit that evening.

Rolling onto my uninjured shoulder, I looked over at the king and asked why.

A few moments of silence followed. Then he answered. "We are hiding, Cadwalador. A Casse sub-chieftain named Meriadoc has men in the area, looking for us. We dare not give away our location."

Another silence, as I digested his words. We were in more danger than I had suspected. Then he spoke again.

"What became of the lad?"

His question smote me to the heart. "Catuvolcos?" I asked, knowing full well whom he meant.

A nod was my only reply.

"He died in your service, my lord. Slain by the henchmen of Erbin moc Dumnacos."

"A pity."

At morning light, we awoke, the sun streaming down upon the highlands in all of their glory. A beautiful dawn.

We breakfasted upon fish caught in an ice-cold mountain stream nearby. Just as we were finishing, a lad from the slingers of Berdic came running into the camp. He had been one of the sentries placed the night before.

"The Casse!" he exclaimed, out of breath and panting from his run.

My one-handed friend leapt to his feet, staring the boy in the eyes. "Where?"

Aneirin moc Cunobelin came over to our fire, joining us as we looked downhill, to where the lad pointed. A thick column of the Casse wound its way uphill toward where we stood. Hundreds upon hundreds of warriors.

Like the sands of the seas in number. . .

Word of the approaching enemy spread quickly through the encampment. Cador bowed as he entered Aneirin's presence, his hands fumbling to strap on a sword.

"We will cover your retreat, my lord. The *eiras* will stay as you make your way to the boats."

Aneirin shook his head, a strange light entering into his eyes. I stared at him in disbelief. "No," he said finally. "This is where we stand. This is where we fight."

"But, my lord!" I exclaimed.

"But *what*?" he asked, one of the servants helping him with his coat of mail. "I have nowhere left to run. Sixty men are all that can be found in Emain-Macha to support me. I sent my messengers and they slew one of them, though he was no more than a lad. As they killed him, so they would deal with me. No, Cadwalador, it is best this way. Win or lose, we have nothing better to risk." His eyes softened as he looked at me. "Of course, I cannot ask you to stay with me. I have abused your loyalty enough."

I stood there for a long moment, my lips unable to form a reply. He misinterpreted my silence and put out his hand. "Farewell, my brother. May the gods favor you in your new life."

Suddenly angry, I turned away from him, grabbing up my longsword as it lay there by my blankets, enclosed in its scabbard.

My hands were still raw from my descent on the rope at the oppidum of Emain-Macha, but I had engaged in sword-play on the pontomora three days hence, and held my own.

I turned back to him, the naked blade clutched tightly in my fist. "Nay, my lord. My life has been spent in the service of the vergobret. Now, I guess, it might as well be given in the same." A bitter smile crossed my face. "I have nowhere to run, no one to run to. Let us fight, win or die."

The camp was filled with shouting, the bustle and hurry of men preparing for what they knew would be a last stand. Armor was pulled on by those few that had it, largely the nobles of Erain.

I girt myself with a coat of mail and saddled the horse of Catuvolcos, which Aneirin had given to me for this day. The stone-gray warhorse nickered and looked at me through puzzled eyes as I mounted, as though wondering where his master had gone.

We mounted and rode through the front of the slowly-forming line.

I sat there in silence upon my horse, looking out over the hills, cloaked as they were in that purple bloom, the heather of the highlands which I had first seen twenty years hence, in the company of Diedre. My desire to live had died with her, and the seed of her womb, Faran. All those I loved had died. I would join them soon.

Our forces came together at last, a thin, ragged line on the brow of the hill. As nothing compared with the hosts that advanced against us. Aneirin sat upon his horse only feet from me, his face unscarred by worry. An incredible peace seemed to illuminate his countenance, untroubled in the face of death.

A brave man truly, I realized at long last. Oi neamha. As worthy of that title as his adoptive father, if not more so.

From the hill where we sat upon our horses you could look back, see the ships waiting there to carry us—to safety?

Aneirin was right. No refuge was to be found there. Only a postponed demise. Our part was to die as men, not as rabbits, running before the wind.

The Casse came closer, ever closer, shaking the earth with the rhythm of their march. Berdic's men opened up on them with their slings, slaying many with stone and lead.

Closer and I saw the *eiras* brace, their javelins in their hands, waiting for Cador's order to fire. The merchant stood at their side, his face impassive. I heard his order as through a dream, saw the *eiras* fling their javelins down the hill into the host.

Many died, the slope was carpeted with the slain, the grass bedewed with their blood. But it was not enough. More men advanced, stepping into dead men's shoes, taking their place. Dying in their stead.

The *iaosatae* retreated behind the line, still plying their slings as they fell back. Berdic waved to me as they passed, that rakish smile still on his face, a sword in his one good hand.

The enemy spread out, sweeping toward and around both flanks. Our line was in danger of being crushed in their pincers. Aneirin looked at me, a grim smile crossing his face as he gave the order to charge.

We swept down upon the enemy axemen, scattering them with the impetus of our onslaught.

Cador's nobles joined with us, desperately trying to hold that flank. The *teceitos* of the Casse broke, fleeing to the rear, but more took their place. We were bogged down within moments.

Several of Aneirin's bodyguards fell to the ground, never to rise again, their horses hamstrung by the foe.

Another few moments, and we pulled back, whipping our horses to higher ground. Many of our number were left behind, dead.

The *balroae* of the Calydrae broke, interpreting our withdrawal as retreat. Outnumbered heavily, they were butchered as they ran.

Aneirin rose up on his steed, his sword brandished high, a scream of defiance on his lips. His attempts to rally them failed and then the *eiras*, the brave nobles of Emain-Macha, ran, flanked on all sides by the Casse host.

Our army was falling apart, only Berdic's men holding true, still pouring a stone rain upon the enemy from their position farther up the hill.

Berdic. Always to be counted upon in a fight. I had known that as a boy, and what had been true of the child was doubly true of the man.

Back we plunged into the melee, Aneirin cursing those who ran, our spears lancing through the enemy warbands. Warriors with brilliant blue patterns of woad etched upon their chests rose up to meet us, blocking our advance.

My spear was shattered by a Casse blow and I tossed the useless shaft away, drawing my sword. I glimpsed Cador fighting among the Casse, a rock amidst the breakers. His blade rose and fell with a lethal rhythm, breaking heads, severing arms. And then he crumpled to the ground, his blood staining the heather. I was too far away to help, to aid the man who had rescued me from the clutches of Erbin Dumnacos. I thought of his daughter, a fleeting vision of her face now cloaked with grief at his death. The cost of war.

My sword flashed in the sun, glistening with the blood of my enemies. I saw fear in their eyes as they disappeared beneath the hooves of my steed, the horse of Catuvolcos. I fought until my arm had wearied, till my hand clave unto the hilt of my sword. Kill—kill or be killed. There was no end of it.

Then we were riding, away once again from the carnage, toward the next crisis. The Goidils had returned to battle, battling Casse axemen in a grove of trees. They were hard pressed, fighting unto the death. In loyalty to Aneirin moc Cunobelin.

Without hesitation, we too plunged into the fray, with Aneirin riding at our head. I caught a glimpse of him as we charged, riding tall, his helmet and armor flecked with blood. Unbidden, my mind flickered back to another time, another man. Another vergobret. Ictis.

Tancogiestla oi Neamha. It was as though I was seeing it all again, Tancogeistla charging to his death in the midst of his enemies. Oi neamha. The berserker come again.

There were scarce a dozen of us now, the last companions of Aneirin. Perhaps just as well that Catuvolcos had not lived to see this day. Young warriors crept beneath the stamping hooves of our warhorses, hamstringing the beasts with their shortswords. Pinned beneath their own mounts, the fallen *brihentin* were easy to dispatch.

The *iaosatae* charged into the grove behind us, their stones exhausted and knives drawn for killing work. I saw Berdic for a moment, pride upon his countenance, a sword in his hand, leading his men into the enemy host. Washed away like sand before the waves of the ocean.

They disappeared for a moment, time lost in the fray as I cut down an enemy soldier. A moment later, my horse fell beneath me, disemboweled by a spearman. I threw myself from him at the last moment, losing my sword in the confusion. I stumbled backward, losing my balance and falling to the ground. All around me, people were dying.

I struggled to rise, weighed down by the mail. As I did so, the heaving mass of men seemed to part and I looked. The *iaosatae* had been massacred, faithful Berdic among them. I saw his corpse between two of the enemy, the sword still clasped in his lifeless right hand.

I was alone in the midst of the foe, alone and unarmed. I heard a shout from behind me and looked, seeing Aneirin moc Cunobelin still seated upon his rearing charger. With an unintelligible cry, he threw his sword toward me, the blade glistening as it spun through the air. I reached out, the hilt landing in my hand. He smiled a last, fateful smile, his lips forming a fare-thee-well.

And then he disappeared, his horse falling beneath him.

The enemy closed in, hiding him from my gaze. A strangled cry broke from my lips and I plunged into the Casse ranks, the sword of Neamha in my hand, hewing a path.

A speartip buried itself in my shoulder, the same one wounded by Cavarillos. I screamed like a wounded bear, turning and disemboweling the spearman with one blow of my sword. He crumpled to the ground, clutching at his middle.

A shortsword glanced upward off my coat of mail, sliding across the side of my neck. I thrust my body into the youth, driving him backward as I smashed down his guard, slicing his shoulder to the bone. He disappeared, trampled by his comrades.

I felt something warm soak the collar of my jerkin and put my free hand up to my neck. It came away sticky with blood. I felt suddenly weak, a hundred enemies surrounding me, like dogs worrying a predator.

More men fell under the blow of my sword, but I could go no farther. I dropped to one knee, supporting myself by a hand as I struggled to beat off their attacks.

I never saw the final blow, a sword slicing deep above the mail. I fell slowly to the ground, my cheek pillowed by the flowering heather, my eyes gazing sightlessly upward to the heavens. *Aneirin moc Cunobelin, I am dead. I hope it was enough. . .*

Epilogue: End of an Empire

Upon receiving news of the demise of Aneirin moc Cunobelin, Praesutagos lost no time declaring himself Vergobret and ruler over all Erain.

The uneasy alliance between Praesutagos and the Casse lasted precisely a year and a half. Then, in the summer of 242 BC, an army of the Casse sailed across the waters and landed in Erain, bent on avenging the suspicious death of their emissary, Cavarillos.

Laying siege to the oppidum of Emain-Macha, they settled in, seeming intent on starving the defenders out. Panicked by the incursion, Erbin oi Neamha ordered the sacred temple sanctuary of Teamhaidh Cnocinhaofan plundered to provide monies by which he could raise an army.

Howbeit, in the sixth month of the siege, the Casse launched their assault, battering down the walls with three huge rams. The Goidils put up a stiff fight at the oppidum, but Erbin's heart failed him and he ran, fleeing from the town and up the hill of Teamhaidh.

Two days later, the Casse found him there, clinging to one of the altars he had desecrated and beseeching the gods for mercy. Whatever mercy the gods might have deigned him, the enemy warriors chose to show none and his craven blood was spilt on the slopes of Teamhaidh.

Emain-Macha fell to the enemy.

Alarmed by the fall of his northern hold, Praesutagos ordered levies upon all the villages surrounding Ivernis, calling their men together to defend what remained of his father's empire.

But the Casse did not oblige, contenting themselves with subjugating the countryside surrounding Emain-Macha for the next year.

Then in the spring of 241 BC, a warchief of the Casse, Meriadoc moc Maglocunos by name, entered Erain at the head of a large army, twelve hundred strong. A Brigante by birth, he quickly established alliances with several of the Goidilic clans of Erain, flocking to his banner as he moved south. Toward Ivernis.

Once again, Praesutagos responded to the threat by calling upon his people, Aeduans and subjugated Goidils alike, to rise to arms. However, this time the response was not as great, and he succeeded only in levying a scant four hundred and fifty men. Little enough in the face of the approaching threat.

Now himself betrayed, the traitor took the drastic step of adopting one of his young officers as a son, his own heir being only three years old.

And so, Mabon moc Morbhe took his place as the "Chosen Superior", the Taoi Arjos of the Aedui. An Aeduan himself, one of the few left from the migration, he at once set to work at the direction of Praesutagos, strengthening the defenses of Ivernis.

It was all to be in vain. In the late fall, the forces of Meriadoc moc Maglocunos laid siege.

The months passed, then *ogrosan* laid its icy grip upon Erain, and the brave defenders of Ivernis. Skirmishes erupted between foraging parties on both sides and men died, their blood staining the pure white snow.

By spring, hunger was making itself felt upon the garrison. Several deserted, making their way over to Meriadoc to report upon the desperate nature of things inside. And in the self-same spring, the Casse chieftain launched his assault.

Twelve hundred men against four hundred and fifty. An almost three to one advantage.

234

But Praesutagos was the son of Malac, and his treachery was matched only by his bravery. Under his leadership, the defenders of Ivernis fought like wolves, bringing down scores of their opponents.

But all was in vain. At the end of the second week of the assault, Ivernis fell to the Casse. Praesutagos and Mabon both died fighting like men, swords in their hands. And with their death, so died the resistance.

The Aeduan kingdom of Erain had lasted a mere thirty years. . .

The End

30547093R00144

Made in the USA
Lexington, KY
08 March 2014